WEREWOLF'S REVENGE

Ferrel D. Moore

ISBN-13: 978-1-958557-23-5

To my lovely wife Beth,
My two children Kate and James
And my brother Thom and his wife Joyce

CHAPTER ONE

Professor Meridian Leaves a Message

Hauck gave hand signals to the group of six that immediately split up and began clearing the ground floor of Professor Meridian's mansion. The Instructor waited impatiently by his side and checked the driveway for hidden snipers. His eyes were constantly roaming, trusting nothing. When the all clear was given, Hauck had one of the six men stay at the front door, one at the back. The other four followed him through the massive lobby to the study door that hung on one hinge, the other having been broken off by the Instructor when he was in his werewolf mania.

Bodies were strewn everywhere and half eaten limbs and headless torso littered the floor. Dried blood was pooled on the floor. A half eaten head was stacked near the study door. Furniture was knocked about like a cyclone had been through the mansion. Claw marks lined the walls like a tiger had rampaged through there.

"Through here," whispered the Instructor.

The four men entered the study, their AK-47's drawn. Hauck had his favorite Czech CZ-P10 S out , and the Instructor had his Mossberg pump shotgun at the ready, but they waited at the door. Four bodies, or what remained of them, lay where they had been thrown inside of the study. Chairs and a table were knocked sideways and were partially splintered. A secret door lay knocked off its hinges where the Instructor had chased Professor Meridian down the stairs to the shadowy world where he had kept Sasha prisoner.

Hauck motioned for two of the men to stay at the door to the secret entrance, and sent two of the men, Arkady and Nikolay, down the stairs. Now Hauck knew, and so did the Instructor, that the most likely time that they would be attacked would be at the bottom of the stairs, as they went in. They would be given enough time to make sure that they were the only ones coming, and then the firing would begin. Perhaps from the long row of doors that made up the first of many floors. Hauck had sent two of his best men down the stairs to ensure their chances of survival.

One man at the door motioned they had reached the bottom of the stairs, and with hand signals told Hauck they were going in. Hauck nodded his understanding. Less than sixty seconds had passed when a tremendous explosion rocked the passageway leading to the surface. The two men guarding the door were blown back across the study. Hauck and the Instructor attempted to turn away, but not in time to prevent them getting a face full of dust and particulate matter from the blast. They coughed and choked.

"Shit," said the Instructor.

Two men came running to the door to the study, but Hauck waved them over to check on the other two men. Hauck looked up in time to see one man shake his head. The two men would guarded the secret entrance were dead. The two who had gone down first were dead as well.

Hauck's ears were ringing. So he motioned for the two men to get gone before the police arrived, while he and the Instructor did the same.They ran out to the twin SUVs, and the two men loaded into the car and pulled away. Next, the Instructor and Hauck made it to their car. Hauck turned the key in the ignition, backed up and went down the side streets to West Jefferson, turned left, and just kept going.

"Man, that hurt my ears," said the Instructor.

"Speak louder," said Hauck.

"I said, that hurt my ears," shouted the Instructor.

Hauck only nodded.

"You think that means Meridian got away or what?" yelled the Instructor.

"I don't know," said Hauck.

"Yeah, I think he did. Shit. I should've popped him that next morning."

"It was more important to get Sasha out of there. You did the right thing. I was thinking about poor Arkady and Nikolay. Terrible way to die."

The Instructor grunted, but Hauck couldn't hear him. His ears were still ringing from the explosion. They drove further down West Jefferson, passing police cars with their sirens going.

"I've been thinking," said Hauck, "that we should pull up stakes before we get caught. Meridian's got to have everybody in town looking for us."

"Could we pull over and get something to eat? I'm starving. Hey, there's a 7- Eleven. Let's pull over there."

Hauck pulled the car over and parked in front. He waited for the Instructor to go inside. Sveta was still recovering. It was an inconvenient time for a move, but it had to be done. Hauck checked his cell phone to see if Sasha was still on the premises. According to the tracker he had implanted in Sasha's clothing, he hadn't left. It was 50-50 with the young man. He never knew if he would stay or leave, but at least he knew where he was at all times. Provided that was, he didn't find out that Hauck had implanted a tracker on him. But he also implanted a tracker in his shoes just to be certain that he would know where he was at all times. Just then, the Instructor returned from the 7-Eleven with an armload of beef jerky.

He got into the car, closed the door behind him, and said, "Let's go. You want one? "

Hauck shook his head.

"So you want to move, right?"

"Yes."

"So you got a place in mind?"

"Drogol's laboratory."

"Yeah, I was wondering when you would think of something to do with that place."

"It's got everything we need to research how to cure the werewolf's bite."

"Okay, but we got nobody that knows what the hell is going on with that equipment."

"We've got Dr. Jimmy and Brittany. And Yuri. And maybe Charlene can help."

"That little pissant?"

"She seems like a bright young woman to me," said Hauck.

"Not her," grinned the Instructor, "I meant Yuri."

"I'm worried about moving Sveta, though."

"What? Don't be such a baby about moving Sveta. It should be fine. It'll do her good to get out and walk around a bit. A little fresh air now and then will do her right."

Hauck looked over at the Instructor.

"Are you serious?"

"Yes, I'm serious. Sure she can't walk, but that's what canes are for."

"You are," said Hauck, "the most insensitive guy I have ever met."

"Yeah," said the Instructor, "but that's part of my charm. So anyway, you want to move to Drogol's laboratory, but you want to keep it secret, am I right?"

"Exactly."

"So that means that we have to do the moving, right?"

"Yes."

"So that means Sasha has to help, right?"

"Correct."

"So let me get this straight — that means that I've got Yuri, Sasha, and Charlene to move everything we've got in three days?"

"Yes, the four of you."

"While you babysit Sveta?"

"Until we can move her, yes, which should be as fast as possible, so we're not caught unawares with Meridian."

"How about if the three of them move and I ride shotgun?"

"Deal."

"But I can only work the hours between ten and four. I got an appointment with a cage."

"You wish. Since the planetary alignment's passed, you werewolves only turn on the night of the full moon. That means you can work all night if you wish."

The Instructor dug into another beef jerky.

****

4

"I can walk," said Sveta.

"You can only limp," said Hauck. "Let me at least get your cane."

Sveta waited patiently at the door of the SUV while Hauck got her cane. She tried to get out of the SUV while Hauck hovered over her.

"I'm fine, I'm really fine," she said, when it looked as if Hauck were getting too close.

She made it out of the SUV, just a bit unsteady on her feet, but otherwise just fine. Her last memories of where she stood now came flooding back in on her. Drogol had led her through this maze, past the iron door now blown off its hinges, into the world below. She didn't know if she wanted to go back down there, but it was the only place that Hauck felt safe.

"Come on," urged Hauck gently, "let's go join the others."

Cautiously, Hauck waited for her at the SUV, ready to help at a moment's notice. He walked alongside her as she hobbled to the door and squeezed through with her to the iron door which lay on its side like so much discarded detritus. She picked up her cane at the stairs and leaned on his arm as they made their way down. She remembered the pistol she had put to Hauck's head when she discovered who he was for the first time and smiled at the memory. Down the stairs she went until she faltered stepping onto the first landing, but Hauck was there to catch her. She didn't look up at him, but she knew he was staring at her with concern in his eyes.

"Hey, come on," yelled Yuri from the bottom of the stairs. "We've got a bed made up for you and everything. The lights are on and the computer is fired up, and we've got food, and, well, you've just got to see the place."

Sveta looked up at the wonders that surrounded her. She had been focused on one foot in front of the other and hadn't glanced up at Drogol's laboratory. Golden globes of enormous size hung everywhere around her. Towers of chrome and coils of stainless steel filled the room. And the bells, now some of them scattered around the floor where they had been shot down by Mishka's men. She saw glassware distillation columns, globes of glass each as large as a hot-air balloon, electrical towers, substations and glistening black cables, gears big as tractor trailers and rows upon rows of shiny brass and silver bells, some large as small planes and others tiny as a child. And amid that wonder stood an antique train, complete with an engine, five cars and a caboose, upended on a track that seemed to run the length of the place and then disappeared at both ends into rock walls. The light came from the air itself, which was electrified by what means she did not know.

She smiled and waved, looked at Hauck, and then made her way down the remaining flights of stairs, using the railing on one side of her, and Hauck, the ever watchful Hauck, always at her side. As she neared the bottom, she stopped and looked over towards a big dial gauge and some lockers nearby. One of those lockers would contain the remains of Mishka, long since dead through starvation. She smiled to herself, remembering the brutal beating he had given to her at the warehouse, and how he came after her with hordes of men and machine guns, breaking through to this place, and how he had ended up in that locker.

Up ahead, she saw the platform that Drogol had hoped would break the werewolf's curse. She remembered Zoe throwing the switch to power it up, with him inside that large glass cylinder, and Mishka's men blasting away with machine guns to kill Drogol, but by mistake hitting the machinery. They had accidentally shot the control mechanism that controlled the output of the machine so that poor Drogol never had a chance- instead; he had become a monster werewolf on steroids.

Strange days, she thought.

When they reached the bottom of the stairs, Yuri was waiting for them. He was full of excited energy, and hugged Sveta and turned to hug Hauck, but saw the look on his face, and decided to not. He turned back to Sveta.

"Sveta, you've got to see the new computer setup that Dr. Jimmy gave us. It is so sweet that I—well, let's just say that I almost cried—I, a grown man."

Sveta smiled.

"Is he here?" she said.

"Yes, he's still here."

"Good, let's get going. I feel the need, the need for speed," she said, smiling.

"Is Trisha here?" said Hauck.

"No, unfortunately she had to go to work."

"Sasha?"

"Yes. He was a big help in getting things moved, too, Hauck. Oh yes, and Dr. Jimmy installed Brittany on our computer system. She is available for anything that we need. Isn't that great? I am back on the Internet, with no restrictions."

"Hmm," said Hauck.

Sveta moved, and Hauck grimaced and caught up to her.

"You've got to wait for me," he remonstrated.

She ignored him and kept on walking.

On past the amazing equipment that Drogol had accumulated over the years. Originally, this had been the storehouse of powerful men who collected these technologies to control them. They hadn't counted on Drogol coming along and claiming it for his own. Their bones were probably stacked up somewhere in some forgotten corner of this underground world.

This place was a virtual wonderland, she thought, and it was.

She hobbled on past it until, finally, tired but stubborn, she reached the cabin that Drogol had used as a centralized command center. Hauck was right by her side.

"Hey, Sveta, how's the leg?" asked Dr. Jimmy, who was fiddling at something with the computer.

"Better," she said.

"Let me get you a chair," said Hauck.

"No, I think I would prefer to lie down. Can you take me to my room?"

"I don't know where it is," said Hauck.

"Good. Yuri?" she said.

"I'd be pleased to," he said. "Follow me."

"But—" said Hauck.

"I'll manage just fine, Hauck, thank you. Yuri, lead on."

Hauck watched her nervously as she hobbled away.

"I tell you," he said, "that woman is the stubbornness woman I've met in all my life."

When Sveta was out of earshot, Dr. Jimmy spoke up.

"It's good that she's not around to hear this."

"Hear, what?" said Hauck.

"Professor Krikor Meridian is alive and well."

"Great."

"And he left you a message on the Internet," said Dr. Jimmy.

"What's that?"

"He said, and I quote: 'I will find you and feast on your bones.'"

CHAPTER TWO

Professor Meridian's All Seeing Eyes

Prof. Krikor Meridian looked at the assembled men before him. They were hard men, assembled from all over the world. But were they enough? No, he decided, they were not enough. He needed a khylsty from the tribe of Ivan the Terrible, and with a motive for killing. That was what he needed, and he would arrive within half an hour. That would make for a fitting end to Hauck and the Instructor. Of all the things he could not have foreseen in his wildest dreams was that the Instructor would be a werewolf. He should have killed him the moment that he walked into his house. He should have chopped off his head when he was in human form.

"You will all report to Akim," he began. "He should be here within the hour. Your assignment will be to find Hauck and to kill him. Also, you will find and kill the man named the Instructor, a short little man who is deadly. You will also kill anyone associated with them. Is that understood?"

One man in the back raised his hand.

"Yes, Heinrich?"

"Sir, how will we know what they look like if all we have are first names?"

Meridian found Heinrich to be an irritating man. It was true that he hadn't snapped a picture of him, but he had memorized every line, every feature of the man's face and his beautiful assistant, and the Instructor was engraved upon his mind. But he would wait until the khylsty arrived before he made that information available.

"You will wait until Akim arrives before I answer that question. He will have all pertinent information on the subject."

A woman raised her hand, this time in the middle of the group of twenty men and five women."Yes, Camila?"

"Do we have full authority to kill anyone that gets in our way?"

"Yes. You do."

The professor liked Camila. She got right to the point. Yes, he liked her very much indeed.

He was blind without the Book of the Dhole, which had been destroyed in the werewolf's rampage. That was another thing that he owed the instructor for; that book was centuries old. And now it was ruined beyond repair by the werewolf's claws. He had lost his magical edge and there was nothing to replace it.

And there was a special place reserved for Dr. Jimmy, Tricia, and Marty in hell. They had killed the Dhole, and that was unconscionable. The Dhole was his lifeline, his master, his very reason for being, and now it was dead. Yes, they would burn for their violation of all that he held dear, but first he had to find and destroy Hauck and the Instructor.

The khylsty would now have to be his eyes and ears, for they had special ways of seeing. The khylsty were true shamans. They had magical powers and would be a fitting match for a werewolf.

With his last words having been said, he departed the room. To his surprise, one person did not stay behind, waiting to meet Akim. Camila followed him out.

"Professor, a word with you," she said.

They were in what used to be a hanger built far away from Detroit City Airport. In fact, it was so far away that the airport had refused to claim it as their property when the thoughts of an expansion were shut down because of the City Council. Since then, it had been abandoned, except for the secret ownership of Professor Meridian's group. The hanger was subdivided into various conference rooms and separate rooms, for secretive meetings and special things. Hauck would never find him in the hangar.

"Yes?" he said and stopped walking.

Camila was a beautiful woman of Spanish descent who was as

lethal as an Indian krait. She had long, black hair that she wore to the side in a braid, an oval face, dark eyes, and a full, ripe mouth. All the right equipment for a lethal killer such as herself.

"I was wondering," she said, "if there was a bonus?"

"A bonus?"

"Yes, a bonus for the one who arranged for the death of Hauck and the Instructor?"

Professor Meridian stroked his chin and rearranged his eyepatch.

"Why yes, Camila, I think that could be arranged," he said.

"Good," she said, and turned and walked back into the meeting room.

She was definitely a young woman to watch. Professor Meridian checked his pocket watch. It was precisely nine o'clock at night. He looked up at the hangar door in time to open fully. A tall, thin man walked in. He was followed by six men carrying his assorted luggage and a large steel box. The tall thin man was dressed all in white, and had white hair that swept back beyond his temples. Four men struggled under the weight of the steel box, with four air holes on each side. The remaining two carried his luggage.

The professor waited where he was, waiting for the tall man to join them, while the other four men put down the steel box and the remaining two put down his luggage. The tall man walked over to them, stopped, and bowed. Professor Meridian bowed slightly at the waist and then straightened to look the man over.

The man had pale skin and pink eyes. He wore polarized glasses that changed color with the differing amounts of light he was exposed to, and even his eyebrows were pure white. He wore a white suit, and a white shirt, and white shoes. His overcoat was white. He was an odd-looking man. But there was something about his face that communicated not to tangle with the man, lest you get hurt.

"So good of you to come," said Professor Meridian. "Please, come with me."

"We will talk here," he said with a strange, not quite Russian, accent.

"Really?" said the professor.

"Yes, really," said Akim.

Professor Meridian glanced around and saw that they were by

themselves, save for a pair of workmen one thousand feet away.

"Very well," he said. "What have you to say?"

"You promised me the head of the one that killed my brother, Ivan."

"Yes."

"And five million dollars US in gold?"

"Yes."

"Good. Very good. Because I want the murderer of my brother badly."

"I understand," said the professor.

"Where shall my men put the chernobog?"

"Pardon?"

The professor glanced over at the steel box, finally understanding what Akim meant.

"You mean, you have actually brought a chernobog here?" he gasped in astonishment.

"I never repeat myself, professor, but I shall make an exception this once. Yes, I have captured and brought a chernobog with me. Now I repeat, where shall my men put the box?"

The professor had never thought such a thing possible. He had only vaguely read of the chernobog. Was it really possible? A chernobog? The professor had read that the Slavic people, according to Helmhold, engaged in rituals surrounding the chernobog, including passing bowls around in a circle, and whispering prayers to protect themselves from him. From Helmhold's writings, scholars had also learned that a chernobog was the personification of evil. He wore a dark cloak and appeared to be a devil.

Suddenly, a horrible scream split the night, and it came from the box.

Professor Meridian shuddered and then, as the scream faded, he smiled. This would be a fortuitous arrangement indeed.

CHAPTER THREE

The Instructor Teaches Sasah a Thing or Two

While Hauck mulled over what Professor Meridian had said, Dr. Jimmy continued on.

"I have to tell you, Hauck, this place is… well, wonderful. I can't conceive of what half of this stuff is, but I would love to try my hand at figuring it out."

"You'll have your hand at trying, doctor. Come, let me show you the single most important piece of equipment there is in this place."

"Sure," said Jimmy.

Hauck led the way through shattered equipment and broken glass, down the stairs, past the control boxes and finally up the stairs again to a raised platform with a shattered tube of more glass. It must have been eight feet tall, with a multitude of wires leading from it to a panel fitted with dials and gages.

"There must have been quite a fight here," said Jimmy.

"You don't know the half of it. Russian Mafiya fighting our Sveta, Zoe, and Drogol, and, of course, when the Mafiya shot this tube-" here he pointed to the broken tube laying on its side- "that was when Drogol turned into the King Werewolf and he went berserk. This tube was the only hope of turning Drogol into a normal man. Do you think you can fix it? Maybe return my son Sasha and the Instructor to normal men again?"

Jimmy got down on one knee and studied it. It was a large tube, big enough to fit two men inside—what was left of it. Jimmy picked up at a piece of the shattered glass and thought about it.

"It's awfully heavy for glass," said Hauck.

"Yes, I know. I think it's some kind of borosilicate. Or, maybe, a vanadium substitute."

"Can you duplicate it?"

"First, I've got to find out exactly what it is. I've never seen anything like this before. I'm just guessing that it's a borosilicate. So if you don't me taking a piece with me?"

"About that…" said Hauck.

"Yes?"

"I would feel safer if you didn't leave this place for a few weeks, doctor. While Professor Meridian is hunting for us, I don't think you would be safe."

"Well, why ever not?"

"Because, doctor," said Hauck, "you killed the Dhole. You remember that, don't you?"

Jimmy's thin face paled.

"Wait a minute- you think that because we killed the Dhole, that I'm in danger? That means Trisha is in danger, too."

"I was going to get to her next. Marty's gone to Angkor Wat in Cambodia for some discovery or other, so he's relatively safe. But as for Trisha, she's exposed."

"I've got to call her, to tell her where I am."

"No," said Hauck. "You can't do that. We don't know if she's already been compromised. Instead, let me send the Instructor and Sasha out to her house to pick her up. That way, we can be sure that she will be safe, and if she's compromised, we'll neutralize whosoever is compromising her. Trust me, it is for her own good."

"But what will she tell her employer? I don't even know if she has any time off at the NSA," he worried.

"She can tell them she has to attend to a personal emergency, and she will be back in about three weeks."

"Is that long enough to neutralize Meridian?"

"I hope so. Otherwise, I'm afraid her days at the NSA are over. And frankly, your days of freedom are over, too. He's a dangerous man, doctor, and neither Trisha nor yourself can protect yourself."

"Oh, God," said Jimmy.

"I'm afraid that He's got very little to do with it, doctor."

"Can't we somehow signal Trisha?"

"What we can do is get the Instructor and Sasha over to her house as quickly as possible."

"Okay, but hurry."

"Let's go find them."

Hauck and Jimmy found them over at a hole in the wall where the Instructor had blown it wide open with an explosive rocket.

"Hey, I was just showing Sasha one of the back ways in to this place that I made," said the Instructor.

The Instructor seemed entirely too happy to be back there. It was like old times to him.

"Oh yeah," said the Instructor, "you see that platform over there?"

Sasha rolled his eyes.

"You already told me—"

"That's where I cut off Drogol's head with my machete."

"Yes, well, I want you and Sasha to go over to Trisha's house, and watch to see if Meridian tries to acquire her there," said Hauck.

The Instructor thought about that.

"You really think he might?"

"We can't take a chance," said Jimmy.

"I didn't ask you, you pencil-necked geek, I asked Hauck."

"Yes, I do. That's all the more reason to have Trisha go down the rabbit hole to this place for three weeks."

"Yeah, but what if they try to snatch her before she gets to her house?" said the Instructor.

"He's got a point, much as I hate to admit it," said Sasha.

"Where does she live?" asked the Instructor.

Jimmy gave them the address. He looked worried. In fact, he was worried about Trisha.

"You ready for some action, junior?"

"I told you to quit calling me that," said a clearly agitated Sasha.

"Me and junior are ready," said the Instructor.

"Good," said Hauck. "Godspeed."

"Come on," said the Instructor, "let's go."

As the two of them headed for the door, Hauck thought back to when the Instructor had taken him under his wings. The Instructor was short, maybe four foot eleven. Arms that were as thick and corded as a braided cable. He had a bald head and a bandy legged walk. But he was the Instructor, so you wouldn't dare laugh at him.

He had been more brutal back then—he was brutal enough now—but back then, he had a punishment ethic that was simply off the charts. Hauck wondered if the old man would take Sasha and turn him around the way he had done Hauck.

Sasha had free flowing black hair, not tied back, shaggy almost. An almost tall body, but not quite. His nose was slightly crooked between a shelf of a forehead. No, that was not exactly right, but close enough. Gray eyes that were deep set beneath bushy, almost feminine eyebrows. A slim, yet muscular physique. Not the way Hauck had envisioned his son. But the eyes, the eyes were like his.

Hauck had shortish hair, salt and pepper in color. He had a wide forehead and firm eyebrows. His ears lay flat against his head and his eyes were gray. Yes, definitely like his son's. But Hauck had broader shoulders, and thicker arms. He was tall and had a narrow waist. And where his son's hands were more feminine, his hands were definitely more masculine. The legs, his were more powerful than Sasha's. Elements of him were scattered throughout Sasha's frame. It was hard to believe that he was his son. All those years alone, on the run, and he would've reached out to Sasha if he had only known.

Jimmy said, "I hope they get through to her in time. You've got me worried sick, Hauck."

When the Instructor opened the door, Sasha look back at Hauck, then followed the Instructor out.

"If anyone has a chance, it's the Instructor," said Hauck.

"I just feel so helpless," said Jimmy.

Hauck nodded his head at that. Sveta was so impetuous, possessed of such a fiery temperament, that Hauck constantly worried about her. He was worried that someday she would get shot, and now he realized he was determined to prevent that.

"I know what you mean," said Hauck.

"You do?"

"Yes, I do. Sveta is a ruthless adversary, but I am concerned for her that she doesn't carry it too far."

"I see, at least I think I see. Trisha is a good deal like that. But I can't stop her and ask her to be any other way."

Hauck could only shake his head at that.

"Hauck?" called Yuri.

"Yes, Yuri?"

"I ran a check on Meridian's name like you asked. This new system is fast, and with Brittany helping me, it's incredible. Come over here so you can see."

As Hauck and Jimmy approached the computer console, a round, three dimensional holographic projection shot into existence. It was of a young woman twenty-six years of age, freckles, red hair, and a slim figure.

"Hello, doctor." said Brittany. "Hauck, and a big hello to you, Yuri."

"Hello, Brittany. It's so nice to see you out of your box."

"I owe it all to Yuri," she said.

"Yes, so what do you have for us?"

"Well, I searched for the name Krikor on the Internet, and I came up with the ethnicity of West Armenian."

"West Armenian, eh?" said Hauck.

"Yes," said Brittany. "West Armenian."

"And the last name?" said Jimmy.

"That's a trifle more difficult," said Brittany.

"Yes?" said Jimmy.

"The nearest I can pin it down is to a town in Iberia, Spain. That's where the name derives from. The West Armenians take the name of a town or place and add the 'ians' to them. Hence the name Meridian. So we can logically deduce that his father came from Iberia, Spain, and the mother from West Armenia," she said proudly.

"No, I don't think that's what it is, Brittany," said Hauck. "The West Armenians also take their last name, if I'd not mistaken, from the father. But thank you for zeroing in on West Armenia as a point of origin."

"You're welcome," said Brittany.

"What does all this mean?" said Jimmy. "What difference does it make where he came from?"

"Any and all facts we can collect on him may make the difference between life and death, doctor. He is hunting us now with God knows what is at his disposal. Do you see?"

Jimmy looked crestfallen.

"All I can think of is Trisha out there alone with maybe him after her," he said.

Hauck hoped that the Instructor and Sasha would be in time.

****

The Instructor and Sasha drove to Trisha's house. It was to the north of Detroit, in a nice neighborhood.

"Wait," called Sasha, "we are going past it."

"What do you think, you moron, we're going to drive up to the front door and announce ourselves? Besides, didn't you see the blinds were half up around the front of the house?"

"So," said a clearly frustrated Sasha, "that doesn't explain nothing."

He threw up his hands defiantly.

"Well, did you ever think that was just a trifle odd?"

"No," said Sasha, just a little more cautiously this time, and he looked away to cover his shame.

But the Instructor whacked him on the back of his head.

"Look, you've got to pay attention. You see that car?"

"Don't hit me," said Sasha. "Yeah, okay, I see it. So what?"

"You see that guy in the front seat?"

"Yeah."

"Does he look like an unemployed lineman to you?"

"A what?"

And Sasha looked carefully at the man, which gave the opportunity for the Instructor to hit him in the back of the head again.

"Goddammit-"

"You don't stare at him, you dumb fuck. Jesus, didn't Hauck teach you anything?"

"Hauck wasn't there. I was there all by myself. Until he told me differently, I thought my real father was killed in the war."

They kept on driving down the street; the car faded into the rear-view mirror. When they had turned twice, the Instructor stopped the car.

"Look, I can't be babysitting you all day. I've got to take out that guy in the car that was outside of Trisha's house and then kill all the people inside. Are you with me, or are you going to keep acting like a dumb fuck?"

Sasha's response was to be sullen and stare out of the window.

"Look at me," commanded the Instructor.

Sasha turned his head to look at him. That's when the Instructor hit him square in the nose. Blood gushed out of his nostrils and Sasha put his hands to his nose.

"Good," said the Instructor, "that's what you get for being a little pussy."

"You hit me in the nose," said a disbelieving Sasha.

"Now that I've got your attention," said the Instructor, "I want you to reach into that glove box and bring out some tissues. I said now."

Sasha hurried up and did as he said. He found the tissues in the glove box as the Instructor said.

"What do I do with them?" asked Sasha.

"Duh—you put them on your nose to stop the bleeding, you dumbass. Christ on a pony, do I have to tell you everything?"

After a minute of fruitlessly trying to stop the bleeding, Sasha spoke up and said that the tissues weren't working. The Instructor thought for a minute, and then said, "You put your finger on this spot, right beneath your nostrils."

The young man looked exasperated, but willing to try anything. He reluctantly pressed on the spot, and sure enough, in a few seconds, the bleeding stopped.

"See? Now's this is where you say thank you."

"You punched me in the nose," Sasha said indignantly.

"You want me to punch you again?"

"No."

"Then say thank you," said the Instructor.

Sasha cringed when the Instructor raised his hand as though to strike him again, and said quickly, "Thank you."

"For what?"

"For stopping the bleeding," said a clearly confused Sasha.

"Oh that? That was nothing. Now we've got to figure out how to take out the driver of that one SUV. He's the key to this entire operation, but he's sitting there with no other cars around him and it's still broad daylight."

"Why don't we just drive by him and shoot him?"

"Of course. Why didn't I just think of that?"

This time, when the Instructor raised his hand, Sasha ducked.

"Nah, I was just fooling. Now look, dumbass, that doesn't work. What if you pull the trigger and he's got bullet proof glass? Did you ever think of that? Well, did you?"

"No."

"Good, now you're not being a pussy, making excuses for being wrong."

"But—"

"Anyway, here's the way I see it. I drive up next to their SUV, while you're hanging onto the outside edge—on the back of our SUV, you got it?"

"I don't see what—"

"And then, I'll engage the guy in conversation, savvy? You got that? Now, while I'm talking to him, you sneak up to the guy's door, open it, and then shoot him in the face. Then you take his radio or whatever and climb back into our SUV and we park at the next house over. You got that?"

"Wait a minute. What if he sees me and opens the door and shoots me?"

"Well, I never said the plan was perfect, did I?"

"What?"

"Hey, I'm in as much danger as you."

"But the glass in our car is bulletproof, and I assume the body is too—"

"Details, details. Is that all you can think about on such an important mission? Trisha is counting on us, and she don't even know it."

"Yeah, but—"

"Look, you don't want that poor girl getting killed when she comes home, do you?"

"What about me?" said Sasha.

"Your the hero in this story, champ. Didn't you ever want to give up your gangster ways and be a hero for once in your miserable little life?" asked the Instructor.

"I—" but then Sasha stopped and thought about it for a few seconds.

"All right," he said, "I don't know what I'm doing this for… but—"

"Hey, champ, you forgetting something?"

"What?"

The Instructor grinned and pulled a Beretta 9 millimeter 92X Performance out from beneath his coat and handed it to Sasha.

"Good hunting, kid. You might want to flip the safety to its on position first. Oh yeah, you might need this to keep the noise down, too. And you might want to take those papers out of your nose, because you don't need them anymore."

The Instructor handed him a noise suppressor, which Sasha affixed to the end of the barrel.

"Now good luck, kid. Hurry up, get out of the car."

CHAPTER FOUR

Professor Meridian and the Chernobog

Professor Meridian had four men staking out Dr. Jimmy's home and four men staking out Trisha's home. They were, he felt, the key to the operation—they were the only contacts of Hauck that he knew for certain. Eventually, Hauck would contact them. He was sure of it. It was only a question of when. But on the chance that they knew something, that was why he was having them abducted at their house.

He fiddled with his eye patch. It enraged him that the Instructor was still walking around while he had to wear a black patch over his eye. Fah! It was unacceptable.

Satisfied that it was on straight again, he looked in the mirror. He was, he thought, a handsome man who looked like he had only just turned sixty years old. The prime of his life, really. He still had jet black hair, a wrinkle-free face mercifully, and was six feet tall. His posture was still straight, and that was a blessing. His all black suit was tailored just so to fit his imposing frame. Yet, what was the use if he lacked a magical edge?

The Dhole, his whole life had depended on the Dhole coming back to life, and Hauck had put a stop to that. That was the key to his future power over the world, but Hauck and the blessed Instructor, Dr. Jimmy Harlen and Trisha, had killed it. He didn't know exactly how, but they had. And with that went all the power... unless, that is, unless he had a substitute. He could say that Akim and the chernobog were his right hand. It could work. All the contacts he had developed over the years of pursuing the Dhole's magical powers could be conferred on him—that was the way it was supposed to happen. But the Dhole had died at Hauck's hand.

He had heard the legends, vague though they were, of what the chernobog was, and what it could do. The mythology concerning the chernobog was a cross between Dracula and the devil. Supposedly he wore a black cape, too, when he traveled about, but that was about all that there was to know.

How Akim had trapped him in a box was beyond his understanding. What power did he hold over the chernobog that allowed Akim such mastery? He would have to find out.

The Book of the Dhole, that magical tome that read the future if consulted periodically, was destroyed in the werewolf's attack. It was shredded beyond repair. That was the Instructor's doing. The Dhole was dead and his magical book was reduced to mere scraps of paper. Unless he had the chernobog. Yes, he would have to find out what hold Akim had on him, how he forced a chernobog, as feared as it was, to do his bidding. Then, if he could not force Akim to be under his control, he would have to kill him. After, that was, after he had killed Hauck and the Instructor, after he had destroyed Dr. Jimmy Harlen and that Trisha, too.

A sudden knock at his door brought him out of his reverie.

"Yes, come in."

In came Akim, a striking figure by any standards. His white hair was swept back and away from his forehead, and he had red albino eyes. In his white suit, white shirt and white socks and shoes, he cut a striking figure. His skin, though, was the most captivating—it was a pale, white shade and even his eyebrows were white.

"I thank you for the money in advance of the contract being fulfilled, professor, it was much appreciated."

"Your entirely welcome. Have a seat, why don't you? You must be tired after all the many miles on the road."

Akim looked upon the luxuriously furnished apartment that sat nestled in amongst the warehouse and smiled. He selected a chair and sat, crossing his legs as he did so. Professor Meridian chose a matching wing-backed chair and sat down opposite him.

"Tell me about this Hauck and his Instructor," said Akim.

The professor steepled his fingers. He knew what he wanted to say, but he felt the need to embellish it a bit and see which way Akim played it, too.

"I knew your brother well, Akim. He was a fine man who did his craft well."

He waited to see the albino's reaction, but there was none, so he continued.

"As I said, Ivan was a fine addition to my team. In fact, if he had not been killed by the cowardly Sasha in werewolf form, he would have risen to the top of my organization."

"Wait, you say someone called Sasha killed Ivan? Why didn't you say so to begin with?"

"Because I had to have you here in person, so that I could tell you."

Professor Meridian studied the albino carefully. He waited for the professor, listened to what he had to say, and then seemed ready to listen more.

"Who is Hauck?" continued the Professor, "Hauck is the devil incarnate, and the Instructor is his handmaiden who does his bidding, and together they caused Sasha to bitten by a werewolf. While they watched, Sasha then transformed into the loup-garou and he tore your brother Ivan to pieces. So you see, all three men are responsible for your brother's death."

Akim nodded at the news. Remarkable, thought Professor Meridian. I have just told him of his brother's death, and he takes it as just another piece of news. He observed him carefully for telltale signs such as anger; he only saw a cold, simmering rage.

"But I haven't told you the most disturbing piece of information yet. It appears that Sasha is Hauck's son."

"What?"

"Oh yes. It appears that the doctor who performed the test deliberately mixed up the test results, making it appear as though Hauck was not the father, that Drogol was. But that was a lie, it was Hauck who was the father."

"Wait—Hauck tolerated his own son being bitten by a werewolf?"

"Not only tolerated, he caused the entire thing, at great peril to his son. Ivan, must I say, was his son's first meal."

Now the professor saw it—the first glimmer of a boiling rage taking hold of Akim. A slight narrowing of his eyes, a flaring of the nostrils. Yes, he had him now.

"There was nothing left of Ivan save bones. Nothing at all."

"Hauck, the Instructor, and Sasha," said Akim, "what do we have on them?"

"I've got men staked out at Dr. James Harlen's house and Trisha Dayton's house also to acquire them. They are our only clue as to how to get a hold of them. When they have been captured, they will be brought here for questioning. I assume you will handle the questioning yourself?"

Akim smiled an evil little smile.

"Yes, I should think that would be satisfactory," he said. "We will feed them to the chernobog after that."

CHAPTER FIVE

Trisha Comes Home to Chaos

Sasha hung onto to the back of the SUV for dear life.

The Instructor drove around thirty-five miles per hour, which Sasha tried not to think about. How did he ever get into this mess? One minute he was the son of the queen of the Russian Mafiya, the next in line, the organizatsiya builder. People reported to him, and yes, even feared him. He was Sasha, his mother's enforcer.

He was afraid of her—she could be a cold-hearted bitch—but he thought she felt something for him. That was until she had him Tasered and thrown into a cage by that son of a bitch Ivan.

The car stopped suddenly, and Sasha leapt off the back of the SUV, pulled his Beretta, affixed the suppressor to its barrel, took a deep breath and took off running to the other SUV, but Sasha heard the pfft pfft of silenced shots and stopped.

"Get his radio," barked the Instructor.

Sasha approached the car carefully, but when no shots rang out, he looked inside. One dead man was all he could see.

"And get his cell phone while you're at it. Hurry up, will you? I ain't got all day," said the Instructor.

The man in the car was tilted sideways with his head facing the front of the car, like a twisted mannequin. In the exact center of his forehead was a round hole. On the opposite, spreading across the seat, Sasha estimated there was a bloody mess. He opened the door and stuck his upper body inside. He tried not to look at the man's head as he felt around for the man's phone and his belt radio, neither of which presented itself. Where could they be?

"Hurry up, will ya?" yelled the Instructor again. "I haven't got all day."

Underneath him, he figured. They would be underneath him on the seat that he lay sprawled on. He unlocked the other side door, got out of the car, and went around to the other side. He opened the door, and seeing the man lying there, he picked him up so that his head fell to one side. Sasha glimpsed the man's shattered back half of his head and almost retched. He looked down at the last moment and saw the phone on the seat, covered in blood. Sasha hesitated, then said, "Fuck it" under his breath and picked the phone up by two fingers. He looked all around the dead man's body, even roughed the person up, but could find nothing.

"No radio," called Sasha.

"You got a phone?"

He held up the bloodied phone.

"Get in, and hurry it up," said the Instructor.

Sasha closed the door, walked around the SUV, and got in his own vehicle and shut the door. He was still holding the phone with two fingers. The Instructor took off.

"What should I do with the phone?" asked Sasha.

"Christ, do I have to tell you everything? First you wipe it off, and then you hold on to it. Now look, we've got to get next to Trisha's house and park the car out of sight. Any place good come to mind?"

He looked around for napkins in the glove box, found some, and wiped the phone down. Rolling down the window, he tossed the bloodied mess out the window.

"Nice going, champ," said the Instructor. "Do you know how much the fine is for littering here?"

"No."

"Well, let me put it to you this way—if you ever do anything so stupid again, I'm going to stomp your face in. You hear me? What if some policeman saw you do that, or what if some stupid YouTuber caught video of you doing that and contacted the police?"

"I—"

"Water under the bridge now, but be careful. Now, do you see any place where we can park?"

"How about there?" Sasha asked, pointing at an embankment at the back of the house.

"Yeah, now you're talking. I like it. See, you don't have shit for brains after all."

"Look, I don't have to—"

"You see our side of the house?"

"Sure, but—"

"They got blinds in place, and curtains covering the blinds."

"So what?"

"So that's the way we'll approach the house, dummy. C'mon now, load up and let's get going."

"But—"

"But what? Look, could they open the drapes and peek out the blinds and see us? Sure, but we'll have to take that chance. And we don't have much time until Trisha will get home and the cops start checking out his car and find a dead body in it. So, let's quit talking and get to it. You just follow me."

Reluctantly, Sasha got out of the SUV and followed the Instructor to the house. Their pistols were holstered as they approached the house casually. They took them out after seeing no one around, and the Instructor led the way to the back door, which he tried and found locked. Sasha watched as he took out a thin blade and shouldered his pistol.

"You watch over me, okay?" he whispered. "Anybody moves, you blast them. And put that suppressor on. Jesus, I do I have to tell you everything?"

As Sasha hurriedly affixed the suppressor onto the barrel of his pistol, the Instructor finished picking the lock, put away his blade, and taking out his own pistol, he gently pushed the door open. They found themselves in a small laundry room. The Instructor listened carefully before going any further. Nothing. And then, a small noise was dead ahead. Sasha waited nervously for the Instructor to make the call. Finally, he did, and advanced, with Sasha following close behind.

A man was making a peanut butter and jelly sandwich in the kitchen, his pistol lying on the countertop beside him. Surprised, the man looked up at them, dropped the jelly knife and reached for his pistol, but the Instructor shot him right between the eyes. The man fell forward onto the Formica countertop and then slid back onto the floor. Another man came into the kitchen, and before he could even raise his pistol, the Instructor shot him in the throat. He crumpled forward and dropped his pistol, trying fruitlessly to stop the bleeding with both hands. The Instructor moved to the dining room.

Sasha had seen nothing like it. The eighty-four-year-old man was a killing machine. He didn't hesitate, and he moved like a young man. It was incredible. His pistol wasn't needed. He was just along for the ride.

The dining room was connected to the living room, and the Instructor stopped there to listen. Suddenly, he whipped around the corner, dropping until he was only two feet of exposed man. He fanned the area, but nothing caught his attention until he heard the bathroom flush on the second floor. Then he took the stairway two steps at a time, catching even Sasha by surprise.

A key turned in the front door lock, just as the Instructor made it to the second floor and two quick, suppressed shots were fired. Trisha backed into her front door with bags full of groceries in her arms. She turned and started when she saw Sasha with his pistol out and stopped. He quickly took off his suppressor and holstered it.

"You remember me? I am Sasha. We are—"

"Hey, Trisha," broke in the Instructor from the top of the stairs.

"What is the meaning of this?" said Trisha.

"You don't want to go upstairs. There's a body up here."

"A what?" said Trisha.

"Look," said the Instructor, "these four guys were waiting to kidnap you, and they're all dead now. We don't have a lot of time. We've got to take you to Hauck and Dr. Jimmy, so leave your groceries and let's get going."

"Wait a minute, you're not just going to leave their dead bodies here at my house," said Trisha.

"Please, we've got to hurry. There may be more of them on the way," said Sasha.

"Yeah, like the kid says. Come on, we've got to hurry."

"But I—"

"Dr. Jimmy's waiting for you, and we don't have a lot of time."

"Do I have time to pack?" asked Trisha.

"Every second's delay gives time for Professor Meridian's men to get here," said the Instructor, "so short form answer is no. Sasha will ride with you in your car, and I'll follow behind in the SUV. Let's go."

"Please," said Sasha.

"All right," said Trisha.

She didn't know why, but she turned and walked back out the door with Sasha in tow. He looked back over at the Instructor as he left. The Instructor smiled encouragingly.

Then, he went out into the garage, got some gasoline and returned to the house and began to systematically splash it around the house. He took a lighter out of one of his many pockets, sparked it to flame, and lit the gasoline on fire. Quickly, he exited by the back door, got in the SUV, turned the key in the ignition, and drove away. In the rear-view mirror, flames were already consuming the house.

"Well," he said with a chuckle, "you used to have a place to live."

****

"You what?" said Trisha.

The Instructor looked surprised.

"I torched the place," he said. "What are you so upset about?"

"So upset about? So upset about? I'll tell you what I'm so upset about—that was my house you burned down. I lost everything, everything."

Jimmy tried to comfort Trisha by putting his arm around her, but she pushed him away.

Yuri turned away to keep from laughing. Hauck was already resigned to what was coming next. Sasha seemed vindicated and Sveta, well, she was as furious as Trisha.

"You could at least given her time to pack her things so that she could have something to wear," said Sveta.

The Instructor, ever nonplussed, said, "Maybe next time you could let her pack, huh? We had to kill four men that were waiting for her at that house, and we didn't know when there could be more coming. So we had to get out of the house as fast as possible and torch it so that there wouldn't be any clues for them to follow."

"But did you have to burn everything?" demanded Trisha. "Every single blessed thing? I've got nothing. I have only the clothes on my back."

"So? You buy new ones. Christ on a pony, I've never seen a bunch of whiny babies."

Sveta hobbled over to where Trisha was standing. Trisha looked like she was going to cry.

"I told you he was an evil little prick," said Sveta.

"Yeah, well, whatever," said the Instructor.

"Well, what do I do for clothes?" asked Trisha.

"We'll go shopping. Yuri will come, too."

Yuri was about to object, but one look at Sveta's face told him it was pointless.

"Yuri, get the SUV," said Sveta.

Just then, Charlene came in to join the group. Until then, she had been fiddling with the new laptop that Jimmy had brought her.

"Did I hear shopping?" she said. "I'm up for it. I'll go with."

"Good, that settles it," said Sveta. "And Hauck, not a word from you about me not going, because I'm not well. Besides, if I tire, I'll have Charlene and even Trisha to lean on."

"I wasn't going to say anything," said Hauck. "But Sveta?"

"Yes?"

"Take some guns with you, will you?"

When they were gone, the Instructor said, "Touchy, ain't she?"

"Well," said Jimmy, "you did just torch everything she held dear to the ground."

"No choice," said the Instructor with a shrug.

"He didn't have," said Sasha. "That's why he stopped her car after we had gone a mile or so and abandoned it, and had us ride in the SUV. In case they already had a tracker in her car, right?"

"Yes," said Hauck. "You see Jimmy, we just couldn't take a chance. That's why the Instructor abandoned her car in such a seedy part of town, so they would strip it down and sell the parts."

"I told her we would go back and get it later," said the Instructor. "She was freaking out as it was."

"You did the right thing," said Hauck. "She'll come around."

Jimmy was silent for a minute and then said, "Yes, I guess so. But still…"

"Look, you want her dead? Cause that's what you could be looking at if we wasted one more minute at that house than was called for. Period. And as for her car, well, that's the breaks. We didn't have anymore time to fiddle with it to see if there was a tracker on that car, do you understand?"

Jimmy looked to Hauck, who seemed to agree with the Instructor.

"Well, why didn't you burn down my house, too?"

The Instructor grinned at him.

"Bait."

CHAPTER SIX

The Glass Tube

The Instructor threw Rasputin, Sveta's giant wolf, another piece of meat. He gobbled it down.

"Now don't say I never gave you nothing."

Hauck looked over at the Instructor and then at Dr. Jimmy, who was deep in Drogol's notes.

"Did you find anything yet?" he asked.

"Come on," said the Instructor. "You asked him that same question less than an hour ago. Why don't you just say that you're nervous because Sveta's been gone like three or four hours."

"Actually, I have found something," said Jimmy. "Tesla theorized that the human body is comprised of vibrations, or rather, he found that the human body reacts to a creative lifetronic force. This life force, he hypothesized, was vibratory in nature. It was subtle, though, and would only respond to delicate vibrations. In other words, we have to supply the etheric vibrations to the body to achieve all sorts of results. He gave a chart with the desired outcomes and the etheric vibrations. What your Drogol did was to extrapolate the values with the established harmonics of the human body. Fascinating."

"Yes fascinating," said the Instructor, "but what the hell does that mean?"

"It means that I think there's hope," said Jimmy.

"You think I can be a normal human being again?" said Sasha.

"Yes, Sasha, if I can reconstruct the tube that Drogol used, I think you can be returned to a normal human being. Mind you, I said, I think. But there will be risks, because I've never done this before. There's no way to test it either except on human subjects. In other words, there are no guarantees."

"But what are the chances?" said Hauck.

"Well," said Jimmy, "like I said, Hauck, it's going to be a fifty-fifty tossup. There is no way really to tell how effective it will be, or if it will cause any effects whatsoever. I just don't know without a lot of testing."

"How long would that take?" asked Hauck.

"It could take years to get a definitive result. Even then, the type of testing we would have to do would require many werewolves to test it on. And unfortunately, we only have two."

Hauck knew that Doctor Jimmy was right. He didn't have anywhere else to turn, though. Drogol knew that the tube was his only chance. So desperate was he for the cure that he was willing to take a chance with his own life.

Rasputin whined for more meat. The Instructor looked around to see if anyone was looking, and threw him another piece.

"I'm willing to take the chance," said Sasha.

"Are you?" said Jimmy.

"Yes, I am. You don't know what it's like to be transformed, you just don't know."

"What about you?" said Hauck to the Instructor.

The Instructor looked down at his feet for a moment before answering. It was a hard decision for him.

"So the first guy is a guinea pig, am I right?" said the Instructor.

"I guess you could look at it like that," said Jimmy.

"Huh."

"I won't lie to you," said Jimmy. "I don't think this will be dangerous, but we're going to be fooling with the molecular structure that makes up what we are as a human being. Do you understand?"

"Yeah, I got you," said the Instructor.

"What are you thinking?" asked Hauck.

"I was thinking that maybe I ought to be the first one to try it."

"I see."

Now, Hauck could see what the Instructor was planning. He was going to be the first to try the transformation. If anything went wrong, he would take the hit. The Instructor was old now, eighty-five if Hauck remembered correctly, and he thought that was only appropriate.

"On the other hand," said the Instructor, "since I got bit by the werewolf, I feel fantastic. I feel young again. So how long do you figure a werewolf will live? Drogol was nearly two hundred years old. Look, so what if I've got to spend three or four nights per month locked up? What's the big deal? You guys lock me up, and I howl for a few nights and that's that. So what?"

Well, thought Hauck, so much for chivalry.

"Are you crazy?" said Sasha. "I would give my right arm just to live as a normal man."

"Yeah, well, speak for yourself, kid. When you're as old as I am, you might think differently. I only got like twelve years left to live and the bulk of that is as a doddering old fool. But now, because I've been bitten by a werewolf, I got like what, another hundred years added to my life? Naw, no thank you, I think I'll stay exactly as I am. You're on you own, slick."

"I understand," said Jimmy.

"You do?"

"Yes, I do. Sasha, you want me to continue?"

"Yes, please," said Sasha.

It occurred to Hauck that if the vibrational tube could make a man who was a werewolf not a werewolf, could it actually turn a normal man back into a werewolf? It wasn't the intention of the inventor of the tube, who was Tesla, or of Drogol, who changed it for this use, but was it possible? What else could a man be modified to be?

"All right, then. By the way, Hauck, it's made of ordinary borosilicate, so it shouldn't be hard to machine. In fact, I will look around for samples of the glass to work with in the machine shop here. Have I told you how wonderful this place is?"

"Sasha, go with the doctor, please," said Hauck.

"Yes, come with me Sasha," said Jimmy, "and we shall go on the great borosilicate hunt."

Hauck watched Jimmy and Sasha head off, and he turned to face the Instructor.

"Yeah?"

"I was just wondering if you had thought this through is all," said Hauck.

"Sure I have. What's there to think about? I've decided, and that's that."

"Okay."

"What, you think I shouldn't want to live?"

"I didn't say that."

"Go ahead, say it. Just say what's on your mind. Spit it out."

"Nothing, I was just wondering is all."

"Goddammit, just say what you really mean. Come on, out with it."

"All right. I was just wondering if it was worth it, is all. A few extra years of life for your… your soul."

"My soul? Shit."

Hauck chose his next words carefully. He was treading on unknown territory here. The Instructor, though, seemed open to what he was saying.

"Look, don't you feel different?"

"Yeah," said the Instructor, "I feel healthier, better. I feel like I'm twenty years old again."

"Don't you wonder if there's a price to pay for that?"

There it was, now out in the open. There was always a price to pay for everything. Sasha was young, and yet he instinctively felt that there was a price to pay and he wanted nothing to do with it. Sometimes, wisdom was with the young. The elderly wanted to hang on to life at all costs.

"Nah. You think too much."

Hauck had to smile at that, for now. The Instructor was the Instructor.

Suddenly, Rasputin lifted his head and tore off toward the entrance. Sveta was back, being helped by Trisha and Charlene, while Yuri carried the bags. That wolf could scent Sveta a million miles away. Hauck saw Sveta, and he smiled. Sveta looked up at Hauck and she smiled, too. Suddenly, Hauck had the feeling that everything would be all right.

He forgot all about Professor Meridian, and he didn't know about Akim and the chernobog.

****

Charlene found life with Hauck and Sveta fascinating. She spoke to Yuri about it frequently. At first he seemed reluctant to talk about them, but he gradually opened up. She found Sasha cute, too, but he didn't seem to have time for her. He was too busy being bossed about by the Instructor.

"This is exciting," she said to Yuri.

"What?"

"You know, Dr. Jimmy found a replacement borosilicate tube. He's machined it so that it will fit into the Tesla device, and, well, we're off to the races. Sasha could be a normal person by the end of the day."

"Or," smiled Yuri, "he could be dead."

Charlene glared at him. Of all the times in his life, you'd think he would be happy for them. It would be a success like they never dreamed possible.

"Dr. Jimmy warned of the consequences. We haven't tried it on any human subjects yet. And here's another downer—we don't even know if it works. Last time it was experimented on was someone named Drogol, and he turned into the King of all Werewolves. I'm not saying that it was the machine's fault, because it was all shot up during the firefight with Mishka's men. I think Zoe fell on the control lever when she took a bullet. But that's all beside the point. It hasn't been tested."

"Jesus," said Charlene, "well I didn't know all that. Now I wish I hadn't talked to you."

Charlene and Yuri were sitting down on the control panel near Trisha, Sveta, and her giant Siberian wolf. Up on the platform were Jimmy, Sasha, and Hauck. The Instructor sat one step removed from everyone, wanting to appear disinterested, yet fascinated enough to keep an eye on the proceedings. Charlene watched, now nervous about the outcome, as Jimmy explained the risks to Sasha.

"Now, I'm going to start slowly with increasing the vibrations, okay? We've only got Drogol's notes to go by, after all, and we're not even sure they were all that sane. You got that? Good. Now, I'm going to gradually increase the vibrations, like I said, taking them one step at a time, monitoring what it does to you."

"Yes, you have explained that to me many times, doctor."

Jimmy frowned.

"I just want you to understand that I don't know what this technology will do to you. Hauck, do you understand that this is something to which there is no experimental evidence?"

"Yes, Jimmy, for the hundredth time, I understand. But you've got to understand how desperate Sasha is to return to normal. And there are no other werewolves that I am aware of to experiment on. And my son is a grown man, capable of making his own choices. I honestly don't know what I'd do in his shoes. We just will have to trust that our good friend Drogol knew what he was doing and pray for the best outcome."

Jimmy looked from Sasha to Hauck and back again. They were resigned to the outcome, whatever it was. He was not so sure. Glancing at Trisha, she nodded at him. Resigned, he smiled and returned to his work. The excitement that he had found a replacement borosilicate tube, no three of them, that could be machined down to his tolerances was amazing. He was ecstatic. And the repairs to the control module had been minor by his standards. The power-generating system down here was truly amazing. Jimmy didn't understand it yet—it was prepared by the great Nikola Tesla himself—but he would. And how did this wonderful world go all this time undiscovered? It made no sense.

But enough stalling.

He looked one more time at Trisha, and she understood. He glanced at Sveta and she nodded, too. He looked at Charlene, who seemed awash in indecision, and Yuri, who shrugged. When he looked at the Instructor, though, he got his final approval. A slight nod of his head was all he did, but it was enough. If Sasha truly wanted to be returned to normal, then this was his best chance. What he didn't see was that the reason that the Instructor had sat apart. It was so that he could conceal the Danline Tranquilizer Dart Gun, and the SIG Sauer Semi Automatic MCX Rattler with silver tipped mercury bullets, too. The Instructor was prepared for anything, although he didn't show it.

"Okay, get in the tube. Do you want to goodbye to anyone?" said Jimmy.

"Yes," Sasha said. To the Instructor he said, "Goodbye, asshole. See you on the other side."

To Hauck, he took a little longer, and it seemed a little more awkward.

"Look, I don't really know you, but you saved me from Professor Meridian and now you've given me the chance to be free of this curse, so I guess... I mean..."

"Good luck, son," said Hauck.

"Yes, that's what I meant to say."

"Good, now will you hurry and get in the tube before I change my mind about doing this whole thing?" said Jimmy.

Sasha grinned and stepped into the tube. It was altogether about eight feet tall and with a diameter of about four feet. Jimmy swung the door to the tube closed, it clicked into place and Sasha looked for all the world like a giant specimen encased in a test tube.

Jimmy next stepped down from the platform, with Hauck following him, and together they walked over to the control panel.

"Well, here goes nothing," said Jimmy, as he flicked the manual switches on the control panel.

"I hope not," said Hauck.

The panel board lit up as Charlene gasped and Sveta reached out and squeezed her hand, then let go. Jimmy watched some gages and then turned a rheostat up a small amount. When no changes were seen, he turned it up some more. Through the top of the tube, a micro-vibration could be seen to distort Sasha's features. All eyes were on Sasha, who stood in the tube erect, but a little nervous. As Jimmy increased the frequency, he paused at every interval to see what effect it was having on him.

He kept turning the dials as Sasha twisted and rotated, and the micro vibrational field kept descending upon him. Jimmy was fascinated by the tourbillion-like movement of its descent. It seemed to progress down the young man like a slow motion whirlwind. Colored waves cascaded down his face, his chest and his legs as though they had a mind of their own. Sasha shook uncontrollably.

Jimmy checked the rheostat. They were at the halfway mark, with fifty percent left to go. Ever so slowly, he turned the knob. He glanced over his shoulder at Hauck, who stood there impassively. The man must have nerves of steel. That was his own son that they were essentially running an experiment on, and yet he stood there leaning up against a post, calmly watching as his son was running through the demented process. Now, Sasha's whole body was blurry, but Jimmy still had to go twenty-five percent of the way further.

It was sheer torture watching Sasha contort under the ululating waves of vibrational force. Jimmy didn't know whether to shut it down or play it to the end. He looked toward Trisha, but she was fixated on Sasha. He pushed the limit and prayed to Jesus, please don't let this boy die, please. Sasha wrenched in place, and Jimmy closed his eyes. Please don't let anything happen to this young man. He opened his eyes and saw that it was right at the mark it was supposed to be. He looked up at Sasha, who had spun around again as though in a blender.

How long was he supposed to leave him at that mark? Jimmy didn't care. He shut down the micro-vibrational tourbillion as slowly as he could stand it. It seemed to take forever to go down. But the blur that was Sasha didn't immediately stop. Oh, please God, please make it stop. He shut off the rheostat completely and rushed up to the top of the stairs with Hauck hot on his heels.

Sasha quit spinning at last. He slumped against the side walls of the tube and collapsed.

CHAPTER SEVEN

The Chernobog

Professor Krikor Meridian slammed his fist down on his desk in frustration. Akim sat directly across from him, his ever-watchful eyes fixed on him.

"Four good men down," he raged. "Four, and still Hauck and the Instructor run free. They shot them and then burned the house down."

"Which house?"

"What?"

"I said, which house did they burn down? The woman's or the man's?"

"The woman's."

"Interesting," said Akim.

"Interesting? Is that all that you have to say is interesting? Four of my men are dead and that's all you have to say?"

"I would say that it is time to let the chernobog loose to find him."

Akim stood then, and Professor Meridian was again impressed by the sense of dread that the man gave off, almost like a tangible thing that you could feel.

"Come, it is long past time when you meet the chernobog," said Akim.

There it was again, that odd sense of distant superiority. Professor Meridian decided to be very careful about how he treated this killer. Perhaps he should do a little more research into the khylsty. As far as he knew, they were the holy men of Siberia who only killed when they had a reason. Ivan, he understood. He hated Drogol, the werewolf man, because he had deserted their order when he was afflicted by the bite of the werewolf. It was his mission to track him down and destroy him. The money was secondary to him.

But Akim gave off a different energy. It was lethal and cold, like Ivan's, but he seemed to be testing him. And the money, the five million dollars in gold for the head of Hauck and the Instructor, and all of those associated with him, he wondered about that, too. At the time, he had been so enraged with the destruction of all those Sanzars and Abarrans, created by the Book of the Dhole, and his having to hide for his life, locked in that underground room—he shuddered with rage when he thought of that—that he had gladly paid the five million in gold, but now he wondered. What would Akim do with all that money?

Akim turned on his heel and walked out of the room, and Professor Meridian followed. As they walked down the hallway, the professor made a note to check out Akim more carefully. If the khylsty ever suspected that he was being checked out, however, there would be hell to pay. He tried to think how many people he could trust in Siberia, truly trust among the tribesman.

He followed the Siberian down the hallways, down the doglegs, until he came to a door that he knew well. It was an old motor pool door that had not been opened in years.

"A suitable place for the chernobog," he said approvingly.

"Yes," said Akim.

The door was locked and chained. Akim took out a key from his pocket and unlocked the bond, and let the restraining chain swing free. He then pocketed the key.

Before he opened the door, he gave Professor Meridian the once over.

"Now, professor, you are about to meet the chernobog, yes? A word of warning, though, first. You must never, I repeat, never turn your back on him. Do you understand?"

The professor nodded impatiently, almost peremptorily. This ridiculous show was for the weak minded.

"I see you have not grasped the solemnity of the occasion. What is the name of one of your most trusted allies?" said Akim.

Professor Meridian thought for a minute. Finally, he decided on a name. Heinrich. Yes, indeed.

"Heinrich," he said.

Akim smiled.

"No, professor, give me the real name."

"All right. Camila is my choice for loyalty and determination."

"Good. Then call Heinrich and Camila over here, if you please," said Akim.

What would Akim want with them both? Finally, though, the professor did as he was bid.

"Heinrich. Camila. I want you both over here," he called.

They both came over.

Heinrich was a portly man for a killer. He was known, however, for his excellent work with a gun. Balding, a trim mustache and a slack face, a pot-belly, he was every woman's worst nightmare. Camila was the opposite. She was trim and youthful, with short hair and a beautiful face. She had a narrow waist, firm breasts and was only five foot six inches tall, but she radiated a kind of animal power.

"Yes," said Heinrich.

Professor Meridian turned to Akim. He was curious to see this play out. What on earth would he wish that both of them could experience?

"Come," said Akim, opening the door, "and meet my chernobog."

The lights were out in the room, so that only the open door provided light to see by and all was in darkness. Akim and Professor Meridian entered the room first, followed by Heinrich and Camila. They stood there for a moment, shrouded in darkness and eerie quiet.

"There doesn't seem to be anything here," objected Heinrich.

But then, almost as soon as he had spoken, a man who shimmered in the enfolding darkness stepped out. Shackled hands and feet, He yet walked with dignity. A prominent forehead and black hair swept back from his head in the European manner. He was tall and slender, with an almost muscular build. Black clothes were all that he wore; black coat, black shirt and black pants were his entire ensemble.

"Hello," said Akim. "I would like to introduce you to Heinrich and Camila."

"How do you do?" said the chernobog, with a vaguely Eastern

European accent.

"Yes, hello," said Heinrich.

But Camila said nothing. Some long-lost faculty was broadcasting a warning to her to be silent. That this man represented a danger that she could not see or taste or hear or even touch was nagging at her subconscious. Her hand stole silently to the Springfield Armory Hellcat 9mm Micro-Compact 13-Round Pistol holstered at her hip. The chernobog seemed to notice and smiled at her with a mouth that seemed vaguely cruel.

The professor was oddly aware that he had not been introduced to the chernobog, but he, too, kept silent. The tension seemed to build in the room, like an invisible noose tightening around their necks.

"What would you have me do, Akim?" asked the chernobog.

"First, let's take the chains off you, shall we? Camila, I would like you to remove the chains from him, if you please," said Akim.

Camila shook her head "No."

"Camila."

This time, Akim's voice was more forceful. Professor Meridian did not like where this was going. But he knew enough to keep quiet.

"I will unchain him," volunteered Heinrich.

Akim looked long and hard at Camila and then shrugged.

"Very well," he said and gave the key to the lock to Heinrich.

Heinrich strode over to the chernobog as though there was nothing to be afraid of, and when the chernobog offered his hands to him, he unlocked them. Next, however, came his feet, and Heinrich pulled out his holstered weapon and gave him the key.

"Unlock your own damn feet," he said. "I am not a fool."

Heinrich backed off a few feet. The chernobog smiled understandingly. He bent down and unlocked his feet. The chains fell away from him entirely. Heinrich kept his pistol trained on him.

"Now what?" said Heinrich.

"You may put your weapon away, Heinrich. You won't need it."

Professor Meridian watched with interest. He was not sure what game Akim was playing. He half considered, perhaps, it was his morbid streak, that the chernobog would kill and eat Heinrich.

Reluctantly at first, Heinrich did as he was told. Akim gave a nod to the chernobog and suddenly, the man was a vaporous mist that enveloped Heinrich. Camila reached for her pistol, but Akim laid his hand on hers and merely shook his head. As the mist completely surrounded Heinrich, Heinrich screamed and twisted. Men came running from the surrounding area, but stopped when they saw Professor Meridian's hand out. Akim did not look about, but kept his eyes fixed on the spectacle unfolding before their eyes.

The smoke that wrapped itself like a glove around Heinrich's body convulsed, and Camila could see the vaguest of outlines of the chernobog with his suddenly sharp teeth fixed on Heinrich's neck, sucking the lifeblood and fluids out of him. Camila watched in horror, unable to take her eyes off of him. Heinrich's face seemed to collapse in on itself. In fact, his whole body seemed to writhe and contort until it was an empty shell of himself. The chernobog grew clearer, as the now lifeless body of Heinrich was thrown away like so much used garbage.

Finally, the chernobog stood alone as the smoke disappeared. With the back of his hand, he wiped the bloody mess from his chin. And then he smiled, a cold, lifeless smile.

Akim turned to the assembled men outside the door.

"Listen to me, everyone of you. Today, we lost four men and our enemy got away. That will not happen again. Do you all, each one of you, understand?"

Slowly, the men nodded, as did Camila.

"Camila will be the chernobog's liaison. What she tells you, you will do. She will control the chernobog in all matters. Should one of you disobey or fail her, then what you saw here tonight will happen to you. Is that understood?"

Again, quicker nods.

"Now, we will begin the hunt for our adversaries. The chernobog will sniff them out, wherever they are. They shall not escape us. Now go to your rooms and get some rest. In the morning, we begin the hunt."

Akim held on to Camila's arm as the others departed.

"Why in such a hurry, Camila? Now you shall truly meet the chernobog."

Professor Meridian was shocked, but pleased, very pleased. Finally, a match for the Instructor and Hauck. Finally, he would get his revenge. He noticed that the chernobog was smiling at him.

CHAPTER EIGHT

Sasha Recovers

Charlene sat by the bed that Sasha lay on, monitoring him to see if he would wake up. Sveta and Trisha were in Sveta's room, Sveta with her leg propped up on the bed, three pillows underneath her foot. Out by the platform, Yuri and the Instructor walked around the tube's platform, talking. And Jimmy and Hauck stood by the control panel, each wrapped in their own thoughts.

"What do you think the chances are that it will work?" asked Hauck, after what seemed like eons.

"I honestly don't know," said Jimmy. "I didn't expect him to go into a coma after being exposed, that's for sure. Are you certain we shouldn't take him to a hospital?"

"No, he knew the risks. Besides, it's too risky to go to the hospital with him. If Professor Meridian should find out where he is, we couldn't protect him. It's really out of the question to take him there."

Hauck sounded cold, but Jimmy knew that inside, he was hurting. He tried to imagine what it would be like to have a son that you didn't know about for all those years. It must be like having a hole open suddenly before you and falling in.

"Thank you for what you did, Jimmy."

Hauck extended his hand to Jimmy and Jimmy, although he didn't know what he had done. He preferred to wait awhile for the results of the Tesla tube. Reluctantly, he shook his hand.

Just then, Charlene shouted, "He's awake. Sasha's awake and

feeling fine."

Jimmy and Hauck exchanged glances, then hurried up to where Sasha was sitting up on the edge of a cot.

"See, I told you he would be okay," said Charlene.

Trisha and Sveta came up right after that, and Sasha nodded at them weakly from his bed.

"How are you feeling?" asked Trisha.

"Like I've been run over by a Mac truck," said Sasha.

"But other than that?" said Sveta.

A weak smile from Sasha. He looked up at Sveta, almost grateful to be alive.

"I'm fine, thanks to Dr. Jimmy."

Jimmy seemed hesitant to accept the praise. He still couldn't accept that it had actually worked. But Sasha seemed okay. The young man was in good health, and that surely helped. His long hair tumbled down to his shoulders, and seemed dirty, in need of washing, but other than that, he seemed fine.

"I'm glad you're okay, Sasha," was all that Hauck could think to say. "But two nights from now —"

"I know. Into the cage I go."

At that moment, Yuri and the Instructor came in.

"Hey, well, you made it," said Yuri. "I always knew you would."

Here, Yuri winked at Charlene, who just scowled back at him.

"So, you made it through the whole mess, huh?" said the Instructor. "How do you feel, kid?"

Sasha brightened considerably that the Instructor was paying an interest in him.

"I'm feeling fine. A little tired, I guess, but other than that, okay."

"You ready to go in the cage?"

"Yes, I guess so."

"No guess about it, Pancho. You'll got in the cage for three nights to make sure, you understand?"

"He understands," said Hauck.

"No, I want to hear him say it."

Sasha flashed red hot for a moment. Who was this little man, anyway, who kept pushing him around? Why did he always have to keep pushing at him? But gradually, under the Instructor's unrelenting stare, he broke. He understood.

"Yes, I understand," he said.

"Good, because you're going to be in that cage listening to me howl for three nights, whether or not you like it. Jimmy and Hauck and all the rest of these people may be convinced that you're cured, but not me. I want to see what you turn into on the full moon."

"Hey, lay off the kid," said Sveta.

"I'll cut you some slack, girlie, because you're recovering, but what makes you think that radiation has not turned him into something far worse than he was before? Jimmy is thinking the same thing, aren't you, Jimmy? Don't bother denying it. I can see it in your eyes. Am I wrong? Because tell me right now if I'm wrong."

All eyes turned to Jimmy. It was an uncomfortable feeling. Hauck was unreadable, but the others were alarmed.

"I... just don't know," said Jimmy. "I mean theoretically, Drogol's calculations were correct. They certainly seemed to be correct, but you've got to understand—there was simply no way to check them out."

"We've been through all this before," said Hauck patiently. "Enough."

"Just remember to make sure that the cage is bolted nice and tight, you hear me? Nice and tight."

And with that, the Instructor was gone.

"He's nice and cheery," said Yuri.

"Don't worry about it, Sasha. You're going to be fine," said Charlene.

But Hauck looked after the Instructor and wasn't so sure.

****

Hauck walked Sveta back to her bedroom, careful to keep out of the way of her cane. When they arrived, Sveta climbed into bed while Hauck plumped up the three pillows that she had earlier used to put her foot on, and placed it on again.

"You're okay?" he asked her.

"I'm fine," she said. "How about you?"

"I'm okay, too."

"Goddammit, you're lying to me again, just to keep me from worrying. Now sit down, and tell me what's really on your mind."

He looked around the room uncomfortably.

"I should let you sleep," he said.

"You should sit your ass down and explain it to me. So sit."

Hauck was uncomfortable with this, but he sat in the chair at the head of the bed.

"Before you start, you've been treating me like a china doll since I got attacked by that mass of pop-up killers. And it's not that I don't appreciate, but you've got to stop it. I've got to know what's going on around here. I can almost walk again without help, and I'm ready to be cut into the action. What gives with Sasha?"

"You really want to know?"

"Yes, I really want to know. I wouldn't ask if I didn't."

"All right, what's got me bothered is this—the Instructor is rarely wrong. I know, I know, he's a pain in the ass to work with—and that's on a good day—but he's rarely wrong. If he's worried about Sasha, then so am I."

"That's it?"

"And I've got a bad feeling about this, too, Sveta. A terrible feeling. I don't know how to describe it, but yes, something's bothering me about this whole thing and I don't know what. It's got something to do with Drogol, but I can't put my finger on it. Drogol set the machine where he thought it would cure him. Is that how it went, Sveta? You've got to tell me, because I wasn't there."

Sveta thought back. It seemed like a long time ago. She tried to imagine just how it had happened in her mind.

"It was like this," she said. "You got the first part right. He set the dials in the places where he thought it would cure him. And then Zoe was supposed to goose it up to that location, but then Zoe got shot and fell on the control mechanism, which took it way past where it was supposed to go—to the limit, I think."

Hauck thought for a minute.

"What if," he finally said, "Zoe was supposed to do something else to the mechanism before the end of his exposure?"

"I suppose that's possible, but we'll never know, will we? Zoe was dead when she fell on the switch."

"And that is the basis of my conundrum. What was it that turned Drogol into a raging King of the Werewolves? Was it just that he was fed too much energy from the Tesla tube, or was Zoe killed before she could complete her assigned duties that would make the transition to a regular human being complete? I don't know if that's what's bothering the Instructor, but that's what's bothering me. Do you think that I'm worrying too much?"

Sveta reached out and took Hauck's hand. It was very warm to the touch.

"If I thought you were worried too much, I would tell you. It's been bothering me, too. The way that he spun around in that machine like he was in a giant blender, that was creepy."

She squeezed his hand gently.

"I just—"

"Just go to sleep on it. You'll feel better."

"I would feel better if I stayed right here, watching over you."

She laughed, a silvery bell-like laugh.

"You've watched over me enough, Hauck. Now go to bed."

"I'm serious, Sveta."

And he pulled out his CZ AccuShadow 2 and laid it on his lap. He flicked the safety to the off position. Sveta grew concerned.

"What exactly are you afraid of?" she whispered.

"I don't know, Sveta. But I almost lost you once to the pop-up killers, and I'm not about to come close to losing you again. So I'll keep watch over you, if you don't mind. I'll sit right in this chair. I won't make a sound, believe me."

Sveta thought it over for a moment, pulled out her SIG Sauer pistol and did the same with it.

"I think I'll sleep better knowing that you're there, Hauck."

"Good, then go to sleep, Sveta."

****

Jimmy couldn't sleep, so he wandered through the maze of scientific equipment and marvels that were the underground world. He stopped by the bells, the giant bells, two of which lay cracked and on their side, and three of them were intact and in their original positions, but which had been peppered with bullets during the fight with the Russian Mafiya. They were magnificent specimens, mementos of a bygone technology. He wondered for what use they were put to when they were in their heyday.

He walked on past steampunkish technology that littered the landscape until he came to the train, half of which was knocked on its side by Drogol in his werewolf form. It still had yet to be straightened out—if it ever could be made right again. Yet there it sat, a train that went to nowhere, on tracks that ended in a stone wall. How in the world had it come to be there?

"Can't sleep, huh?" said the Instructor.

Jimmy started at the voice.

"You startled me," he said, after getting his breathing back to normal.

"Yeah, well, ain't it the truth? Anyway, that Drogol sure packed a wallop of a punch, didn't he? Knocked two cars of this train off their tracks by just ramming it. I'd call that pretty amazing, wouldn't you?"

"Yes, yes, I would. He must have been possessed of incredible strength."

"Anyway, what's got you up and worried, doc?"

Jimmy looked at the Instructor to see if he was serious. He was a hard little man to read. Volatile, incisive, brutal and funny at the oddest times. He finally decided he was serious.

"What you said earlier. That's what's got me up. I keep wondering if I read all of Drogol's notes, I wondered if Drogol was right in his calculations. I wondered if there was something else that needed to be done to... to ensure that everything would work together to bring him back to human transition."

"And?"

"I don't know, Instructor; I just don't know. I've racked my brain a thousand times, but I still can't be sure. Maybe the last step to freedom—maybe Drogol did not write that down because it was so simple. Just a little thing, you understand? That maybe he had just told Zoe to do it. I don't know… am I making any sense?"

The Instructor stared at him. It was so hard to guess what he was thinking.

"Yeah, you are. You're afraid you've fucked up by missing something. I get that. Now all we can do is watch and wait. I don't think that whatever has happened to him—and look, Doc, he turned out perfectly normal, but I feel it in my gut. This was just too easy. Let me ask you this: what if Drogol had taken some drink beforehand, before the Tesla device kicked in? Like a pre-op drink or something. I don't know, but a drink to make the experiment go in his favor. Is that possible?"

"Like a drink to insure the experiment's success? Thats certainly possible…"

"What? Tell me what you're thinking."

"It's nothing really… it's just that all of this time that I read the notes on the machine, I never, ever thought of what came before the machine. I poured through his notes on the device, but sweet Jesus, I read Tesla's notes and Drogol's notes. I studied the diagrams of the machine. I should have read his alchemy notes to see if…"

"Yeah, well, you better get to it to see if there's something you missed, because, Doc?"

"Yes, I don't think we have a lot of time. I can feel it in my bones that something is going to happen. Soon."

****

Sasha was left alone in his room. Charlene had made sure he was comfy, and when she was sure that he wanted nothing else, she left him alone. But she made him promise that if he wanted for anything, if he felt dizzy, if he felt sick, he was just to call out for her and she would come running. She had developed a liking for him in the short time that she had been exposed to him.

As she went from the room, Sasha said, "Good night, Charlene. Thank you for staying with me after the treatment. It means a lot to me."

She turned, smiled at him and said, "Good night, Sasha. You sleep tight, do you hear me?"

And with that, she was gone. Sasha was alone with his thoughts. He felt secure for the first time in his young life. Gradually, he drifted off to sleep. But his sleep was filled with wild and terrible dreams.

He was in a dark world of horrors. A world of dark caverns and ever burning liquid rocks. A sulfurous, smoky mist hung in the skies and pale-skinned monsters with glowing red eyes and leprous skin hunted in the eternal night of that wretched landscape. Always, they hunted, and he knew he was no longer on this earth. It was a world where herds of animals were running from gibbering creatures. Screams bloodied the night like the red phosphorescent fungus that grew everywhere. And he cried out for help, but there was none forthcoming. What was this world of dark terrors that he was thrust into?

But it was more than a nightmare world that he was thrust into, more than an ephemeral place of crepuscule that he was trapped in. There, lying in his bed, was no longer Sasha, but a pale-skinned monster with glowing red eyes. It blinked in surprise, but rapidly went into kill mode. Eight feet tall and with four arms, it was truly monstrous to behold, and with teeth that were as sharp as a blade, polished and ready for the kill. It leveraged itself off of the bed when it suddenly was hit by a flash of lightning.

Just then, Charlene burst into the room to find Sasha sitting on the edge of the bed dazed and confused. He had to hang on to the side of the bed to steady himself.

"Are you all right?" she asked, out of breath from the sprint from her room to his. She took his arm and steadied him.

"Yes, yes, I'm all right. Really, I am fine. I just had a horrible dream. There were all sorts of monsters in it."

The reality of the dream was shocking to Sasha. Never had he dreamed in such vivid Technicolor. Most of his dreams were forgotten as soon as he woke up. But not this one.

The entire group was there by this time. There were consolations all around. Yuri said it was just a bad dream, and Charlene was quick to agree with him.

But the Instructor noticed some green slime on the floor, and he looked at Hauck and Jimmy and just shook his head.

CHAPTER NINE

Camila and the Chernobog

"You understand, Camila, what a substantial burden this is and what a great opportunity this is, too?" asked Professor Meridian.

"Yes."

"And you accept the charge?"

"Do I have a choice?"

A faint smile creased Professor Meridian's face. Akim sat on a corner of the professor's desk while Camila sat on the opposite side.

"Camila, you have a choice," said Akim. "You will either accept this assignment or I will feed you to the chernobog."

Silence in the room for a long, drawn out time.

Then:

"I accept," said Camila.

"How delightful," said Professor Meridian. "Camila, I want Hauck and the Instructor dead. Sasha, too, but I want the driving force in this whole affair, Hauck and the Instructor dead, and I shall have it. Do you understand?"

"Yes."

The professor's face had a dark edge to it. Camila didn't know who frightened her the most, the professor, or Akim, or his chernobog. Akim had an air of danger about him and the chernobog terrified her, but the professor had about him the tint of madness, and that genuinely horrified her.

"Then there are certain things you must know about the

chernobog," said Akim.

"I'm listening," said Camila.

"First," continued Akim, "you must never turn your back oh him. Let me make that perfectly clear—he is always to be in front of you. He will try to maneuver and trick you to go out front, but you must never, ever be in front. Never."

"May I ask why?" she asked.

"Because the last person to get out in front of a chernobog was never heard of again. Does that answer your question?"

Camila felt a chill go through her body. She merely nodded her response. This had turned into the goat rodeo from hell.

"Yes," she said, but she wondered what had happened to that individual.

She remembered Heinrich. He had been a despicable human being, but once you got past his essential lack of humanity and his aggressive nature, he was an okay person to work with; at least he was a known quantity. But what she had seen the chernobog do to him sickened her. No one deserved to die like that, and how exactly did he die? What was the chernobog? And most important to her, was when Hauck, the Instructor, Sasha, and the rest were all killed, would Professor Meridian and Akim then clean house? Would this be a case of leaving no loose ends, such as herself, to tell tall tales of a chernobog monster?

"Second," said Akim, "and this is very important. The chernobog must eat once a day—do you understand this?"

"Yes."

"I think not," screamed Professor Meridian. "The chernobog must eat once per day, Camila, means that he must eat one person every day. Now is it clearer? Every day at sunset, the chernobog must eat, and you must be very certain, very certain to have a man or a woman that you can feed to him, or else you will become his next meal. Now, do you fully understand this?"

Camila paled. This was madness. She had to find some way to get out of this.

"But how do I—"

"You simply will capture a sufficient supply of Detroit's homeless to feed him. If the hour of sunset approaches and the chernobog must eat, well, I leave that matter to you," said Akim.

"You said he must eat once per day at sunset, correct?" asked Camila.

"That is correct," answered Akim.

"How many times a day may the chernobog eat theoretically?"

Akim leaned over on his corner of the desk. His eyes were dead, and his face was a mask.

"The chernobog may eat endlessly, Camila. Endlessly."

Camila felt her stomach drop. This was worse than madness. She had to find a way out of this mess that she found herself in. She had to.

"How do I make certain that he does not eat me?"

"The chernobog obeys my commands. I will simply tell him not to eat you. Unless, of course," said Akim, "you object to that?"

Panic hit Camila like a freight train. All that was between her and disaster, horrible disaster, was a command by Akim. She tried not to show her feelings.

"No, I most certainly do not," she said.

Akim smiled a predatory smile.

"Now the third thing, and this is the most important of all."

Camila dreaded the third thing, whatever it was. She cringed at the thought of it. She looked over at Professor Meridian, who had a wild glee in his single eye. Never before had his eye patch looked so sinister as it did in that moment.

"The chernobog can read thoughts. It is the way he will track down Hauck and the Instructor. Their thoughts will be like a homing beacon to him. When they think of the professor, as think of him they must, that will be his cue. He will mercilessly hunt him down and then execute them."

"He reads thoughts?" asked Camila.

"Does that terrify you?" asked Akim.

She had to tell him the truth. Something in his merciless albino eyes warned her against the lie that she was just about to speak.

"Yes. Yes, it does," she said.

"Good. Good," said Professor Meridian. "It should terrify you Camila, because it terrifies me. But don't be afraid, my dear, because what the chernobog divines from your thoughts, it keeps to itself. Not even Akim knows, right Akim?"

Akim turned his head to the professor and seemed irritated by the comment. It was as though he had slipped up in telling him about the chernobog's mind reading acumen.

"Yes, that's true, but that's slight consolation for our victims, yes? But guard your thoughts carefully, Camila, for the chernobog is dangerous in ways you cannot even imagine. I have had control of this chernobog going on seven years and I still do not know even half of what he can wreak on this world of ours. He can change forms on a whim from a vapor to an animal to a man, but when he fastens his true teeth on your neck, you are quite finished."

"You don't know all of what it can do?"

Camila did not want to think of the chernobog fastening his teeth on her neck.

"All I know is that it is a treacherous beast that must be dealt with harshly for the best results."

"But what gives you the power to control it?"

Akim stood at the exact moment that she asked the question, and Camila thought she had gone too far. But she noticed Professor Meridian perk up at his question.

"In my native land of Siberia, is where you will find the khylsty, the warrior saints. You perhaps have heard of us?"

He turned his back on her before she could answer.

"We are the guardians of the seven worlds, the gates of which are forever opened and forever closed to mere mortal men. We rarely, if ever, travel—we have no need. All the harvested power of the seven worlds is ours to control. Why should we ever go anywhere but out homeland? But when we had extended an offer—which we never to did to an outsider, Drogol was the first and the last—to become a priest defected, nay chose his religion over the faith in the old gods and vanished from our midst, we swore an oath to leave and capture this man, this Drogol, as he was known.

"My brother Ivan was chosen for this mission, and when we were contacted by Ann Kazakova with his location, it was his calling to hunt him down. But he was killed by a werewolf, this Sasha that your Professor Meridian hunts, and the people responsible for him being a werewolf were Hauck and the Instructor. So your Professor Meridian contacted me to... how do you say? To finish the job."

Akim held up his hand.

"As I told you, we are the protectors of the seven worlds, and this monster, this chernobog, was trying to flee our world to go to another world. He came to this world by accident, and he did not belong. I... trapped him in this world, and I will not let him pass until he serves me for seven years. That time is almost up, when I shall have to abide by my word and let him go to the next world. I have struck a bargain with him that if he will do this one job for me, I will set him free. This one job is to avenge my brother's death. And I want their bodies drained of all their life energy. Is that clear?"

Camila, for the first time in her years of killing, was afraid.

"But the chernobog can only live for a time out of his cage. He can only hunt at night. Do you understand?"

"Yes."

"Therefore, you must go out and gather evidence for the chernobog to... read... and when we learn where they are, we will take the cage to that location, and together, we will turn him loose to... to feed."

The way that Akim said "to feed," she felt very sorry for the intended victims.

"Now, go get a homeless person for him to eat," said Akim.

CHAPTER TEN

The Monster

"I'm telling you, Hauck, I saw that green slime with my own eyes," said the Instructor.

The room was full of people. They were in a room that Drogol used for spreading out all his drawings. It was nighttime in the world outside. The moon was three quarters of the way toward full and riding high in the sky. But inside, you wouldn't know it; it was a world of never-ending daylight with the floating globes giving off their golden radiance and the very air itself giving off a soft luminescence. In the room itself, however, the Instructor held court in sepia tones, with the aura of the globes blocked out by pulled shut curtains and closed double doors.

"And the sounds coming out of that room he was in wasn't normal, neither. I'm telling you there's something wrong with him."

"Like what?" said Hauck evenly.

"I don't know, but I think we should place him in a cage until we figure it out."

Dr. Jimmy looked at Trisha and then Sveta. Yuri was in the other room, watching Sasha.

"Are you sure that he—" he began.

"Yes, I'm sure, goddamit," the Instructor cut him off. "Do you think I'm nuts enough to say something like that if I wasn't? Fuck man, where's that big brain you're supposed to have? We've got to cage him now."

Hauck got out of his chair and began pacing. Sveta could tell that he was frustrated. How to tell your own son, who just was thanking you for saving him from the curse of the werewolf, that he might turn into something worse?

"I don't like this," he said.

"Yeah, well, you'll like it a lot less if he turns into some hideous monster right before your very eyes."

Hauck looked at Sveta.

"He's right, Hauck. You'd never forgive yourself if something happened," she said.

"Yes. Lock him up. That's all you can do until we sort this out," said Trisha.

The decision was simple, but hard, Hauck thought. This would crush Sasha, but it couldn't be helped. Everyone else's safety was at stake.

"Let me tell him," said Hauck.

"No, you can't tell him alone," said Sveta.

"I should go, since I'm the one that botched the Tesla machine," said Jimmy.

"You didn't botch it. We just don't know what went wrong. I should have listened to you and waited," said Hauck.

"We can figure that out later for cryin' out loud. Let's just get it over with and get him put in the cage, okay?" said the Instructor.

"He's right," said Trisha. "Let's all go. It will be easier that way."

"All right, let's go," said Hauck.

"I'm taking the tranquilizer gun and the Mossberg. The rest of you better go armed."

"Is that necessary?" said Jimmy.

The Instructor looked at him as though he were stupid.

"Suit yourself," he said, "but me, I'm going armed. Now come on, let's go."

They were halfway to the door when Yuri broke in breathless

"Hauck, I—I... he just turned. Right in front of me, he just turned into this awful... monstrosity," said Yuri.

Hauck looked at the Instructor. He grabbed his pistol and the Kel-Tec KSG Pump Action 12 gauge that was on the table and some shells and said to the others, "Stay here."

"The hell I will," said Sveta.

"Sveta, I'm not going to argue with you. Arm up the lot of you and wait for us here."

"But—" she began.

That was all she had time to say before he heard a terrible screaming howl from somewhere outside. It sent chills down his spine in a way that Hauck had never felt before. The Instructor opened the door and Hauck didn't have time to argue with Sveta anymore. They went out of the door and closed it behind them.

They looked around and couldn't see anything out of place. So they waited for a moment, then advanced in the direction to where they had last left Sasha, to their left, towards the control panel. But a hideous growl, the sound of jaws snapping, and a wolf's barking and bay told them that Sasha was not there, but straight ahead.

"That's Rasputin, the dumb dog. Man, but he's stupid," said the Instructor.

"Over there," said Hauck. "Come on."

Rasputin was dancing around the train that had been knocked on its side by Drogol and split in two. The wolf was running and spinning around the half that had been rolled over obliquely to the track. That was what Hauck and the Instructor ran towards. Past control panel boards and tubes and wiring, past floating tubes and wires, down the stairs, and then to a dead stop. About fifty feet from the train, the wolf dashed out, just beneath a pair of monstrous paws.

"My God," breathed Hauck.

The Instructor raised the Mossberg and advanced, while Hauck did the same with the Kel-Tec pump. They advanced cautiously as Rasputin ducked around the train, and then the beast showed itself. It had walked on two feet and had four muscular arms. A wide scaled chest and a deformed head. Its mouth distended in a wild, howling scream beneath its four eyes and hairless head, while the rest of its body was covered by wiry, curling hair. It was green and purple and looked nothing like Sasha, and it was eight feet tall. When it came fully into their sight, they could see it had a long, spiked tail that twitched back and forth restlessly as it came after the wolf.

"Aw shit," said the Instructor, as he switched from the Mossberg to the tranquilizer rifle, sited and fired off a shot just as the creature turned and caught sight of them.

The tranquilizer dart miraculously embedded in its throat, but it kept coming straight at them. Hauck went to the right and the Instructor dove to the left, loading another tranquilizer dart in his rifle as he did so. The four armed monster went barreling past where Hauck and instructor and stood only seconds before. The Instructor leaped to his feet and fired another dark into its hide. It screamed bloody murder and turned to look to see where the dart had come from. By that time, the instructor had loaded another dart. The beast screamed, spread its four arms wide and opened his hideous mouth with its rows of razor-sharp teeth. The Instructor fired another dart, and it stuck into its shoulder.

Hauck covered the creature with his Kel-Tec pump, ready to fire, but not pulling the trigger. When the Instructor had fired his third dart into the creature, though, he pulled the trigger and sent a blast winging by the monster's head.

The beast felt the breeze and heard the blast. It turned to where the sound came from. Hauck fired another shot, missing his head by just inches. The beast roared and beat its chest in a challenge. Just then, the Instructor fired another dart into its back and it whirled again in exasperation. It thundered a bellowing cry and attacked. Running at full speed, it was an awe-inspiring sight, its four arms with claws outstretched and its ghastly mouth with its razor like teeth it extended. Hauck fired off another shot, but it didn't respond, so intent was it on reaching its goal, the little man who dared inflict pain on it. The Instructor tried to load and fire another dart, but there wasn't time. He dove behind a control panel.

The frustrated creature swung at the metal control panel, but it was too well constructed and it just tore a piece off. It swung again, with the same result. Hauck fired two rounds over its head and it spun around and shrieked with an ear-splitting, bawling sound. In the meantime, the Instructor had time to reload and tried to fire another dart into the monstrosity, but the dart jammed in the barrel. The Instructor swore and ducked back behind the panel again, trying desperately to fix the mis-fired dart. Hauck fired a third and fourth shots at the creature, and this time, it sized him up and bore straight down on him.

Hauck had never had anything seen anything so frightening in his life as the beast barreling down on him. He looked around for something to hide behind, anything. Just then, the Instructor fired his last dart at the horror. Hauck raised his shotgun for a kill shot that he desperately did not want to take. Fifty feet, thirty feet. Hauck braced himself, aimed, and suddenly the beast became woozy and stopped in its tracks. It stood there for a moment, with Hauck and the Instructor both now pointing their shotguns at it, and staggered about in circles.

"That's it, come on you bastard, fall," yelled the Instructor.

Hauck still stood with his shotgun fixed on what he was convinced was his son.

"Come, fall already, damn you," roared the Instructor.

The beast wove, then dropped to its knees. The Instructor moved in quickly and clubbed it on the head with the Mossberg stock, using the barrel like a grip. It finally dropped.

"Well, shit, that was close."

Hauck nodded.

"It was indeed."

"Come on," said the Instructor. "Let's get moving before the tranquilizers wear off. I don't want to be around when this thing wakes up. Let's haul him to the cage."

Now they regretted having moved the cages so far away, but they got to it. They slung their guns over their shoulders and lugged him as far as they could.

"Damn, he's too heavy," said the Instructor, panting heavily after only fifteen feet.

Hauck called out for Jimmy and Yuri. The door opened cautiously and Yuri poked his head out.

"Come on," Hauck yelled, "we need help to move him. Hurry up and bring Jimmy."

Yuri and Jimmy came on the run, followed by a limping Sveta, helped along by Trisha. When they got there, the Instructor gave his tranquilizer rifle to Trisha.

"It's all loaded and don't hesitate to use it, got it? And follow close behind us, too," he said.

Trisha nodded. Sveta had her Ruger PC Carbine Black 9mm along with her, just in case.

"All right, let's get hauling. Jimmy, you're with me on the top and Yuri, you're at the bottom. We've got to hurry, because we don't know how long these tranquilizers will hold."

They made an odd procession, the four of them carrying the knocked out body of the beast, with Trisha following close behind, rifle pointed at it and Sveta limping behind. Around the various control panels, past the fallen giant bells and the shot up gages, past the lockers and through the cavern until finally they arrived. Hauck lowered his end, took the key from his pocket and unlocked the cage door.

"Uh—Hauck, I think he's waking up."

Hauck hurried up and swung the door open. They tried to swing the beast in the cage, but they got hung up with one of his four arms catching on it.

"Shit," cried the Instructor.

The monster began to wake up.

The Instructor slammed his arm in, and the beast woke up, giving a sudden ear-shattering roar. Hauck slammed the door shut and jammed the key toward the lock, but missed.

"Oh, no," cried everyone simultaneously.

The beast slowly turned around in the cage, fixing its eyes on them. Finally, Hauck got the key in the lock and turned it and he and the Instructor leapt back as four arms reached to grab them and missed by inches. The beast howled in rage.

While the rest of the people backed up, Trisha fired another dart into the creature, and its furor shook the ground.

"Well, yell, you bastard. You can't get out of that cage and we've soundproofed the thing," the Instructor laughed and slapped the ground.

Hauck closed the soundproof door and locked that, too.

He turned around and looked at the others.

"Everyone is okay?"

"I'm a little shook up," said Jimmy, "but I've got to say, I was sure glad when Trisha fired that last dart into it."

"Thanks," said Trisha, giving a nervous smile.

"This job sure has its interesting moments," said Yuri.

The creature was quiet behind the bars in the soundproof room, presumably having fallen asleep.

"I thought I told you to fire that rifle when we needed you, not when we'd already locked the thing up," said the Instructor to Trisha.

"Well, you and Hauck were in the way," said Trisha.

"Yeah, yeah," said the Instructor, as he started walking toward the room.

Hauck smiled a grim smile and looked at Sveta.

"How about you, Sveta? You okay?"

"Look, my leg is damaged, not useless," she said and alternately stomped and limped away.

Hauck had a bad feeling about the way that this would turn out, and now it was coming true.

CHAPTER ELEVEN

A Conversation with the Chernobog

Akim and Camila walked into the room where the chernobog was held captive. Akim had to unbolt the door and slide it back to permit entrance, but once he had, they entered. There was a comfortable chair in the room, and two folding chairs facing it. The chernobog sat in the comfortable yet straight-backed chair with his black hair swept back in a European style, his hands folded in his lap and his long legs crossed. He smiled, but his eyes were coldly calculating, almost ice blue. His cage sat on the floor behind him.

"Good evening," he said.

"Good evening, Gregor," said Akim.

Camila said nothing, eying the chernobog warily.

"You have met Camila. She is to be your new handler."

The chernobog's eyes traveled to Camila. He looked her up and down.

"You are eager to get back to your world," said Akim.

Suddenly, the chernobog was animated.

"You have kept me here for nearly seven long years. You must let me free," he said savagely.

The chernobog stood up suddenly and his countenance was enraged. He stood there threateningly, but was held back, as if by an invisible thread. Camila could almost see the distortion of his features as he struggled. He began to change to a black smoke with red eyes, swirls of a tourbillion in ever-expanding circles. Camila cringed away from his terrifying form.

"I will do nothing of the sort until you have fulfilled your obligation to my order," said Akim quietly.

Slowly the chernobog calmed down, and his form changed again to a man. But his eyes remained as scarlet as his rage. Camila was thankful for whatever hold Akim had over him, for she knew that without it, the chernobog would have devoured them both.

"Good," said Akim, "now Camila will be you new handler, and you will not eat her. Camila, tell the chernobog what he will do."

Camila was almost afraid to talk. The chernobog stared at her, as though taking her measure. Slowly, his eyes returned to their normal color. Or was his normal color the blazing red that she had glimpsed? She honestly didn't know, and she was too terrified to ask. The monster—for that was exactly how Camila thought of him — sized her up, as though she were a side of meat, which to him, that was all she was. She gathered her courage and spoke.

"You are to find three people for us," she said, trying desperately not to betray her nervousness. "They are called Hauck, the Instructor and Sasha. We have no last names, but here is a likeness," and here Akim handed sketches over to the chernobog. "Professor Meridian has prepared sketches of the three, as there are no known photographs of them. Study them carefully. Now Akim tells me you will track them by their thoughts of the Professor. Is that correct?"

"That is correct," he said coldly, "for as much as you say."

She wondered if he was telling her the whole truth. Deciding to press him on this, she asked him, "What am I not saying?"

The chernobog inclined his head.

"Very good, very good. I can not only track him when any of them thinks of the Professor but also by objects they have touched."

"Really?"

"Really, Camila, he tells you the truth," said Akim.

"Then we will go to the one they call Dr. Jimmy's apartment, and we will bring you back some objects of his that he recently touched. You will then tell us where he is, and we," here she looked at Akim, "will take you to him and turn you loose on them. Is that understood?"

The chernobog laughed, a terrible bass din that Camila could not bear to hear. She was about to scream that he stop, but he turned into a miasma of mist and floated into his cage again. The door closed with an awful screech behind him.

CHAPTER TWELVE

The Aftermath

Hauck didn't sleep at all that night, and neither did Yuri. It was their job to sit up through the night, guarding the monster. It was a lonely vigil, and it was quiet, except for the faint humming of the globes that lit the place. The monster. Try as he might, Hauck could not wrap his brain around how that was possible.

"Well, Drogol was a hybrid, right?" said Yuri, at about three a.m in the morning.

Yuri was initially nervous when watching the soundproofed cage the monster was locked in. When he found out it didn't break free, Yuri relaxed enough to sit down on some cartons.

"So?" said Hauck.

"Not a hybrid, exactly, but something that came through him from another dimension, I guess, for want of a better word. What if, by tuning the Tesla machine to the right frequency, Sasha got a dose of the same thing?"

"What thing?" said Hauck impatiently.

"What I'm saying is what if that vibration attuned him to the right frequency to admit something through to this world? Maybe Sasha is trapped in another dimension, where these things are from."

Hauck thought about it. It made sense to him in a sort of weird way, but the thought of Sasha trapped in another world, being at the mercy of things like that monster, made him profoundly uncomfortable. There was no way known to science to get him back safely.

"No, I don't buy it," he said at last.

"Why not?" asked Yuri.

"Because that would mean he was trapped in a world where we can't help him. How are we going to save him?"

"You'd rather think that he was turned into that horrible creature for good?"

"No."

"What then?"

"We wait until morning comes and then look into the cage. If we're lucky, he'll turn back into a person."

"And if he doesn't?"

"We'll give him some more time. It's all I can think of to do. That, and hope that Jimmy will come up with a solution."

"If anybody can, Dr. Jimmy can. He's one smart dude."

"I hope so," said Hauck.

With that, they fell silent for the longest time. Yuri was used to staying up all night. He survived on very little sleep at erratic hours. Some times Hauck would find him at his keyboard asleep during the day, but he would wake up with a start, stretch, have a cup of coffee and get right back to it. Now, he fiddled with his phone looking things up, always exploring different avenues on the Internet, hoping against hope to find some valuable information about any other cases like Sasha's, but finding nothing.

"The only thing I'm finding is nothing," said Yuri, looking up from his phone. "The only person in the universe who underwent a transformation similar to Sasha is Drogol."

"I know," said Hauck. "Only Sasha is different. Drogol turned into a monstrous werewolf, whereas Sasha turned into..."

"A monster?"

Hauck looked pained. But yes, his son had turned into a monster. There was no denying it. In trying to cure him of the werewolf disease, they had only made him worse. He should have listened to Jimmy. He should never have let Sasha go ahead with the experiment. What kind of father was he, anyway? In giving him what he thought was the freedom to choose, he had condemned him to life as a monster. One that could never be let out of a cage because they never knew what was going to happen to him or when. At least with the werewolf curse, he was only in a cage three days out of a month. Now he was condemned to being locked up forever.

"Yes, a monster," Hauck agreed reluctantly.

"Well, why didn't Drogol turn into one of those things, too?"

"Because when Tesla's ray caused the Tunguska explosion, Drogol was near the resultant explosion. When Drogol looked up, he was being attacked by a giant wolf, so Drogol somehow fused with the wolf to become a wolf man. That's all I know, really."

"Yeah, I guess so," said Yuri dubiously.

"What?"

Yuri scratched at his mustache for a minute. He considered something, but rejected it.

"I just don't know," he said at last. "Something doesn't make sense, but I'll be damned if I know what it is."

"Well, when you think of it, let me know, will you?"

They drank coffee for the longest time in silence. Hauck played with his tranquilizer rifle after setting aside an FN P90 submachine gun. He would prefer to use the tranquilizer , but if he had to... could he really use a submachine gun on his own son? He set down the tranquilizer rifle and picked up the FN P90 again. It was hard to contemplate. But he thought of Sveta, exposed to the monstrosity that was his son, and determined he would never let that happen.

At around three thirty in the morning, just when Hauck was getting yet another coffee, the Instructor showed up. He was fully armed and Hauck noticed that this time, he didn't carry a tranquilizer rifle.

"Hey," said the Instructor, "I couldn't sleep."

"There's a lot of that going around," said Yuri.

"Who asked you? Did you hear anything from our boy?"

"No, not after the initial thrashing around," said Hauck. "That thing is soundproof, but the sound still gets out. He quieted down about a half an hour after you left."

The Instructor grunted and had another sip of coffee. Then he gave up and drained the whole cup.

"You got any more?" he asked.

"No, that's the last," said Yuri.

"You think you could get anymore?" said an irritated Instructor.

"Well, I—"

"Hurry up then, will you? I'm falling asleep on my feet just listening to you."

Yuri left for refills, mumbling something incoherent under his breath in Russian.

"You ready to open it up and see what's what?"

Hauck was not ready to open it up to see what was what. He wanted to know, but he didn't.

"I—"

"Come on, open it up, you know you want to," said the Instructor.

"You're right. But we should wait for backup to wake it up."

"Look, this isn't going to get any easier the longer you wait. While Yuri's getting me getting coffee, let's just get it over with."

Hauck stood up, stretched, and then set off for the cage. The Instructor followed. When they got there, Hauck took out the key to the steel door and soundproofing that formed the second cage and got ready to open it.

"Now remember," said the Instructor, "at the slightest hint of movement, just move out of the way and let me do my thing."

The Instructor lifted his SIG Sauer machine gun and placed the stock against his shoulder, reader to fire. Hauck inserted the key in the lock and turned it. Gritting his teeth, he swung it open and stepped back. It was dark in the enormous cage, but the admitted light revealed a horror asleep in the back part of the cage.

"Look," whispered the Instructor, "If I kill him now, he'll never feel a thing. It'll be all over except for the shout."

Hauck looked back at the Instructor in surprise. He was actually arguing for a merciful death for Sasha. But what if Sasha was trapped in one world, having traded place with a monster from another world? Or maybe Yuri was right. Maybe that just didn't make any sense at all. Maybe the experiment had just changed him permanently into a monster.

"No," said Hauck.

"I'm just saying," said the Instructor.

The monster's eyes snapped open. It blinked, then stared directly at Hauck.

"Last chance, til later."

The creature lunged at Hauck. Hauck stepped back before the onslaught. Three of the hellion's arms reached through the cage, and flailed around wildly at Hauck, while forth held purchase on the bars. Hauck grimaced. This was his son in there grasping at him. Or was it?

The cage was a double cage affair with an additional level for sound proofing. There was no danger of him breaking free, as it was built to contain Sasha as a powerful werewolf. Its bars were made of titanium steel and were unbreakable. There was no chance that he would get out, none. The beast suddenly snarled a blood-curdling cry.

"Go on, howl you bastard, scream all you want," yelled the Instructor. "You ain't going nowhere. Shut the door—I don't want to listen to him for the rest of the day. Jesus, he's giving me a headache."

Reluctantly, Hauck swung the outer door shut, the beast bellowing louder until the door was closed all the way.

Yuri came running. "Did he—"

"Hey," said the Instructor, "you forgot the coffee. Can't I trust you with anything?"

"But I heard—"

"Yeah, yeah. We checked in on the beastie and found out our boy was still a beastie. Now go get the coffee."

"But—"

"And hurry it up, will ya? And tell anybody else that it was a false alarm and go back to bed while you're at it."

A clearly frustrated and frazzled Yuri headed back toward the office.

"Cute kid, but mouthy," said the Instructor. "Come on, let's go sit down again and see what we can figure out."

Hauck nodded, and they walked back toward the row of boxes that they had been sitting on. They sat down, just as Jimmy, his hair all messed like he'd just gotten out of bed, came running up.

"Hey, relax," said the Instructor, "didn't Yuri tell you it was a false alarm?"

Jimmy bent down and caught his breath. He wiped his glasses off on his shirt and put them back on.

"I know," he said between deep breaths. "I couldn't sleep."

"Join the club," said Hauck.

"What? No, that's not it, I've been thinking. I followed every direction in Drogol's notes to the letter."

Jimmy took another deep breath and sat down on a wooden box. He ran his fingers through his hair while looking desperately at Hauck.

"Yeah," said the Instructor, "so what'd you come up with? Any bright ideas?"

"No," admitted Jimmy.

"Great. You can go back to bed now."

"But, I've got a theory."

"Go on," said Hauck.

"Well, it goes like this," he said. "I followed Drogol's instructions to the letter. I checked and rechecked every single scrap of paper that he had, and it all makes sense."

"Yes…"

"That's just it. I followed every single line of instructions that I could find. But what if, it's just an if, mind you, that somewhere in this place, there's another journal with more instructions? Hidden — maybe Drogol hid it away so that no one else could find it. He was a paranoid guy, wasn't he?"

Hauck thought about it. Was Drogol a paranoid person? Paranoid enough to hide a journal that held the key to his salvation? He was secret enough to hide it in this fabulous underground laboratory, that much was certain. But did he honestly think that someone would break into this place, that was so hidden that no one could find it, and steal his formula? Wait, the Russian Mafiya had found it — was it that impossible that someone else would?

"Go on," Hauck said.

"If he was that paranoid, where would he hide it?"

Where would he hide it? Hauck cast his mind back in a desperate bid at forgotten memories. But nothing came to him. The truth was, he didn't know Drogol well enough to guess where his secret hiding place was, if he had one. He had been hunting him for most of his life, and that was all that concerned him. He was drawing a total blank on that.

"I don't know, Jimmy. I really don't know. Someplace down here, but where?"

"Shit, there's a thousand cubby holes around here that he could hide it in, maybe a million," said the Instructor.

"Think hard," said the Jimmy.

Hauck closed his eyes to block out any distractions, just as Yuri came back with three cups of coffee. He passed them out to Hauck, the Instructor and Jimmy. Hauck drank from his, then closed his eyes again. Somewhere in his brain, he must know something. His eyes suddenly popped open.

"Sveta," he said, standing bolt upright. "She spent the most time with him of any of us. If there's any chance, she might know."

Just then, a faint beeping sound could be heard coming from the office area.

"What's that?" asked the Instructor, immediately shouldering his rifle.

Jimmy listened for a minute and then looked alarmed. He shouldered past the Instructor on a run.

"That's my remote terminal," he said. "Someone's breaking into my house."

CHAPTER THIRTEEN

The Break In

Camila led the team of three men at exactly four fifteen a.m. in a descent on Jimmy's house. Two men guarded out front while the remaining three went in with Sveta. Two covered the back door and broke in while Sveta and another went in the front. Each of them moved silently on rubber-soled shoes. They were all dressed in black and carried Heckler and Koch submachine guns. Dark hoods, gloves, and night vision goggles completed their gear. Camila gave the signal and her man went silently up the stairs, followed by another of her men. The remaining man spread out and checked the main floor.

She walked through the living room and the kitchen and paid attention to all the little details of how Jimmy lived. No one was expected to be home- Jimmy had cleared out, and the watchers she had placed on the house saw that no one had returned for anything. But he had left in a hurry, that was for sure. He had to have left in a hurry, because not long after Professor Meridian had been freed from his house, he had sent a team over after him and came up empty. The house had been completely vacant since then.

Minutes passed, and the men returned to the kitchen, where she was waiting for them. They all shook their heads.

"All right," she said, "stand guard while I go through his stuff."

So, while the men took up guard positions, Camila began the slow process of rifling through Dr. Jimmy's things. There were the normal bills and things on the kitchen table. There wasn't a phone anywhere in evidence. He must have used a cell phone or two. Nothing in the downstairs bathroom—wait, there was an electric shaver in the bathroom. Camila pulled out a plastic bag and put the shaver in the bag. That would be what the chernobog could read. What an odd word. Could the chernobog really gain a psychic fix on Dr. Jimmy on his whereabouts just by touching the shaver? He had said to bring just a few personal items belonging to the man with her, so that's what she was doing. She searched through the rest of the downstairs, finding nothing of value, and went upstairs.

This was a gold mine. There were clothes he had worn in a hamper, and she dug out a particularly worn T-shirt and bagged that, too. Next, she searched through his drawers. Just a bunch of clean clothes were all that was there. But her attention was drawn to four pictures on the dresser. His mom and dad were both dead. He had a framed picture of the two of them smiling up at the camera. But there were three pictures of the same young woman- one as a young girl with three other boys, one of her as a teenager and one of her all grown up. She recognized that young woman. One team had been sent out to retrieve her. Her name was Trisha... Trisha Dayton, yes, that was it. Grabbing another plastic bag, she retrieved the photo and then left the bedroom. She just did a cursory search of the other rooms. No, she had what she needed for the chernobog in the three items.

"Are we going to torch it?" asked one man.

She was about to say yes when her eyes were drawn to a corner of the ceiling of the living room. There was a blinking light there.

Well, I'll be damned, she thought.

"No," she said. "Change of plans. Let's go. Clear out."

As they exited the premises, she couldn't resist one more look back at the corner. It wasn't a security system, that much was for sure. They'd been in there too long. If there was a security system in play, then they would already be busted by now. No, that was a camera. Someone was watching them.

She closed the door behind her and walked to the SUV, thinking that Professor Meridian and Akim would be very interested in that piece of information. As she got in the SUV, she thought the chernobog would be as well.

But the chernobog worried her. What Akim had said about him

eating an unlimited amount made her think Akim would clean up—by having the chernobog devour every one of them when they were no longer needed.

Driving down the highway on the way back to the shop, she thought about why Akim would kill them all at the end of the job. Surely, Professor Meridian had enough money to afford them. It couldn't be that. Was it instead that he wanted no one left alive to tell stories of the chernobog? Was it something in their religion that they weren't supposed to talk about him? No, surely that didn't make any sense either. What was she missing? Dare she confront Professor Meridian about it? If she did, he would surely lie if he knew the reason behind the question.

She could make a run for it, but to where? Where could she possibly hide that the chernobog wouldn't find her? The memory of Heinrich was a terrible thing, too. The way that he died was awful.

Then there were the cameras positioned in the ceiling so no one would notice them. Clever, she thought. Could they be private security? No, or like she said, the police or someone else would have come as soon as they broke in. It just didn't make any sense. Unless they were watching to see what they would do—that might make sense—but to do exactly what?

She pulled off on the West Jefferson Avenue warehouse entrance ramp. Activating the overhead door, she drove in and pulled to a stop. The other members of her team would take the side entrance. As the chernobog's keeper, she got to take the front.

As she walked to Akim's office, she wondered if she should tell him about the cameras. But she knew that she would have to tell him everything.

Lifting her hand to knock on the door, she felt her stomach drop when he answered from inside.

"Come in," he said.

She wondered how he did that; she hadn't actually knocked yet.

CHAPTER FOURTEEN

The Plan

"Look at that," said Jimmy.

The entire group was awake and gathered around Jimmy's monitor. Sveta, Trisha and Charlene had joined them and Hauck, the Instructor, and Yuri were crowded at his workstation.

"I count four of them," said the Instructor, "and the lead is a girl."

"Can't you ever—" said Sveta.

"Okay, okay," said the Instructor. "I mean a woman. There, you happy?"

"That's odd," said Trisha. "She's picking up random things. That doesn't make any sense."

"It doesn't," said Hauck. "So far, she's picked up a shaver, a T-shirt, and a picture off of Jimmy's desk. You're right, Trisha, that's really odd."

Jimmy looked angry. That photograph that she had taken off of his dresser was of Trisha. Now what would they want with a picture of her?

"That was Trisha's photo," he said.

"That was a picture of me they bagged up? They took a picture of me?" said Trisha. "What would they want a picture of me for?"

"I don't know," said Jimmy, "but it's making me angry."

Hauck thought about this. Of all the things to take, she took a shaver, a T-shirt and a picture of Trisha. He clearly was missing something, but what?

"Look, there," said Jimmy. "She's staring right at the ceiling cam. Now she looks away and pretends she didn't see it."

"She wants you to know that she knows," said Charlene.

"How so?" said Hauck.

He was genuinely interested in Charlene's opinion on this. So far, she had proven that she was both smart and resourceful.

"It's more like she doesn't care if you know. She's been caught, and she's thinking, 'So what? I got what I came for.'"

"Go on."

Jimmy was interested, too, as were the others.

"Well, let's see… she bagged a shaver, a T-shirt, and a picture of Trisha. I'd say that the shaver was for DNA, the T-shirt is clearly for DNA and the picture I'd say was for… for DNA, too."

"How do you figure?" said Hauck.

"The picture was because she thinks that he's touched it a lot, I figure. It's on his dresser, so… I don't know, that doesn't seem right. What would they want Jimmy's DNA for?"

"Setting him up at a crime scene maybe?" said a suddenly animated Yuri.

"Maybe," agreed Charlene.

"Dogs," said the Instructor, "they want his scent."

"Good," said Hauck.

"You really think that is it?" asked Jimmy. "The clothes I could understand, but not the shaver and the picture."

"You got any better ideas?" asked a sarcastic Instructor.

"No."

Hauck turned to Sveta, who sat down in a metal folding chair and shook her head. He closed his eyes for a minute, hoping to clear his head. The Instructor's idea for dogs was good. That might explain the shaver and the T-shirt, but what would she want with a picture of Trisha? Charlene's idea of DNA could explain things better, but if that were the case, she could have just taken a bundle of clothes from his hamper and called it quits. Maybe a combination of the two? And what about her staring right at the camera, all the while pretending that she didn't see them, or acting like she just didn't care? Curiouser and still more curious. Hauck had an idea, but when he opened his eyes, it seemed ridiculous. It was like they were trying to get a fix on

Jimmy, and that made little sense. What could his shaver, his T-shirt and a picture of Trisha have to do with any of that?

"What?" said the Instructor, "give."

"I'm not comfortable with—"

"Come on, goddammit, what do I have to do? Pull your teeth out of your head before you speak?"

Sveta, for some reason, found that tremendously funny. She laughed out loud. The Instructor gave her a look.

"All right," said Hauck. "I was thinking, mind you, this is just thinking, that what if the Professor were employing a psychic?"

"A psychic?" said Charlene. "Yeah, that makes sense. Someone to track him down using objects he touched frequently. Yeah, okay."

"That would explain why she took Trisha's picture, because that's something I think of a lot," said Jimmy. Then, when he noticed everyone staring at him, he blushed.

Trisha came over and hugged him.

"I think that's sweet, Jimmy," she said.

"Yeah, Jimmy, that's sweet," said the Instructor miming her voice. "Jesus, I think you're on to something, Hauck."

"That would explain her bagging them up, too, so as not to contaminate them with another's psychic energy. Still, it's just a theory. But she's taking them back to their pocket psychic to get a read or a fix on where Jimmy is."

"Can that really be true?" asked Jimmy.

"Like I said, it's just a theory, and who knows if it works, but Professor Meridian must be desperate to find us to try it."

"Yes, but could a psychic track me down that way? I mean, here, underground, that is."

Hauck shrugged.

"I honestly don't know," he said. "It's possible, I guess. But it doesn't seem likely."

"But I could be drawing them right to here."

"Hauck, it would explain a lot," said Yuri. "We torched Trisha's place so they couldn't take anything from there. They didn't have anything of yours, mine, the Instructor's, Sveta's or Charlene's that they could lay their hands on, so that left Jimmy. I think your idea, crazy though it seems, makes sense. And I think Jimmy's right. He could be drawing them right to us."

"That would have to be an extraordinary psychic, Yuri," said Hauck.

"I've heard of such people," said Sveta. "They are called… psychometric, I think. Or they practice psychometry."

Hauck's eyebrows went up.

"Don't look at me. I hate it when you look at me like that."

"I'm sorry, I'm just surprised, is all. How did you hear of it?"

She looked at him suspiciously, as though he were making fun of her. This was a touchy subject with her. It was her mother who had the gift, as it was called, of just by touching something that belonged to someone else, she could tell things about that person. Like where they had been that day, or what they'd had to eat. Sveta didn't enjoy talking about it.

"Why? Are you going to say I'm crazy?"

"Sveta…"

"It was my mother that had the gift."

She stared at him for a moment, as though she were daring him to say something. When he didn't, she continued.

"When she touched objects that belonged to someone, she could tell things about the person."

"What things?" asked Jimmy."

"She could tell where they were, whether they were alive or dead, what they'd had to eat—"

"Whoa, back up," said the Instructor, "what's that part about telling where a person was?"

"Yes, she could see that person. She could see the places he had been, where he was. A famous psychic once told her she had the gift of psychometry. That's what he called it. She would have to put her hands on the object, though."

Hauck looked at the Instructor and he looked back at him. They both had the same idea, though.

"How accurately could she tell someone's location with this… psychometric gift?"

Sveta looked at Jimmy, who was watching her carefully. He was leaning forward in his chair and white knuckling the table, as though his life depended on it. As well, it might.

"I see what you mean," she said to Hauck. "She was never called to locate someone below ground, though."

"How accurately?" Hauck asked again.

"I don't know because she never had to locate… fairly accurately, I suppose."

"Think, Sveta, did she see street numbers ,or did she have visions of things the person saw?"

This was going back years in Sveta's memories. Her mother had died when she was fairly young, and her father had taken over as the primary caregiver. They never talked about her mother's special gifts for finding things and people. Her father was a career military officer, one of the privileged few who could have his own dacha off of base. Sveta was raised after her mother's death by a succession of nannies who knew next to nothing about her mother, and Sveta had kept her memories of her mother close. She had never shared those memories with anyone, which is why she found it painful to talk about, and painful to revisit. But Hauck and the others were depending on her now.

"I think she saw visions of things that they saw."

Hauck considered his next question carefully.

"Were those only of the past, or were they current memories?" he asked at last.

Everyone was staring at her now, and Sveta was increasingly feeling their pressure. It didn't help her remember any better. In fact, it made it harder to think. Finally, she closed her eyes to blot them out. Once, she remembered a woman who had come to her mother with her full family , including her mother and father. They had been looking for their son, and they could not find him. They had been to the police, but though they looked for him high and low, they could not find him. But her mother found him. They brought her a scarf of his. They found him being held captive by a local pedophile bound and gagged in his garage. Sveta couldn't understand how it was possible to find a blindfolded boy with no knowledge of where he was. She couldn't see his surroundings with the blindfold in place…

"It wasn't like that," said Sveta. "She could locate him in real time without the subject even knowing where he was. She could… it was like she had a map in her head that she could follow straight to him. Does that make sense?"

"It's too late to get Jimmy out of the way," said the Instructor. "No offense, Doc, but you've already caused the damage. The psychic will know right where we're at, whether we're underground or above ground."

"Maybe I could shield myself? Sort of a lead cocoon... so the psychic rays that she uses won't be able to get through?" said Jimmy.

Hauck shook his head. The Instructor was right; they were already too late for that. Jimmy had already stamped the akashic record with where he was. They could all make a run for it, but where could they go? And Sasha... Hauck didn't think he would transport well.

"We take a stand here," said Hauck.

"You sure about this?" said the Instructor. "Tomorrow night and for three days after that, I'm not any help at all. I'm locked up, remember?"

"We can't run, we're too vulnerable on the move, and besides, the psychic will find us."

"Yeah, forgive me for saying so, your down Sasha, right? All that leaves you is a crippled Sveta—"

"I'm not crippled," said an angry Sveta.

"Yeah, sure you're not. Anyway, for guns you've got Doc Jimmy, whose shit is useless. Charlene, do you know how to handle a gun?"

"I know which way to point and pull the trigger," said Charlene.

"Great, okay you've got Miss point and pull, here and you've got Yuri, who isn't the best in a firefight, no offense. You've got Trisha, who's okay, and you've got you. So basically, you've got Jack and shit, and Jack's left town. Me and Sasha will be locked up in cages, and we're your best men. So it's basically you versus... what? Meridian's entire army?"

"I can fire a pistol. I trained at Quantico," said Trisha defensively.

"Get real," said the Instructor. "You've got a desk job, don't you? How many times you fire that pistol?"

"Enough to keep up my certification."

"You see what I mean, Hauck. Look lady, you may have kept up with the Joneses in pistol firing protocol, but we're talking submachine guns to the eye teeth, because that's what they'll be firing at you."

"I can fire a submachine gun," maintained Trisha.

"Sure, but it's different when they're firing back at you. And how about three or four?"

Trisha didn't answer.

"So, you see, Hauck, you've got a problem."

The Instructor was right. They had a problem and damned little time, if Hauck was correct, to prepare for it.

In his wildest dreams, though, Hauck could never have imagined the horror that would be coming after them soon.

The chernobog.

CHAPTER FIFTEEN

The Hunger

Professor Meridian was fascinated, no obsessed with Akim's control of the chernobog. How did he do it? What was the controlling mechanism? Akim seemed to have the chernobog on a chain somehow, and he was desperate to know what held him.

Hauck and his ilk had killed the Dhole. They had destroyed the Book of the Dhole, and Professor Meridian had been stripped of his power. Without it, he could no longer see the future or hope to have his greatest dreams realized—control of the world and everyone in it.

This enraged the Professor and he could barely contain his hatred. He paced behind his desk and thought to himself, if only he controlled the chernobog, he would have power again. To be so close to that power without knowing the answer to what controlled it was maddening.

There was a polite knock at his door. He must get himself under control. It wouldn't do to give away his secret lust for power.

"Come in," he said, sitting down in his handcrafted chair made of leather and wood as naturally as he could.

The door opened slowly, and it was Akim, Camila and a street person who they had picked up along the way. He looked lost, yet preternaturally docile. Camila carried with her three plastic bags.

"You said, Professor," began Akim, "that you would very much like to see the chernobog divine Dr. Harlen's thoughts from objects he has touched."

"Yes," said a suddenly interested Professor Meridian, "I very much would."

"The come and see. I think you will be impressed."

"Certainly."

As the professor stood up, a troubled look came over his face.

"And who is this, this man?" he said.

"You shall see," said Akim, and with that said, he departed, followed by Camila and the man.

Professor Meridian didn't like the answer, but he was eager to see the chernobog simply by touching the objects to divine Hauck's location, so he went after them.

The man was obsequious and followed Akim like a lost puppy. He had wild hair and glasses, the lenses of which seemed to be missing. Of an angular, gaunt build, he walked with a shambling gait. It suddenly occurred to the professor that this man was food for the chernobog. Camila seemed distinctly uncomfortable with his presence. Perhaps she did not approve of the chernobog's eating habits. What a cold-blooded killer such as herself could find to object to in the death of a street person intrigued the professor.

They arrived at the room where the chernobog was held, and Akim unlocked the door and went in first. He beckoned the street person to follow him, which he did, showing little trepidation, but the professor noticed for the first time the man's eyes. They were bloodshot, with the pupils severely dilated. The man was drugged.

He wore rags, with one sleeve of his coat in shreds and his pants were full of holes, with his red underwear showing through. A frayed army coat was on his back, wide open at the front, revealing a green and black checked flannel shirt beneath.

Camila seemed to shrink back from the man, which the professor observed with a detached interest. He thought again how odd that someone who killed for a living should have such a reaction. It was almost as though she saw… then the professor had it. She was afraid for herself—that something she did not comprehend like the chernobog should be turned loose on her. Yes, that was it exactly. She was afraid that when they were all through with Hauck, that Akim would then set the Chernobog on her and her men.

"Meet Gregor," said Akim. "You may advance on him and shake his hand."

The man seemed hesitant at first, as though some sixth sense warned him that the chernobog was a danger to him. He turned and looked at Akim, who only stared straight ahead at the chernobog. He looked at the professor, who smiled encouragingly. Slowly, unsteadily as the professor observed, he shambled towards the chernobog. When he got close to the chernobog, the chernobog smiled. The man stuck out his hand.

"I'm—"

But the street person stopped when the chernobog grasped his wrist. His smile suddenly terrified him because the chernobog's entire body was turning to mist. He couldn't quite grasp what was occurring. The man in the black clothes was dissolving in front of him.

"What—" he cried.

His cries were cut off when the chernobog reappeared on top of him. The chernobog was now a grinning demon. Its red mouth stretched wide to reveal huge vampire like teeth that came down fast and clamped down hard on his neck. The street person couldn't move, he could only shake like a fish caught by a hook. He screamed once—a long, howling scream. He flailed his arms as though trying to fight off whatever held him, but the chernobog was fastened onto his neck like a fantastic leech.

Professor Meridian felt a dreadful fascination at the man's suffering. He noticed, though, that Camila did not. Then the Professor looked at Akim, and was shocked to see that his eyes were as black as the chernobog's. He tore his eyes away from Akim as the street person gurgled his life away. Blood spurted out of his neck into the chernobog's hungry mouth. It seemed to go on for an endless time, with the man's struggles growing ever fainted until he collapsed and lay limp in the chernobog's embrace. The chernobog was now a vaporous mist that encircled the man, wrapping him in its grasp of a roiling smoking embrace, his mouth all the while cleaved to his carotid artery. When all the man's fluids were drained from his body, the chernobog dropped him.

Slowly, the chernobog formed out of the mist, a fiend now with the figure of a man dressed in funereal black from head to toe. His all black eyes seemed to shimmer with the excitement of having fed. With the back of his hand, he wiped his mouth.

CHAPTER SIXTEEN

Nowhere to Run

"We're sitting ducks," said Hauck.

"That's what I'm saying," said the Instructor. "The best you could do is split up, but that gives Meridian what he wants. Separated from your team, he could hunt you down one at a time. Of course, you could kill the doc here, no offense doc, but it's too late for that."

Jimmy looked at the Instructor to see if he was kidding, but he wasn't.

"You're serious?" he asked.

The Instructor acted hurt.

"Serious? Me?" he said. "Of course I'm serious, but it's too late for that, so you don't have to worry."

"Thanks," said Jimmy.

"Don't mention it," said the Instructor. "Now, where was I? Oh, year, the best you can say is you've got a funnel going for you."

"A funnel? How so?" asked Hauck.

"Look at it this way. This entire underground complex has got only one way in and one way out."

"We still haven't finished blocking off the back way in yet," said Sveta.

"Yeah, but the doc here don't know about that yet?"

"The back way in?" asked Trisha.

"Hauck and the Instructor, the first time they came after Sveta," said Yuri, "blasted their way in from a sewer tunnel."

"But now you've told Jimmy about the tunnel. Now he knows," said Sveta.

The Instructor grinned at that. Sveta thought he had to be the strangest man she had ever met.

"That's true," he said, "but he doesn't know where it is yet. And besides, you've got to slog through a lot of water to get here. No, my bet is they'll take the easy way in—through the front door. They'll come through with guns a-blazing."

"You're saying that the one way in could be an advantage," said Hauck.

"I get where you're going with this," said Sveta. "We could booby-trap the entrance, while using the back way out as an escape hatch."

"Bingo," said the Instructor, "smart girl."

Hauck noticed Sveta beamed when the Instructor called him a smart girl. She didn't even stop to correct him for calling her a girl. Things were looking up.

"All right," said Hauck, "that could work. But we've got to allow them to get fully inside before we pull the trigger."

"We brought enough explosives," said Yuri. "I'll start mining the entrance. Good thing we brought enough food to last us several weeks, though."

"Get to it Yuri," said Hauck. "Trisha, you help."

"What about me?" said Jimmy.

"I need you," said Hauck. "Sveta, you've just been itching to get back in the fight, right?"

"Yes," said Sveta, "I'm not an invalid, you know. I can—"

"Find a secure sniper's nest," interrupted Hauck. "That's where you're going to be stationed. And Sveta?"

"Yes?"

"Load up with lots of ammunition," said Hauck, "you're going to be there for the duration, and we don't know how many men will be coming. Make it far enough away from the explosive force that Yuri sets."

Sveta nodded. She seemed invigorated at the thought. For too long, she had been limping along with nothing to do but heal. She wanted something to do, anything. But now, with their very lives at stake, she was being called on to do something that meant something. She stretched and stood up and leaning on her cane, although less than before, she headed out to look for a safe place to act as a sniper's nest.

"Charlene?"

"Yes?"

"I've got an important job for you," said Hauck.

"Fire away."

"First, I'm going to give you the extra keys to the cages."

"Okay, but why?"

Charlene was a little bit overwhelmed as fast as things were moving. One day they were ushering Sasha into the Tesla tube, fully expecting to be cured. The next thing she knew, Sasha had turned into a monster, and they were filling him full of tranquilizer darts and locking him up in a cage. And now this. When she joined up with Hauck, she never had imagined it would be this exciting.

"Because when all the shooting is done, someone has to let the Instructor and Sasha, if he's cured by then, out of their cages."

"Yeah, and you better not screw it up," said the Instructor, "because I don't want to be in any stinking cage for the rest of my life."

"But," said Charlene, "what if Sasha isn't cured by then?"

Hauck looked pained. The thought that his only son would be trapped in that monstrous body was unthinkable. What kind of father was he, anyway?

"That is a stupid question," said the Instructor. "If he's not cured, you don't let him out. Sorry, but that's how it is. Isn't there anything to eat around this place? I'm hungry."

Charlene just stared at the Instructor as though he were from another planet.

"Yes," said Hauck, "if he doesn't change, or is cured, then don't let him out. That much should be obvious."

"Well, what about you and everybody else? Why me?"

"Everyone else will probably be dead by then, Charlene," said Hauck.

She looked from first Hauck, then the Instructor, and then Jimmy to see if they were serious. When she couldn't see any daylight between them, she gulped.

"Now look," said the Instructor, "I don't plan on being dead, so you've got to stay alive to let me out. Someone's got to take revenge on Meridian. You got that?"

"I got it," said Charlene.

"Just for the record," said Jimmy, "I don't plan on being dead either."

"Yeah, but what are we going to do? To hear the Instructor talk, they're going to come through that door with their machine guns blazing, and all we've got is Sveta and a sniper's nest."

"I wouldn't underestimate Sveta," said Hauck with a grim smile.

"And I'm only saying this because she ain't here, you understand," said the Instructor, "but I wouldn't underestimate that girl either. She's hell on wheels with a machine gun, or a pistol, for that matter."

"What we're saying is, we wouldn't want to be in Sveta's line of fire," said Hauck.

Charlene digested that for a minute. She really enjoyed working for Hauck. She was a born Hacker, like Yuri, and the chance to use Brittany, Dr. Jimmy's powerful AI, was really a lot of fun. It's just that she never figured on being shot at.

"Where should I... you know, I feel like a coward. While you guys are being shot at, I'll like what, hide?" said Charlene.

Hauck was suddenly serious.

"Look, Charlene, I'm giving you a grim assignment, I know. Believe me, we could use the extra gun hand, but somebody's got to survive this thing to be alive and to free the Instructor. So your primary assignment is finding someplace that it's safe to hide and that you won't be found. Are we clear on that? You've got to have enough food and water to last several days, in case they stay after they've killed us all. Understood? Your the Instructor's guardian angel, yes? He must be set free to avenge us. You got that?"

Charlene felt the responsibility settle on her like a lead blanket. Her job was to stay alive to free the Instructor. If that's what she was supposed to do, then she would do it.

"I've got that," she said confidently.

"Now, get going," said Hauck.

As Charlene walked away from them, Jimmy said, "All right, we've got what the Charlene does, but what about me? What do I do during all the shooting?"

"You've got to cure Sasha. Sveta, Trisha, Yuri and I will take care of defending the place. Believe me, I want you to fire a gun, too, but freeing Sasha is more important."

"But Hauck, I don't know how," said Jimmy.

"If anybody can do it," and he laid a hand on Jimmy's should, "I'm going to bet on you."

Jimmy looked into Hauck's face for any signs of duplicity. Seeing none, he straightened his back and lifted his chin.

"I hope you know what you're doing," was all he could think of to say.

"I do. I know you'll do everything that can be done."

Hauck and the Instructor left Jimmy to work out problems on the computer. They walked to the far end of the underground complex, to the opening that they had blown through to come for Sveta and to catch Drogol. Stopping before it, Hauck turned to the Instructor, who had been uncharacteristically silent during the long walk.

"Okay, out with it," said Hauck.

"What?"

"What you're thinking."

"Oh, that. Well, okay. Did you ever think of just running out on this whole mess?" asked the Instructor.

Hauck thought about that. Truthfully, had he ever given a thought to turning tail and running? It wasn't in his nature. He had thought about bringing in more guns, but who could he trust with the secret of the underground complex? Answer, nobody. The Instructor was waiting for an answer.

"No, I've never thought about it. I understand the concept of living to fight another day, but it's just not in my nature."

"How about bringing in more guns?"

"No, they would have to be the kinds of people that I could trust with the secret of this place. We would have to bring them in unvetted, so considering the time frame we've got to work with, I'd say there isn't anyone that I could trust."

"You sure about that?"

"Yes."

"Okay, you know Hauck, I've known you a long time, haven't I?"

"Yes, you certainly have. What's your point?"

"You know I'd help you with this if I could, right?"

"I know that."

"You're sure you won't consider just leaving everybody and making a run for it? Meridian would be satisfied with just getting his hands on me, you know. Everybody split up and then let Meridian duke it out with me. Everybody after that is on their own."

Hauck stared at the man who had taught him most of what he knew about fighting. And, truth be told, how to survive while he was being hunted by the KGB. He was a bombastic, complicated and brutal little man. At just shy of five feet and eighty-five years old, he was a wonder as to what shape he was in. He had arms that would make Pop-eye proud. A chest that would be the envy of a bigger man and legs that could run forever. And he was cursed with the werewolf's drive to kill and maim. Hauck owed him a debt bigger than he could calculate.

"No," was all he said.

The Instructor took his time answering. Hauck wondered what was going through that calculating mind of his.

"All right," the Instructor finally said. "You prepared to die?"

"Yes."

"You prepared for Sveta to die?"

Hauck gave a visible start.

"Yeah, I thought so," said the Instructor. "You better go ask her. And while you're at it, you might as well ask the rest of them, too."

"I—"

"Because," interrupted the Instructor, "they're counting on you pulling them through in on piece, you know."

"I—"

"At least one of them, maybe more, is going to die. You know that, too, right?"

Hauck didn't think there was a choice, but there was, wasn't there? Maybe the Instructor was right. Maybe Meridian would just be satisfied with him, and maybe, just maybe, they would risk their lives for nothing. He thought seriously about it. Professor Meridian would never be just satisfied with taking and killing the Instructor. The man would have to kill Hauck as well, and Dr. Jimmy for killing the Dhole. Where did Sveta and Trisha fit in? Would they be safe or not? And what about Yuri and Charlene? Were they just along for the ride, innocent passengers who didn't know they faced probable death if they stayed and they had better chances on their own?

He could see Sveta and Trisha being iffy. Sveta, though, now there was a toss-up. Professor Meridian knew about her, that was for sure. He met her at the book launch party. Trisha he had met, too, had even threatened that he would revenge himself on her. Sveta could disappear. She had papers that could get her outside the country. Homeland Security couldn't penetrate her papers, that was for sure, since they had been prepared by Brittany, Jimmy's AI. Maybe she could lie low in Russia, maybe in her now dead father's dacha. The place was rented out, but Sveta could handle getting rid of the people. She could even pay them off to get them out. But Meridian would eventually find her.

And Trisha? Meridian knew where she worked. She would never make it in the underground life. Hauck mulled that over. Maybe she could get Jimmy to make them. Of course he would. Why was he even considering that? Jimmy would gladly do papers for her. Maybe they could run away together. They'd be safer that way.

What about Yuri and Charlene? Yuri would stay because he trusted Hauck. If he said stay, then Yuri would follow. But Charlene could slip away unnoticed. Disappear into the crowds and then what? Would Meridian come after her, too? He didn't even know she existed. But he soon would know her if she stayed where she was, or maybe she could find a safe place to hide. Maybe. Or was it already too late for her? Did the psychic know of her just by Jimmy seeing her now?

They couldn't take a chance. They had to stay and fight. Meridian would be on their tail, and there would be no peace for them. At least together, they had a fighting chance.

"Don't say it," said the Instructor. "I can see you've decided."

"We've got to stay and fight here. Thanks to Jimmy's computer system, we have an early warning that they're coming for us."

"I hear you. You sure about Sveta?"

"I'm sure. She knows if she asks me, she can leave."

"You better ask, Hauck, it's important to ask. You ask every single person here if they're in it for the duration."

Hauck nodded.

"Is that it?" he asked.

"Yeah, let's go back and get ready for visitors."

But what Hauck and the Instructor didn't expect was the chernobog.

CHAPTER SEVENTEEN

The Vision

"Give the chernobog the items you have collected," said Akim.

Camila nervously approached the chernobog. He was sitting in the room's only chair, waiting. She extended her right hand, containing the large plastic bag full of things that she had collected from Jimmy's house. In the bag were the shaver, the T-shirt and the picture of Trisha. The chernobog took them from Camila without saying a word. Immediately, Camila backed away. The chernobog watched her walking away in silence. Professor Meridian, positioned in the back of the room, observed carefully.

"I want you to read these things, and tell me where the person in question is," said Akim.

The chernobog said nothing for a few minutes, his gaze on Camila, who looked nervously away. Finally, he looked down at the plastic bag and took out the shaver. He held it in one hand and closed his eyes. Camila raised her eyes and looked over the now depleted husk of a man that was the street person, and peered at the chernobog. She wondered what on earth he was.

Finished with the shaver, he laid it carefully on the floor. Next, without giving any sign of feeling whatsoever, he reached into the bag and took out the T-shirt. Again, he closed his eyes. Minutes passed without the slightest motion on the chernobog's part.

Now Camila studied him. He looked like a man, but clearly he was not a mat. He had the power to turn into a mist whenever it suited him, particularly when he closed in on prey. To feed, he extended his jaws and sunk his canines into a victim's neck and literally sucked the life out of him. To Camila, it suddenly became clear. The chernobog was really a vampire.

The chernobog opened his black eyes and stared directly at Camila. He was smiling. It was a cruel, lifeless smile, and Camila involuntarily took a step back.

"Don't be afraid, my dear. The chernobog won't harm a hair on you lovely head. Because, you see, I say not to," said Akim.

It was when the chernobog laid the T-shirt down carefully that he first seemed to notice the picture of Trisha. He took it out with a reverence that Camila found oddly disconcerting.

"Lovely," he said with a quick intake of breath.

"You find her attractive?" the professor said, suddenly interested.

"Yes, I most certainly do," said the chernobog.

"Interesting," said the professor. "She is the girlfriend of the man we seek to find, Dr. Jimmy Harlen."

"See if you can find anything from her picture," said Akim. "We think he handled it frequently."

Considering carefully every word that was said to him, the chernobog slowly nodded. He touched the picture to his forehead and then fell into a deep, trance-like sleep. Time passed as the chernobog dreamed. Camila was beginning to feel, uncomfortably, that the chernobog had fallen asleep, when suddenly his black eyes popped open.

"I see him," he said.

"Good," said Akim. "Now tell us where he is."

"Will you allow me to move on, after this?" asked the chernobog.

"When you have completed your contract," said Akim. "First you have to find them and kill them."

The chernobog seemed to consider that.

Camila couldn't get out of her mind his feeding on the street person. She looked at the dried out husk of the street person. It was an abomination. She was used to killing people with a gun or knife, but this... this was too much. The street person was just a husk of a man lying there. Professor Meridian had her move the man to the side so as not to act as a distraction until his body could be properly disposed of like Heinrich's. They had an incinerator on site to take care of things like bodies. Camila shivered at the thought. She wasn't getting soft. It was just that the thought of the chernobog had her spooked.

"I can tell you where they are, but after my contract is fulfilled, you must set me free," said the chernobog.

"Of course," said Akim smoothly, "of course."

The chernobog suddenly stood up in one fluid motion and walked within an arm's length of Akim. He was a creature of all black, and in the dim light, his movement was frightening.

"You must set me free," he said.

Camila and Professor Meridian both stepped back at the chernobog's advance, but Akim stood his ground, seemingly unafraid.

"When you have completed your contract, I shall set you free. Not a second before," said Akim.

It was amazing to Camila that Akim was not afraid of the chernobog. Yet he stood there, face to face with him. No fear was exhibited on his part, it was as though he were royalty addressing a vassal. For a full minute they stared at each other, without saying a word, and then the chernobog spoke.

"There will come a day when I shall be free of these shackles, Akim, and then I shall drain you dry of all life."

"On that day, you shall have your thoughts fully occupied by something else, I assure you. Your bloodlust will be your undoing."

The chernobog's black eyes flashed a deep scarlet shade, and his fingers grew long, pointed claws. Unnoticed by either the chernobog or Akim, Camila and Professor Meridian backed up until they were up against either side of the door. When they did, they turned and looked at one another, and it was clear to Camila that they would bolt and run if the chernobog attacked.

"Now," said Akim, unruffled by the sudden change in the chernobog, "to business."

Slowly, the chernobog's eyes returned to their normal black, and his claws retracted. Camila and Professor Meridian did not relax. At the slightest sign of hostility, they were prepared to run for it. But the chernobog, was seemingly cowed by Akim. What could his hold over the chernobog be? While the chernobog could clearly suck the life it if him, yet he obeyed him. Unwillingly, of course, but still he did whatever Akim told him. Why didn't he just turn into a mist and surround Akim and suck the life out of him, like he did the others? Camila looked at Professor Meridian, but he seemed as fascinated by the dynamic as she was.

"I will have to take you there," said the chernobog.

"No," said Akim, "tell me first where he is."

"It is difficult to describe. He hides underground, in a place beneath a place. Your man Hauck and the Instructor are there, too. I see other people, two women. One of them is the woman in the photo. The other is a cripple. There is another man there, too. A Russian, I think."

"Where?"

The chernobog leaned over and whispered directions to Akim. When he was through, he smiled at Camila, a smile that told her he would like nothing better than to sink his teeth into her throat.

CHAPTER EIGHTEEN

The Preparation

Everyone was gathered around the big table in the center of the old engineering room, where generations before the mysterious men who had designed the complex met to discuss their plans. The table was swept clean of all their old drawings; they were neatly stacked on shelves to the side.

"All right," said Hauck, "the Instructor thinks I should ask every one of you whether you want to be here. Let's go around the room, and say aye or nay if you would like to leave."

The group looked at each other. It had never occurred to them that Hauck would ask their opinion.

"I think we can short circuit this," said Sveta. "I don't want to be here. I'd rather be on a beach in Buenos Aires. Anybody else?"

"Me, too," said Charlene. "Make that two for Buenos Aires."

Yuri held up his hand.

"Yes, Yuri?"

"Make that three."

"Duly noted," said Sveta. "That's three for Buenos Aires. Anybody else?"

Jimmy and Trisha held up their hands.

"That's four, five for Buenos Aires. Instructor?"

"Nah," said the old man, "I've got a date with a cage."

"Okay," said Sveta. "It's settled. That's five for Buenos Aires. But we're not going anywhere until we make a stand right here, otherwise we'll be running for the rest of our lives. That satisfactory?"

Hauck appreciated the vote of confidence. The group was standing behind him. That had to mean something. They weren't natural born followers.

"That's satisfactory," said Hauck. "What have we got?"

"I found a natural born sniper's nest, and have loaded it up with gear and ammunition. To be completely sure, I have two other places to fall back to, again each one loaded up with gear and ammunition."

"Impressive," murmured Hauck. "Yuri, have you and Trisha finished mining the entrance-way?"

"With enough explosives that there won't be anyone left standing. First they get in, and when they start to spread out—ka-boom. They won't even know what hit them."

"Excellent," said Hauck. "Now, you two have got to be back up for Sveta. Yuri, I know you're not a gunman, and Trisha, do the best you can. But separate, one on the left flank and one on the right flank. That way, you've got an excellent field of fire and won't shoot each other. Understood?"

"Sure thing," said Trisha, seconded by Yuri.

"What about you and Jimmy?" said Yuri.

"We'll give Jimmy a gun, but his main objective is to get Sasha back. And me, I'm going to be the bait that's right in front of their eyes."

"What?" said Sveta.

"I'll let Jimmy explain," said Hauck.

All eyes turned to Jimmy. The Instructor looked particularly interested.

"Well, first of all, I don't know if this will work, but in theory, I'm going to project holograms of Hauck all over the complex."

"Cool," said Yuri. "How on earth do you do that?"

Jimmy smiled. He felt like he was doing something useful. With all the time he had been banging his head against a brick wall aimed at bringing Sasha back, at least now he could contribute something tangible.

"Brittany, my AI, is running the show. I've got a series of eight projectors that show brief video clips of Hauck in action poses.'

"Was this your idea?" Sveta asked Hauck.

"No, definitely not," said Hauck. "It was Jimmy's"

"Actually, it was Brittany's idea, too."

"I like it," said the Instructor.

"We've got Hauck running from place to place, ducking, hiding, jumping so we can have him leaping for cover," said Jimmy. "I've even got sound."

"It was nothing," Hauck said modestly.

"So we've got Hauck in various clothing, too. It should fool them for a little while."

"Meanwhile, I'll sneak in shots," said Hauck. "Hopefully, with enough distractions, I can whittle down the opposing forces."

Yuri whistled. He had to admire the way Jimmy had his own AI. He had to use Brittany more. She was handy for going on the Internet without being identified, but she was capable of so much more. Yuri had to explore the possibilities, provided they got through this.

"How about me?" asked the Instructor.

"You'll be locked up in a cage," said Hauck.

"I know that, you dumbass. I mean, can she project my image along with yours?"

"I never thought of that," said Hauck. "What about it, Jimmy?"

"Yes. All we have to do is—"

"No, hang on, can we do one image of me as a man, but can we also do me as a werewolf?" asked the Instructor.

"We can't get images of you as a werewolf. We don't have any pictures of you as a werewolf. You see what I mean?"

"What about Drogol?" asked Sveta. "Can we use images of him as a werewolf? You've got images of him ransacking Detroit."

Jimmy thought about it for a minute.

"We could try. None of those pictures is of high enough quality, from my recollection of it," he said.

"Well, we don't know how much time we've got," said the Instructor. "Better just do me as a man and leave it that."

"No," said Jimmy, "it's not that. Brittany can easily multitask. It was that I just don't know what quality they'll be, that's all. It's not that hard for her to do. Again, I was just questioning the quality."

The Instructor whistled.

"Man, you're a genius. I'm glad I didn't kill you after all."

"Thanks," said Jimmy, "I think."

"I've got a question. Who's going to be on lookout to tell us they're coming?" asked Trisha.

"Brittany will tell us," said Jimmy. "I've rigged a series of sensors along the way in, and she monitors the streets via our street cams. She never sleeps."

"That's my man," said Trisha.

"Nice," said Sveta. "Now what else can we do?"

"Set traps," said the Instructor.

"What?" said Yuri.

"What are you, deaf? I said set traps."

"No, I mean—"

"Set traps, dummy. Ain't you ever set traps before?"

"No, I—"

"Go on," said Sveta. "Specifically, what kind of traps?"

"Wires. Cable. We only got seven hours' til I've got to go in the cage. You want to set them or you want to yap about them? Come on, I'll show you, Sveta."

"I want to learn to," said Yuri.

"I'll take Trisha. She knows how to keep quiet."

"But—"

"I'll take you, too, but you better keep your trap shut. Come on, hurry it up. What are you waiting for?"

Hauck thought that was the first time that the Instructor had ever called them by their first name, instead of "girlie." As the Instructor left with them, Sveta, Trisha and Yuri in tow, Hauck felt a stab of pride. Then he thought about the danger that they faced, and how each one of them was laying it on the line, and he felt a sudden chill go through him.

"Hauck?"

"Yes, Charlene?"

"I've found a place to hide that I think will work."

"Good."

"So can I go with the Instructor, too?"

"Yes, Charlene. Hurry and catch them."

"Thanks."

With that, she was gone. The Instructor would be in his teaching mode. Teaching them to set traps for the enemy. In a way, that made the old man happy. In fact, he was the happiest that Hauck had ever seen him. At the end of it, though, he would be locked in a cage for three days. The material of construction was titanium steel, and there was simply no way for the Instructor to get out, even in his werewolf form. The sound proofing was a nice touch, Hauck had to admit. It had been difficult to find the people who could construct it, but it had been worth it.

"What do we do now?" asked Jimmy.

"We go check on Sasha. Come on, let's do it while we still have time."

They walked the distance together to Sasha's cage in silence. It and the Instructor's cage were as far away from the living quarters as they could, because the soundproofing wasn't perfect. There had to be air vents, after all. Jimmy stopped when they got to the cage.

"Hauck?" he said.

"Yes?"

"I'm truly sorry for Sasha's predicament."

"We've been through this before. There's no need to be sorry. Sasha's a big man, and he wanted this to be a success more than any of us knew. You warned him of the consequences and, well, he chose to go ahead with the experiment, anyway. Now come on, let's see how he's doing."

Jimmy acquiesced as Hauck took the key out of his pocket, took in a deep breath, and unlocked the door. He pulled it back, and there was no sound from within the cage. At first he thought the beast was asleep, but when his eyes adjusted to the light, he saw a naked Sasha curled up at the back of the cage.

"Sasha," he exclaimed. "You're back."

"Oh, thank God," Jimmy said.

"Sasha, wake up. It's me, Hauck, your father."

Slowly, Sasha woke up.

Hauck was about to insert the key into the inner lock when Jimmy's hand grabbed his wrist.

"Don't," he said.

"What are you talking about?" said Hauck.

"We don't know how fast he turns or when," said Jimmy quietly.

Sasha blinked his eyes, coming fully awake now.

"Where am I?" he said. "Where are my clothes?"

Jimmy held on to Hauck's hand, mindful while he was doing it that Hauck didn't like it. But finally, Hauck nodded and Jimmy let go.

"You're in the cage, Sasha," said Hauck. "Everything is all right now."

Confused and dazed, Sasha got to his feet.

"Go get him some clothes," said Hauck.

"You're sure you're okay?"

"I'm okay. Thank you for stopping me from making a terrible mistake."

"You're welcome. I'll go get his clothes now."

And with that, Jimmy was gone.

Sasha came forward until he was even with Hauck.

"I must have blacked out," he said. "I don't remember anything."

"Nothing at all?" said Hauck.

"Not a thing," said Sasha. "One minute I was lying in bed and then I was having a horrible dream and then the next thing I know, I wake up here, buck naked."

"Jimmy has gone to get you some clothes. You're okay, then?"

Sasha grinned.

"Except for being naked and locked up in a cage. Must have been a full moon last night. Man, I don't remember."

"Sasha, I need you to listen to me carefully, all right?"

Leery now, something in Hauck's voice had tripped the wire.

"What?"

"Do you remember the experiment?"

A blank look spread over Sasha's face. He squinted, and then brightened.

"Oh yes, it was a success, wasn't it?" And then a realization dawned on him. "I guess it wasn't, was it? Otherwise, I would not be waking up in this cage naked."

He seemed downcast, forlorn, dejected. As though, for a while, his high hopes had been dashed. He was introspective for a moment, wrapped in silence.

"No, Sasha, it wasn't a success."

"No, no, we must try again. I can defeat this curse of the

werewolf. We just keep trying."

"It's worse than that, Sasha," said Hauck gently.

"What?" said Sasha, suddenly in an anguished tone. "Tell me, what can be worse than being locked up in this cage for three days? What can be worse than turning into a monster for three days out of the month? To wake up the next morning naked and alone."

Hauck turned away, not sure he could go through with this. How do you tell a young man in such agony that no, he was really fine except on an unpredictable schedule, he turned into an alien monster? And for three nights of the month, he would still turn into a werewolf?? How to tell him that he could never come out of the cage again?

"What father, what is it?"

Hauck turned back to face his son. The son he thought he would never have. The son he was now determined to save, at all costs, to tell him the truth.

"Sasha, it's much worse than that. You see, the Tesla waves did not fail. We don't know if you will become a werewolf yet. We have to wait and see."

A look of relief spread over Sasha's face.

"Then that's good, yes? But why do I have no clothes on?"

"Because, Sasha, we initially didn't see any side effects, but after a while—"

"Yes?"

"But after a while, you turned into something… something alien."

Sasha was confused. A look of disorientation spread across his face.

"What?"

"It took the Instructor five or six tranquilizer darts to put you down."

For a moment, Sasha was silent. Then, his face contorted with despair.

"Why is this happening to me? Why?"

"Sasha, I—"

"Don't Sasha me. You don't care that I'm… I'm a monster."

"Sasha—"

"You don't care. I hate you. I hate you, I hate you."

Having said his piece, Sasha returned to the far corner of his cage and sat down, his head in his hands.

CHAPTER NINETEEN

The Agreement

Professor Meridian sat behind his desk with his hands folded in front of him. The time had come for a decision. He simply must have the chernobog. He had to control the power to make him do what he wanted, the way Akim did. Akim, who would simply vanish with his five million dollars' worth of gold when Hauck and the Instructor and the others were destroyed, leaving the professor with nothing. He would, in theory, set the chernobog free, and then, where would the professor be? What would he have except for the death of his enemies? The chernobog would be gone, Akim would have left him bereft of all the power that the chernobog possessed. If the chernobog stayed, if it were under his control, then he would have all the power he could wish for at his command.

A knock at the door told of her arrival.

"Enter," said the professor.

Camila came in.

"Close the door," the professor commanded, "and sit down."

She did as she was told, and, after closing the door behind her, she sat down in one of the rich red velvet chairs with gold welt detail on black lacquered cabriolet legs. Camila's smallish yet slightly oval face was unreadable.

"I asked you here, Camila—forgive my poor manners—would you like something to drink?"

"No, thank you."

"Are you sure? I have a fine grand cru Montrachet that I can offer you."

"No, but thanks anyway."

"You don't mind if I pour a glass, do you?"

"No, not at all. Please, help yourself."

The professor stood, walked over to his wine cabinet, and took out a bottle and an opener. Then he walked back to his desk, uncorked the bottle while standing up, smelled the aroma, and let it breathe. Finally, he poured himself a glass, sniffed it, and then sipped the wine.

"Most satisfying," he said, and sat down.

He waited a moment before continuing. Foremost in his mind was Camila's fear of the chernobog. How to proceed with that in play. He decided on an oblique approach.

"Camila," he began, "it has come to my attention that you do not approve of the chernobog."

"No, I am afraid of the chernobog. But I think that is only natural under the circumstances."

"Hmm, yes, I see your point. Only, what circumstances are those?"

"Its inhumanity. It's hard to explain, but I feel that it is a danger to us. I am afraid that it will turn on its captors."

"I see. Yet, Akim seems to have it under his control, does he not?"

"I'm afraid... may I speak frankly?"

"Please do."

"I'm afraid that is just an act. I'm that he will turn on us at a moment's notice."

"I see."

The professor sipped his wine slowly, as he considered. It was amazing to him that this rather dangerous woman was afraid of the chernobog.

"No, I'm afraid you don't see at all, professor."

"Oh?"

"Can't you feel it, the evil radiating off of it? The chernobog is not a human being. He may look like a man, but he is most definitely not."

"True enough, but what of it? I need him to locate Hauck and the Instructor, and he has located him with a speed we could not have hoped to achieve otherwise."

Camila leaned forward in her chair. The professor thought that she was desperate to make him understand. But, in fact, he already understood too well.

"But don't you see? Akim is playing a dangerous game. He wants Hauck and the Instructor for his own ends?"

"What is that to me, my dear Camila?"

"Professor, I worry the chernobog won't care. He'll kill everyone —everyone of them, and what's stopping him from coming after us, and you?"

The professor appeared to consider that. In fact, he had thought of that long ago. Akim had no use for the professor's men, and even less use for the professor himself. The professor needed him, though, to point the way for the chernobog to destroy Hauck and the Instructor. But after that, Akim would not need him at all. Of course, there was the matter of the money. The professor had already paid Akim one million dollars in gold as a down payment. The other four million would be transferred to him when he completed his task. It was at that moment that the professor was at greatest risk.

"But what would you suggest I do, Camila?"

"Find out what Akim's game is, how he controls the chernobog, and what is the source of his power."

"But he would suspect me, Camila. He is too guarded around me. Any clue that I was looking for and he would simply clam up. Perhaps you can find out more?"

Camila hesitated.

"I don't know if he will talk to me," she said hesitantly.

"I see," said the professor. "But you could try? Time goes short, you know. Tonight, we assemble and go in."

The professor made a show of checking his pocket watch. He flipped its cover open and could see that there were seven hours to go. He turned and showed it to Camila.

"You see, only seven hours to go. Won't you please try, Camila?"

"I don't know. What would I say to him? How should I approach him?"

"You might try flattery, but somehow I don't think that work."

"No, no, that wouldn't."

"How about if you asked him what the chernobog really is? And from there, you could lead up to how he controls it so well."

"Don't you think that would be too obvious?"

The professor seemed to think about that. He pursed his lips as though considering. At long last, he simply shook his head.

"No," he said, "It is all we have, considering the short time element."

Camila seemed uncomfortable with the line of questioning. But the more she thought it over, the more she thought they had no choice.

"I'll do it," she said.

Professor Meridian smiled.

CHAPTER TWENTY

Desperation

A despondent Hauck turned to the Instructor.

"He won't listen to me," he said.

"Yeah, well, what did you expect? Get real. The kid won't feel any better till he's cured. How would you feel knowing you had to spend the rest of your life locked up in a cage?"

"Thanks for the kind words."

"Well, it's the truth, ain't it?"

Hauck let a long breath. He was miserable.

"Yes, I guess it is."

The Instructor patted him on the back.

"If I can't give you some kind words," he said, "what good am I? Now come on, we've got to lock me up, because we can't take any chances on them attacking at night. They may just attack in the day. I don't think so, but we can't take any chances with me turning into a werewolf during a firefight."

Hauck nodded and walked the Instructor toward the cage. They passed Jimmy on the way there.

"Hey, Hauck, I've got him all locked down," said Jimmy.

"Did he talk to you?"

"Yeah," said the Instructor, "I'm kind of curious what the condemned man had to say."

"No, so far he just sulked, but he'll come around."

"Right," said Hauck.

"Charlene's up there, waiting to see you."

Hauck and the Instructor continued on the winding way up to where the cages were. Charlene was sitting on a crate in front of them.

"Hey, Hauck," she said.

"Charlene," he nodded.

"Hey, Instructor."

"Kid," said the Instructor.

"The Instructors here to go into his cage," said Hauck.

"I know," said Charlene.

"You remember everything I taught you?" said the Instructor.

"Yes."

"Bullshit. All right, Hauck, open her up. I'll see you tomorrow."

Hauck unlocked the first lock to the soundproofing, and then the second lock to the cage itself. He stood to one side and allowed the Instructor to pass. He closed the door, then locked it and closed the second door to the soundproofing. There was a light inside of the cage that was set behind the bars, out of reach to the werewolf.

"He'll be okay, Hauck, believe me, he'll be okay."

"As long as you open the door tomorrow, he'll be fine," said Hauck. "Have you got your hiding place set?"

"Yes, it's—"

"Don't tell me where. I don't want to know. It's safer that way, in case I'm captured and forced to talk."

Charlene looked shocked.

"You don't think that will happen, do you?"

"I don't know, Charlene. Anything is possible, but I don't plan on it. Just in case, though."

She looked relieved, but troubled.

"Okay," she said at last. "But be careful."

"You, too, Charlene. Now, get lost. Vanish to your little hiding hole and good luck."

Hauck then turned around and walked back the way he came. He felt lost that his son wouldn't speak to him. It wasn't his fault. It wasn't anyone's fault that Sasha had turned into a monster. But he had infinite confidence that Jimmy would bring him back. He just had to find where Drogol had put the real instructions. He couldn't believe that they had followed the real instructions, and that Drogol had been wrong. No, he was too careful. He had taken too much time, too much effort that he had put behind them.

Up ahead, he saw the Tesla tube and remembered the disastrous results of Jimmy's first experiment. Hauck flinched at the memory. How could they have been so wrong? Jimmy had followed every word to the letter in Drogol's journal. Could the words have been coded in a code only known to Drogol? It just didn't make any sense.

Sveta.

Drogol, in declaring his love for Sveta, had said something to her that nagged at Hauck's memory. What had Drogol given Sveta before he had the disastrous experience in the Tesla tube which turned him into a giant werewolf? Drogol had been standing in the Tesla tube when Zoe was shot and had fallen against the lever that drove the vibrations to full maximum. No, there was nothing there. It had to be before then. What had Drogol said or what had he given to Sveta that might give any clue?

Hauck had to ask Sveta.

He passed Jimmy on the way to find Sveta, who had something to tell him, but he told him later he had to do something. He walked on past the tubes and wires and other contraptions, that he had no earthly idea what they did until he reached the catwalk where Sveta had her first sniper's nest.

"Hauck," she said as he approached.

"Sveta, I've got something to ask you," he said.

She adjusted her rifle sites as she said, "Ask away."

"Did Drogol try to say something or give you something at any time before the event at the Tesla tube?"

She laid the rifle aside and asked, "What?"

"I can't get it out of my mind that he said something or tried to give you something that might be key to the settings for the Tesla machine that will restore Sasha."

Standing up to face him, she reached up and put both hands on his shoulders and stared directly into his eyes. It was the first physical contact that Hauck had ever experienced with her.

"Hauck, there was nothing that Drogol tried to say or give me that in any way had any indication of dials or settings that had anything to do with the Tesla machine. I'm sorry."

He felt the bottom going out of his hopes.

"I understand," he said.

But Sveta did not remove her hands. She left them on his shoulders.

"You can't fix everything," she said.

"I know," he said.

"Good."

"I'd better go."

"Yes," she said, and she kissed him, long and hard and deep. "That's for luck. We're going to need it."

Hauck was so shocked he didn't know what to say.

"Now go on, you've got the others to check on."

"Yes," he said, and turned and started walking away.

"Hauck?"

"Yes," he said, as he stopped and turned around.

"Now that you mention it, there was something that Drogol tried to give me the day or the night before he was in the Tesla tube. I just remembered. It's probably nothing—"

"What was it?" said Hauck eagerly.

"Like I said, it's probably nothing."

"Sveta—"

"When he was on the train, he tried to give me a picture of me, or Catherine the Great — she looked a great deal like me—and at first I thought it was me. And in this picture, there he was, when he was known as Rasputin. Anyway, he tried to give it to me."

"Where is it now?"

"It's in the train where I left it, I think, in the second or third car before the derailment he caused when he was a werewolf."

"Thank you, Sveta."

"Like I said, it's probably nothing."

Hauck felt renewed. There was hope. It was like Sveta said, it was probably nothing, but it was a place for Jimmy to start. It was all he could do not to run back to where Jimmy was. When he got to Jimmy's table with the computers, Jimmy and Trisha were staring at the screen.

"Jimmy—"

Jimmy held up his hand for silence.

"Just a minute," he said. "I've almost got this."

Hauck waited for a minute, then two, then three and finally, when neither Jimmy nor Trisha would look up, in frustration, he set out to find the train himself. On the way to the train, he found Yuri fiddling with something on the Tesla tube.

"Yuri," he said in passing.

"Huh? Oh hi, Hauck. Where are you off to such in such a hurry?"

"I'm going to try and find something on the train."

Yuri looked puzzled. The train was normally left alone. It wasn't something that normally attracted that much interest.

"What?"

Hauck stopped to explain.

"I think Drogol left something for Sveta. A picture of himself with Catherine the Great that explains the settings that he used on the Tesla tube. Maybe. I'm hoping it is, anyway."

"You want some company?"

"Sure."

So Yuri quit what he was doing and went with Hauck. They went past the controls for the globes that floated overhead, past the seemingly endless rows of parts that, again, Hauck did not know what they did.

"Did you ever wonder about who built this place?" said Yuri.

"Yes," said Hauck. "Drogol said to Sveta that it was built by capitalists, industrialists who wanted to steal technology and hold it hostage."

"But you don't believe that, do you?"

"Let's just say that I think Drogol was biased. If these men were stealing technology to make money off of it, why not just release it into the world and make a killing right then and there?"

"Yeah, I see what you mean. Well, it's hard to imagine that within six or seven hours, this could be the place where we take our last stand."

At last they came to the train. Hauck could never understand how they got it there in the first place. The rails at the far end ended in an impenetrable brick and stone wall. There were seven cars and a caboose just sitting there, mindlessly occupying space. But four of those cars were twisted up and thrown off the track by the impact of

Drogol in his werewolf form. It was unimaginable to Hauck the amount of force that took. The train itself, counting the engine, must have weighed close to ten thousand pounds.

"Man, Drogol sure made a mess of this, didn't he?" said Yuri.

"He did at that," said Hauck. "Fortunately for us, what we're after is in the third car, the last car before the ones he hit."

"You know what kind of strength that must have taken to hurl four train cars off the track?"

"I know, Yuri, I know."

They took the steps on the caboose up to the train's main floor and went inside. Everything was dusty, but serviceable, as if it hadn't been touched in years. What could Drogol have found in this place? Solace of a bygone era?

"This place is eerie, Hauck. It's like from another time or something."

Hauck nodded.

"It was, Yuri."

There were no lights on the train except for the windows, but still they could see the counters where the caboose man had sat. The wooden floor, the wooden superstructure, and a potbellied stove with a coffeepot on top of it were all part of the stifled ambiance. A small built-in couch ran alongside the walls. Pin-up pictures of 1920s and 1930s movie women were along the walls.

Hauck and Yuri continued on. They opened the door to the second car and the repressed opulence was staggering. The royal blue carpet, the red velvet chairs trimmed with gold and elegant woodwork were impressive, even in the muted light that came in through the curtained windows. As they walked down the carpet toward the third car, the overhead hand crafted woodwork of the carriage for luggage caught Yuri's eye.

"This car must have been for royalty," he said.

Hauck agreed. The sophistication of it was unmistakable. They opened the doors to the third car, and they were even more impressed. The third car was the pièce de résistance, its carpeting was a deep scarlet color, trimmed with silver scrollings. There were chairs of blue velvet instead of rows of seats and the woodwork was fabulous. The light filtered in through train windows, whose golden cables pulled back curtains of red satin. At the far end of the car was a large photograph, framed in rosewood. Hauck approached it, with Yuri following down the aisle. It was a photograph of Catherine the Great, with Rasputin by her side. Yuri whistled.

"Boy, that does look like Sveta," he said.

Hauck nodded.

"And that is Drogol at her side. The likeness is undeniable," he said.

The photograph detailed a remarkable likeness of Sveta and Drogol, that was yet marred by age, a photograph that was over one hundred years old. It was faded, and a long, cracked line ran down its length.

"Kind of spooky, huh?" said Yuri.

"It's like Catherine was her exact clone."

He took the photo down and took it over to the window to see it better. He turned it over in his hands.

"Give me your knife, Yuri."

Yuri did so, and Hauck pried the back of the picture off. Hauck handed the knife back to Yuri. He looked at the back of the photograph and the single piece of paper there. With trembling hands, he laid the picture down on a counter and walked over to a window and held the paper up to the light again.

"What is it, Hauck?"

Hauck turned to Yuri and smiled. It was one of the very few times that Yuri could ever remember him having smiled. In fact, it was the only time that he could remember him having smiled.

"It is the key," he said, "to everything."

CHAPTER TWENTY-ONE

The Vampire

In his room, behind closed doors, Akim stood with his feet apart. He was surrounded by a chalk outline of a circle with strange names written around it in an ancient tongue. At each of the four corners, he had placed one of four Tarot cards. The Ace of pentacles to represent the earth, the Ace of swords for air, the Ace of wands for fire, and the Ace of cups for water. Behind each of the four cards, he had placed candles of various colors—brown for the earth, light blue for air, red for fire, and light green for water. In addition, he had also placed a bowl of salt, a feather, an athame, and a small chalice filled with wine.

Standing in his black robe, his long hair hung to his shoulders, his powerful frame was relaxed and his thumbs and forefingers touching in a way that closed the circle. He began the chanting that would also close the quarters. He closed his eyes and imagined a black curtain folding around his circle and whirling around with the rhythm of his chanting.

He stopped and intoned, "I call on the element of earth. Bring stability to my magic today."

Then he walked to the left and said, "I call on the element of water. Bring fluidity to my magic today."

Next, he walked to the south and said, "I call on the element of fire. Bring the light and heat of your transformative energy to my magic today."

Then, he perambulated to the east, and finally said, "I call on the element of air. Bring me mental clarity to my magic today."

Having completed calling in the quarters, he bowed his head in prayer. When he raised his head, his eyes were all black. He spread his arms wide, as though he were drawing in the universe's energy.

"My will," he shouted, "reigns supreme throughout the known worlds. I speak, and the earth trembles. I call the chernobog's very soul into being."

A replica of the chernobog appeared out of thin air as the air before him shimmered. The chernobog was cabled and bound in a way that prevented his escape. The chernobog screamed.

"Let me go," he howled.

"Fah," said Akim, "you have not yet completed our bargain."

"Let me go," repeated the chernobog.

"Complete your bargain, and I will consider your debt to me paid."

"You lie," snarled the chernobog.

Akim smiled.

"Do I? It is to be expected. But this time, it is the truth. If you kill the murderer of my brother and his friends, then our deal is done and I shall set you free."

"Do you give your word? Do you swear it?"

"Do not try my patience. I have spoken. Yet there is one more favor I would ask of you."

The chernobog roared.

He twisted and turned, but there was simply no way for him to escape his bonds. For the thousandth time, the chernobog strained to break free, but he could not. Exhausted, he slumped forward.

"This would be in the way of something you would very much like to do anyway," said Akim smoothly.

"What would you have me do?" asked the chernobog.

"Only that when you are killing and feeding on Hauck and his men, you kill Camila and her cohorts, too. And when we get back, and the payment is made, you will kill Professor Meridian as well."

At this, the Chernobog smiled.

"And then you will let me go?"

"Oh, yes, friend, then I will let you go."

Slowly, the chernobog faded away.

****

Camila found Akim just outside of the door to the chernobog's room. She approached him warily. There was something about the man that unnerved her. He shared in common with the chernobog a brooding silence. The thought of what she was going to ask him terrified her.

"Akim—"

"Are you ready to go?" he interrupted her.

The question startled her, but she answered.

"Yes, we are ready. The men are all loaded and ready to go."

"Good, then we go tonight. We will strike at two a.m."

"Of course, but shouldn't we go over the strike plan first?"

She was desperate to find a way to ask him the question, but there didn't seem to be an opening.

Akim's gaze was perfunctory, but penetrating. He held her with it for a long heartbeat. It seemed as if he could read her very soul.

"You wish to know what the chernobog is?"

Suddenly, Camila found Akim had backed her up into the wall. His eyes turned all black, like the chernobog's. She felt herself unable to breathe. She tried to mouth words, but they wouldn't come. His eyes were mesmeric.

"The chernobog," he said, "is a vampire of a very special type. He feeds on the fluids of the living."

"But—"

"You wish to know how I control him?"

She struggled to come up with an answer. In the end, she merely nodded, struck dumb with fear.

"I control him with the power of my mind and ritual. The mind is a powerful thing, Camila, when amplified by certain occult practices. Would you like to explore them with me?"

"No," she said. "No, I would not. I mean, if that pleases you."

"Oh, but it most definitely displeases me. I would like you to see, to take part in them when we return. Would you pleasure me,

Camila, by participating in them?"

"No. I mean yes, I mean no."

And she slid out from the wall, out from beneath his eyes and fairly ran away.

Akim smiled broadly at her discomfort and felt the pleasure of anticipation at the chernobog's feeding.

CHAPTER TWENTY-TWO

The Setting

Brittany, Jimmy's artificial intelligence, was speaking.

"Hello, doctor."

The AI platform was a four foot in diameter circle of shiny silicon, beryllium and stainless steel wafer. For the first time, Jimmy had hooked it up, and he was rewarded by seeing a full sized woman appear out of thin air, hovering above the circle.

"Nice to finally see you again, Brittany," said Jimmy.

"Nice to see you again, too. Trisha, it's a pleasure to see you too."

"Hello, Brittany," said Trisha. To Jimmy, she said, "She's so... so real."

"I am real," said Brittany. "I am an artificial humanoid."

"Sorry," said Trisha.

"No offense taken," said Brittany. "What have we on the schedule today?"

Brittany wore a simple two-piece outfit. It was gray-black with a high collar and a striking, plunging neckline. Beneath the coat, which had puffed up shoulders, she had on an elegant blouse of pure white. The skirt was a tight-fitting sheath with a natural waistline of pure black. Trisha didn't know if Jimmy picked out her clothing or the AI did, but either way, it was an impressive look.

"First off, is the perimeter clear?" said Jimmy.

"The perimeter is clear of any traffic. I have checked all monitors and they show no evidence of intruders."

"Keep an eye out for invaders. They'll come at us quick, I think."

"Yes, doctor. I am also programmed to watch for drones if you can install four more cameras."

"Hmm—I don't know if I have the time."

"Hey, doc?"

It was Yuri. He had come to see Brittany. Hauck had waited behind at the train.

"Yes, Yuri?"

"Why don't Trisha and I go do it together?" said Yuri. "You can keep an eye out for trouble."

Jimmy was appalled at the idea. He had just got Trisha back, and he didn't want to lose her.

"No, I don't think that's advisable," he said.

"Why not?" said Trisha. "It's a great idea. Brittany's right—drones are the things nowadays to watch out for. Meridian could be scoping out the place with drones right now. Besides, if they already know where we are, we've got to keep an eye out, and what better way than to watch the skies for drones?"

"I—I don't think it's safe for you to go outside," stammered Jimmy.

"I will watch out for her, but you can go with her if it will make you feel better. We can stay in contact with blue tooth connections. Since you boosted the signals, it should be no problem."

"I don't know," said Jimmy. "It's getting late."

It was three o'clock, and the dusk was coming early.

"Come on, let's just get it over with," said Trisha. "Brittany will watch the street for safety's sake, and we'll be done inside of an hour."

"Look, I just don't feel safe—"

"Come on," said Yuri, "by the time we're done talking about it, we'll be through setting the cameras in place. Besides, if you don't want Trisha to do it, I can do it by myself."

"Okay, okay," said Jimmy. "I don't like it, but let's get it over with."

They gathered up the four cameras and two repeaters and headed toward the door. Along the way, they passed Sveta in her sniper's nest.

"Hey, Sveta, we're going outside to put some extra cameras up to watch out for drones," said Jimmy.

"Does Hauck know?" asked Sveta.

"No, but we'll be back before you know it," said Yuri.

"I'd let him know."

"Would you tell him, Sveta?" said Trisha.

Sveta looked dubious.

"Sure, I'll tell him for you," she said at last. "But he won't like you going out without telling him first."

"We won't be long," said Yuri. "We've got to get these up before nightfall."

"They won't help you at night," said Sveta.

"They're thermal cameras, so they can see at night. They'll be a big help," said Trisha.

"Whatever. Hurry it up, though."

"We will," promised Jimmy.

They walked past the big gauge that, unknown to them, Sveta had hid behind when she was stalking Mishka's men. Brass piping and steam wisps, gages and dials, levers and knobs as large as a fist. Jimmy, like Sveta before him, thought they had been taken from the engine room of the Nautilus. Past the fifteen foot pit filled with a phosphorescent liquid that crackled with lightning-like charges through its depths. And finally past the big gauge, that was the size of the Windsor Cathedral clock.

"I can never get over this place," said Jimmy. "It's like a wonderland."

Next came the catwalk up to the surface, and finally they came to the door.

"Brittany, is the door clear?" he asked.

"Yes, Dr. Harlen. The door is clear," she said in his earpiece.

"Here goes," he said under his breath.

"It will be fine," said Trisha.

Jimmy unlocked the door and swung it open. It was a massive affair, with double locks and made of titanium steel. They walked out into the garage and smelled the Detroit air.

"You know, it's odd, but it always smells better down below," said Yuri.

"Come on," said Trisha, "let's get these things installed."

****

Charlene was burning off nervous energy. She was exploring the cavernous expanses of the underground laboratory. It was a veritable maze of pipes and structures that defied imagination. She couldn't imagine a place that was more bizarre.

The intermittent noise from the light globes discharging and pressure relief valves releasing jolts of steam made it hard to hear sometimes. She moved deeper into the place, keeping behind a massive set of horizontal silver tubes resting on a skid. There were towers and globes that lit the place with golden light. There were fewer power beams shooting overhead in their wireless grid. It stopped where the piping dog-legged across the room.

She decided she had to get to higher ground to see exactly where she was and to try to find the ventilation system. Scaffolding bracketed to the side of what looked to be a network of steam and water pipes gave her a secure way to gain some height. Overhead, she could see that there were service platforms roughly every twenty feet. The original engineers and construction people had been kind enough to weld in place a half circle protective cage onto the ladder rungs to prevent anyone from falling backward and killing themselves.

Each of the service platforms was four feet square with a three foot tall sheet metal wall formed and welded inside the curved railing. She crawled out onto it and then shimmied the rest of the way and collapsed onto the diamond-backed floor. This was the place she would wait out the coming gunfight, high up and unseen. She couldn't find the ventilation system, though, and decided to give up the search.

From her unseen perch, she could see the hole in the back wall that Hauck had referenced, and marveled that the beast had blasted its way through it. She had brought up enough food and water to last her three days, which she thought should be enough, and she brought up a change of clothes in her backpack. She packed a toothbrush and plenty of reading materials. Also, she was armed to the teeth.

It bothered her that Hauck had assigned her to this menial job. All right, it wasn't menial. Someone had to be left alive to let the

Instructor out of his cage. It wouldn't be fair to let him just rot in there forever. She thought of what that must have cost him, to have one person—when they had so few people—just one person out of how many? Yuri, Sveta, and Trisha. That was it. And Hauck, of course. Dr. Jimmy was, well, to be honest, shit useless. She wished she could fire a gun, but Hauck's instructions were very specific. No firing unless forced into it.

Still, there hadn't been any shooting yet, but she felt safer up here. But then again, it wasn't night yet. The waiting, she decided, was the worst of all. She just couldn't stand it. What was there to do while waiting? Perhaps that was all part of it.

She thought, how could Hauck stand it? He never seemed to unwind. He always was wound as tight as a bullet. Maybe he was attracted to her. She couldn't tell. He was an older man—forty something—maybe. She was twenty-three, but stranger things had happened. She had always heard of older men and younger women. Maybe he was attracted to Sveta? She thought about it. If he was, they were the strangest pairing ever. Sveta was hot tempered and Hauck was cold, man was he ever cold. But he seemed almost solicitous around her. She would have to give that some thought.

She was about to head down when something caught her eye. It was the strangest thing. Little more than a distortion in the cavern's roof; it was odd. She couldn't be sure that it was even real. The roof of the cavern was solid rock—or so it seemed—but there it was again, a slight wiggling. It was almost as though it was real, but not real.

Walking along the catwalk, she suddenly realized that she was up pretty high. In fact, she was damned high up. She glanced up at the ceiling and it appeared to be light years up higher, but with ladders that went up there, so... wait a minute. The ladders went up to nowhere; they ended in a solid rock wall. That was odd.

Charlene looked down again, not sure if she wanted to go higher. In the end, though, her curiosity won out, and she walked to where the catwalk doglegged to the right. There were a series of handholds there, that if she went up that way, she would see what that odd distortion was. It seemed to be gone, but when she tilted her head one way, there it was again. So she gritted her teeth, and, thinking she had nothing else better to do with her time, she began to climb.

Up and up she went. Looking down, she panicked and clung

tightly to the railing. She had never been so scared in her life. Her breath caught in her throat as she realized she was almost to the ceiling, hanging in the middle of the air, and if she slipped and fell, it was curtains for her. Calming breaths, she had to breathe calmly. She couldn't do it while looking down, so she closed her eyes. Time passed amazingly slowly, and she simply couldn't catch her breath. Oh God, I'm going to die. Open your eyes, but look up, she finally thought. Taking a deep breath, she opened her eyes, careful to look up, and the moment passed.

She was ready to go down now, but just then, the rock wall shimmered again. What was that? For the moment, she forgot how high up she was and started climbing. When she came even with the ceiling, she realized she was looking at a clever illusion. She waved her hand through the opening and it was then that she realized she was looking at a concealed trapdoor.

Boy, did she have something to tell Hauck.

CHAPTER TWENTY-THREE

The Trap

Camila didn't have time to think of Professor Meridian. She had to organize the teams to go in and kill the targets. And she had to oversee the moving of the chernobog.

She had them coordinated in three teams of six. With Heinrich... dead, and her as the responsible person, that worked out exactly. The numbers matched perfectly.

One team was responsible for moving the chernobog's enclosure.

"Get three other men and bring the chernobog to the van," she said. "Akim's men will load him in."

The man stared at her, obviously uncomfortable with being that close to the chernobog.

"Or you will be his next meal," said Camila.

He paled at that and hurried away to get three of his teammates to assist. Camila watched him go with trepidation. She was genuinely frightened of Akim, and she didn't like it one bit. In all her three years as a paid assassin, it had never occurred to her to be afraid of anyone. She prided herself on the fact that she bowed down to no man. That had all changed the minute she had met Akim.

She looked up to see Professor Meridian coming her way. She had nothing to tell him except what Akim had said.

"Well, Camila, you are certainly busy," said the professor.

"Getting ready for tonight," she said.

"Have you time to walk with me a little ways?"

She hesitated. Now not trusting the Professor any more than she did Akim, made it difficult for her. But she decided to walk with him for a ways anyway.

"Certainly," she said.

They walked a ways down the aisle, away from the others, before the professor spoke.

"Do you have anything for me?" he asked.

"He says that the chernobog is a vampire, a very special kind of vampire."

"A vampire? Hmm…"

"Yes."

"But, you say, a very special kind of vampire?"

"Yes."

"What kind of vampire?"

"He didn't say. He threatened me instead."

"Really—how did he threaten you, Camila?"

She thought about it. She felt uncomfortable saying it.

"He controls the chernobog by the power of his mind, and certain occult practices. Does that make sense? He performs certain rituals that he invited me to take part in."

"I see. Did you agree to participate?"

"No."

"That is unfortunate, Camila, for then we should have learned the mechanics of how exactly to control the chernobog."

"If I would have agreed, I have no doubt as to the outcome. Akim would have killed me."

At that, the professor seemed surprised.

"I see."

Camila didn't know how sincere the professor was. He seemed to listen to her, but his mind was far away. He was no doubt wondering what type of ritual that Akim used to control the chernobog. He didn't really care if Akim killed her or not, so long as she learned about Akim's secret ritual. Well, screw that. Camila was more interested in surviving. And she was thinking of killing Akim herself. He frightened her, and that was all the more reason to kill him.

"I've got to go before he misses me."

The professor ignored her.

"I see it now," he said. "He is keeping the chernobog under his control by the power of ritual magic. Why didn't I see it before? But how did he trap the chernobog in the first place? That would be valuable to know. Now, the chernobog can only go a certain distance from his cage to kill, is that correct?"

"Yes, that is, I think so."

The professor waved his hand at her, dismissing her objection.

"So, he only can go so far," he continued, "and I wonder just how far that distance is?"

"I don't know."

"Find out for me, Camila. Your life may depend on it. If Akim… turns on you, you would do well to know exactly how far to run from the chernobog."

Camila thought it over. What the professor said made sense. In fact, it made damned good sense.

"I'm beginning to think that Akim has other plans for us, Camila. In fact, may I say that you must not trust him, no matter what he says. We may both be in danger, whether from Akim or his chernobog, I cannot say, but certainly from him or the chernobog, but now that I think of it, from both. Stay back from the killing field, as well."

"I think he means to kill us all when the chernobog is through. Then I think we are next."

"Then you must sneak away from him and the chernobog. Get as far away as you can, Camila. Sacrifice whom you must as a distraction, but get as far away as you can. You must get outside the limit of the chernobog's influence. Do you understand?"

"You're afraid of him, too. I understand that. I will do my best to sneak away during the chernobog's attack on their underground lair. But what then?"

The professor thought it over for a minute. Camila thought that the professor was finally waking up to the danger that he had invited into the whole affair. It would have been a simple matter to take out Hauck and the Instructor if they could have found them. The chernobog was necessary to find them, that much was certain. No garden variety of psychic could have performed the same feat as he did. But what had he let in?

"You must find a way out of their underground lair, and then you must come back to me here. You must be the edge over Akim that he does not see coming. He has six men here that he will take with him to move the chernobog, no?"

"Yes."

"Then somehow, I do not know how, you must escape the notice of Akim and his six guards and get back to me."

"What about the others?"

Camila knew about the others already. She just wanted to hear the professor say it. The thought of all those men dying was regrettable, but Camila didn't see any way around it.

"They must fend for themselves, Camila. I'm sorry, but you must give them that leeway to fight for themselves."

"Professor, why don't we just kill Akim now, when the chernobog is in his cage?"

"Because we must have him control the chernobog to kill Hauck and his men first," hissed Professor Meridian. "It is only afterward that he and his men are expendable. When Hauck and the Instructor are dead, then, if our men are still alive and the chernobog is locked up, you may certainly kill him. In fact, there will be a bonus for you and your men if you do."

The professor smiled an enigmatic, chilling smile.

Suddenly, Camila felt the world was all right again. Still, she wondered just how easily Akim would be to kill.

CHAPTER TWENTY-FOUR

The Last Night

Jimmy, Trisha, and Yuri came back just in time for the night to be falling. The four aerial cameras were installed at the corners of the outside properties. Jimmy locked and bolted the door as they came in. Then they went down the stairs to the main floor. They stopped at the big gage.

"Well, that's done," said Jimmy.

"Hey, we did it with no problem," said Trisha. "Congratulations, all the way around. We've got the whole outside wired for sound and video, so now we wait."

"Why do I feel," said Yuri, "that we won't have to wait too long?"

"Come on," said Jimmy, "let's get back before Hauck gets worried. You know how he gets if one of us disappears for too long. I'd hate to see him if all three of us went missing."

They walked past all the long tubes and pipes that seemed to stretch endlessly, past the phosphorescent pit that sparked lightning and Jimmy wondered again at who had built this wondrous place. There were the globes that simply floated through the air and lit the place with golden light, high overhead and over in the distance the train car and, standing high and alone, was the Tesla tube on its platform. He didn't notice that he had stopped moving for a while.

"What is it, Jimmy?" asked Trisha.

He didn't answer.

"Jimmy?" asked Yuri. "You okay, man?"

He still didn't answer.

Now Trisha was getting worried. Jimmy was just standing there, a look of wonder on his face. It was as though he had found the Holy Grail.

"Jimmy?"

This time, Trisha shook him. He turned to her with an absolutely beatific smile, lighting his countenance.

"What is it Jimmy?"

"I think I have just figured out how to bring Sasha back."

"Really? Well, what are we waiting for—let's go."

The three of them ran the rest of the way back, past Sveta to whom they gave only a passing nod, and back to Jimmy's table where Brittany stood on the silver platform.

"Hello, doctor," Brittany said. "You seem to be in a bit of a hurry."

"I am Brittany, I am."

Trisha could only watch as Jimmy thought furiously. Something seemed to have caught his attention and caught it big time. What it was, though, she couldn't tell. Yuri laid his hand on her arm, as though to say, "Shh. He's thinking."

"Brittany, bring up the diagrammatic of the Tesla tube," said Jimmy.

She did.

"See there," he said triumphantly, "I knew it."

"What?" said Brittany.

"Well, you see this wire here, the one going to the base of the tube?"

"Yes, I see it," said Trisha.

"I fail to see the significance of it, doctor," said Trisha.

"Where is it?" asked Jimmy.

"What?" asked Yuri.

"Where is it?" repeated Jimmy. "It's in this diagram. But where is it in actuality?"

"You mean where is it, like now? On the... wait a minute, I'll got check," said Yuri.

While Yuri went to check on the cable, Trisha asked, "What are you getting at?"

"I didn't see that cable there," said Jimmy.

"Ah, I see," said Brittany. "You think that Sasha's transformation was ineffective because a cable was missing?"

"Yes," said Jimmy. "It's more complicated than that, but if I'm right and Yuri doesn't find that cable, then we can begin saving Sasha."

For a minute, Trisha just stared at him. This man that she loved, she didn't understand how his brain worked. She didn't know where he got his ideas, but she was just grateful that he did. She kissed him, and she meant it.

"What was that for?" Jimmy asked with a smile.

"Because I love you, that's what that's for."

Just then Hauck came up to them both.

"Jimmy," he said, "I've got something to ask you."

"Wait a minute," said Jimmy.

Hauck looked puzzled and in that time Yuri came running up excitedly.

"The cable in the picture isn't there," he said, panting.

"I knew it," he said.

"What cable?" said Hauck.

"There was an electrical cable in the original diagrams, but it's no longer there. Remember when there was the shootout with Drogol? Well, he must have knocked the cable loose. It went to another motor control box. See this one here? On the diagrammatic I mean, on the computer screen."

"No, I don't see—"

Just then, Brittany made the computer diagram appear before them in mid-air.

"Whoa," said Yuri, "now that is cool."

"How'd you do that, Brittany?" said Trisha.

"I—"

"Never mind the explanation. Just where is the cable?" interrupted Hauck.

Brittany zoomed in on the offending cable. Remarkably, the detail she was able to produce in the spaciousness of thin air. To see it hovering there was truly amazing.

"See it, right there," said Jimmy.

"I'll be damned," said Hauck.

And there it was. Another electrical cable going from one motor control box to the Tesla tube. Hauck wondered what it did. He didn't understand any of it, frankly. That's what Jimmy was for, and he was just glad that he was there.

"Come on Yuri, let's see if we can locate where that cable is, repair it, and get Sasha back to where he was before all this mess with him being turned into a werewolf started," said Jimmy.

"Amen to that," said Yuri.

"You wanted something, Hauck?" said Jimmy.

"Later, it can wait until later. Right now, this is the single most important thing we can do."

Jimmy nodded, and he and Yuri took off.

"What was it you wanted to speak to Jimmy about?" asked Trisha.

Hauck seemed reluctant to talk. He was far away somewhere. Trisha studied his face. He was a most peculiar man, she decided. Distant, yet kindly. Solicitous where Sveta was concerned, but Trisha felt he could be coldly calculating when the occasion demanded. Perhaps that was the key to him—he was never unwound, he was always wound as tight as a bullet. Like he was always waiting for the other shoe to drop. That shoe was a boot, and it was always looking to grind Hauck and his under their boot.

"What?"

"I said, what was it you wanted to talk to Jimmy about?"

"Nothing, really. No, that's not accurate," he said, and he smiled ruefully. "I'm sorry, it's just that I don't really know you, and I have a difficult time revealing secrets to those I don't know. All I know about you is that Jimmy seems quite taken by you."

"Well, look, I didn't mean to—" Trisha began in a huff.

"No, it's my fault, really. I didn't mean to offend you. It's just that for so long, I was alone. Yuri is my oldest employee, and he didn't know who I was until the thing with Drogol started falling apart."

"Really?"

"Yes, no one—except the Instructor, that is—knew who I was until then. Sveta only knows me since the time with Drogol."

"Is that how you met Sveta?"

Hauck seemed to go far away again.

"Yes, that was how I met Sveta."

Trisha glanced over at Sveta's sniper nest, far away. She was little more than a dot in the vast expanse of the cavern.

"Are you two... " she trailed off uncomfortably.

"No... yes... we are a... complicated pair, I guess you might say."

"I see."

"Do you want to sit down?" said Hauck.

"What?"

"I said, do you want to sit down? Can I get you some more coffee?"

Trisha laughed. It was a musical sound in the empty cavern.

"Hauck?"

Brittany's voice startled Hauck and Trisha. They were beginning to take the AI for granted, like she was a quiet fixture that only spoke when spoken to. It never occurred to them she could speak to them on her own.

"Yes, Brittany," said Hauck.

"You have deviated from Trisha's original topic. Were you aware of that?"

"Yes, I guess I have, haven't I?"

"I just thought you should know," said Brittany.

"Why thank you, Brittany," said Trisha. To Hauck she said, "Well, how about it? You going to talk, or do I have to beat it out of you?"

"Wait, I yield," Hauck said, holding up his hands. "I found something remarkable behind an old photograph of Drogol on the train with Yuri. It was an odd cipher that was written in Russian that I just couldn't figure out. The introduction to it was clear enough, it was in plain Russian, not coded, in other words. It said that this was the '...key to everything...' in Drogol's own words. Naturally, I thought it was the settings to the Tesla machine, but now I don't think so."

Trisha thought for a moment, and then shrugged.

"I worked for a while in the coded messages section of the NSA. Maybe I can crack it. Let me see it."

Hauck took a folded piece of paper out of his pocket and handed it to Trisha. She scanned in for a minute before she frowned.

"I don't know... I don't speak a word of Russian, so we're out of luck there," she said.

"I speak Russian," said Brittany.

Hauck smiled. Brittany really was a remarkable creating of Jimmy's. He had to give the man that.

"But of course you do," he said.

"Hold it up so I can see it," Brittany said.

Trisha obliged. Brittany stared at it for a few seconds.

"You may hold it down now, Trisha. I have memorized it."

Trisha dutifully lowered the paper and gave it back to Hauck.

"What does it say?" she said hopefully.

"I am calculating that even now," said Brittany.

Leaning forward, Trisha's and Hauck's curiosity was getting the better of them. What mysteries could Drogol have been talking about when he said "... this was the key to everything?"

"Well, that's remarkable," said Brittany.

"What? What's remarkable?" said an impatient Hauck.

"According to Drogol, there is another journal buried on the grounds that reveals what he only describes as '... the secret to everything.' It's most strange."

"That doesn't tell us anything," complained Trisha. "Now we've got to find the second journal."

"You're right," said Hauck. "We are back to square one. Does he give us any clues as to where the second journal is?"

"Yes, he gives us clues, but Hauck?"

"Yes, Brittany?"

"I have already deciphered his clues, and know where the second journal is. Would you like me to tell you?"

"God-damned right we would," said Trisha.

Brittany smiled a dazzling smile. AI's, thought Trisha, could be very irritating.

"It's under the Tesla tube in a secret compartment on the front. You have to press your palms against it for it to open, but it's there."

Trisha was amazed at the AI's ability to decipher the hidden meaning behind the Cyrillic letters so quickly. Hauck had worked on them for a long time and had given up. She looked over at him.

"Let's go," he said with a grin.

Hauck seemed transformed. At long last, the secrets of this

underground world would be at his fingertips. Jimmy had discovered what was wrong with the Tesla tube. Everything, thought Trisha, would be all right at last. Then her thoughts clouded as she realized that Professor Meridian's gunmen would come tonight. Or if not tonight, then soon. Four people was all they had, against how many men? Trisha didn't know exactly, but she was afraid.

"Sure, let's go," she said.

****

Charlene crawled up into the space and made the mistake of looking down. It was a dizzying drop to the ground and for a moment, her heart stopped. Finally, she gulped and looked up. She found herself on a whole another floor from where she was. There was a short railing around three of the sides of the opening. She supposed to identify it so you didn't fall. Remembering the downside of that, she thought that yeah, that would be a deadly fall.

It was about ten feet of clearance where she was now and seemed to stretch on forever. She realized she was at a false ceiling for the place. It was littered with junk on all sides, and she wondered how she could see with no lights. Charlene was startled to realize that the air itself was alive with light.

"I'll be damned," she said under her breath.

Everything was covered with a thin layer of dust, as though no one had been up here since the false ceiling was put in place. She got to her feet and began to walk. Everywhere up her was equipment that she didn't understand what it was. Fantastic tubes and wires and glass gages. She wondered why they were up here instead of on the main floor. In fact, she was confused. What was so different about these machines that they had to be kept up here, away from down there? Walking through and around the scattered equipment, she looked for a pattern. It would help, she decided, if she knew what things did.

There was an even split between apparatus that were big and on the floor, and the things that were up on tables. She couldn't figure out what they were until she came to a unit sitting on a table all by itself. Awestruck, she ran her finger over the surface, leaving trails in the dust as she did.

It was a long tube of a type of crystal, with wires wrapped tightly around it. At the back end was a black metal box with a gage on it. There was a strap mounted on it, too, that went from somewhere near the end of the barrel until the back end where the box with the gage on it was, and from there it came down into a handle that was maybe a foot and a half long. Affixed to the base of the tube and the top part of the handle was a trigger, complete with trigger guard.

"It's a gun," whispered Charlene.

Suddenly, it all became clear to Charlene. Downstairs was the pure science part of the laboratory, but up here was where all the weapons were. She could understand it now. Jesus, this was where all the guns and weapons were. What an amazing place. Hauck was going to be so excited by this place.

Doubts flooded in, though. What if this was just the weapons junkyard, where all the cool ideas were but none actually worked? She fingered the tube. Would this still work? Only one way to find out. But where was the on switch? She walked around to the other side of the table and saw it. The on switch was on the far side of the box.

She shrugged and then lifted the tube weapon from its resting place on the table and lifted the strap around her neck and allowed it to settle on her shoulders. Who built this wonderful place, she wondered again? Well, she would never know the answer to that one, would she? Still, she wondered. With the weapon still on her shoulder, she looked around at the place again. It would take an army of men to construct this place, she decided. Where were they all now?

Dusting off the weapon with her shirt as best she could, she realized she was nervous about firing it. But, she flipped the power switch to the on position, and, to her surprise, the thing came to life with a faint hum and the gage flipped to full power.

"Well, here goes nothing," she thought.

She aimed at the ceiling and pulled the trigger.

The resulting flash of light and tearing into the ceiling was awe-inspiring. The result was a six feet in diameter hole. Charlene was shocked. Dust came pouring down from the hole she had created.

"Wait until I tell Hauck," she said.

CHAPTER TWENTY-FIVE

The Attack

As they loaded the trucks, Professor Meridian watched. He was most disturbed by the loading of the chernobog onto one particular truck. Akim's six men carried the box with the chernobog inside it, placing it at the back lip of the truck and sliding it inside. Then they closed the door and locked it all under Akim's watchful eye. It was late at night now, and they were almost ready to go.

Camila oversaw the eighteen men loaded into three SUVs while she herself would leave in a black Camaro that was especially outfitted as a muscle car. It would achieve a speed of 180 miles per hour in nine seconds. She wished she could just take off and keep running in that car, but she knew the chernobog would find her. It would be convenient if she could just dump the chernobog box and all into the Detroit River, but the opportunity had not presented itself. When she had offered to drive the chernobog to the location where Hauck was hiding, he had responded with a curt "No."

"I made a mistake inviting Akim into my operation," said Professor Meridian.

Camila nodded.

"That is an understatement," she said.

"Still, you must remember that the chernobog can only go so far from his box, so if you can escape him, then you will be free. He will destroy Hauck and his people, and only then will he turn on you and your men."

"Perhaps I can tell them, warn them of his treachery?"

"I don't think so, Camila. Then they would never go."

"We could take Akim and his men while the chernobog is still locked in his box."

The professor shook his head. He had already thought of that, and it wouldn't work.

"No, because only he knows the location of Hauck and his men. Besides, we still only suspect him of treachery. We don't know for a fact that he will turn on us after Hauck and his men are dead. We just have a bad feeling about him, is all. If only we could be sure of his intentions."

Akim was walking over to where they stood. Camila felt a shiver go through her as he approached them.

"Are you ready to go, Camila?" said Akim.

"Almost. The men will be ready to go in five minutes. Have you any last words you wish to say to them?"

Akim looked at the professor, his eyes now a deep shade of gray-black. He seemed to study him, inviting him to speak.

"No," said the professor, "I have already outlined their jobs to them. I think they are well prepared for the job that they have to perform, each in their own way. Anything I could say to them now would be nothing but a distraction. You might, though, offer them a one hundred thousand reward for the man who shoots Hauck dead and brings me his head."

Camila stared at the professor for a long moment, then she looked at Akim.

"Akim?" she said.

"No, I have nothing to say. Let's get moving."

Camila tried one last time. If only Akim would divulge the location of Hauck and his men, then she would kill him on the spot. Her men would react by killing Akim's men.

"Where will we be going?" she asked.

Akim smiled. She thought, I wonder if he knows? That would be a disaster.

"Just follow me," he said.

"Yes, certainly."

Camila looked at Professor Meridian. It was a no go as far as Akim was concerned. Akim would not reveal the location. As many times and as many ways as Camila had tried, she could not get Akim to give it up. He walked away to get into his car, stopped, and looked back at Camila. He knew she would try to escape him. What did he have up his sleeve? Why was he so certain that she could not escape?

As Akim got into his car, Camila said to Professor Meridian, "I tell you, I don't trust the man. He's got shifty eyes."

Professor Meridian, who observed the reaction between Akim and Camila, agreed.

"Be careful, Camila," was all he said.

It was all that he needed to say. Camila turned and climbed into her car. She thought, "You don't know the half of it."

The garage door opened and the lead van motored off, followed by the three cars of her men. Camila started her car, revved the engine and waited for Akim's car to pull out. With one last look at Professor Meridian, she followed.

It was nighttime in Detroit. The full moon dominated the sky. Like a radiant beacon, its light lit up the streets below. It displayed an immense plain of broken dreams and buildings. The streets were lined with litter and trash and human detritus. Liquor stores and boarded-up buildings with sliding metal gates in front of them dominated the landscape. In the cones of the streetlamps, the occasional homeless person huddled in the cold. Broken beer and liquor bottles cluttered the sidewalks and streets. Empty warehouses lined the way as they moved through the windy, silent roads.

Camila felt the tension building in her as she drove. She tried to think of how to handle Akim and his chernobog. She wondered if he would go in, or stay back from the kill. The mechanics of it were everything. If he went in first, she would hang back and stay out of the way of the chernobog entirely and watch from the safety of her car. But she didn't think that was possible. If he hung back, however, she would have to go in and face Hauck and his guns, a prospect with which she didn't feel comfortable.

An icy rain started up, splashing against the windshield and leaving her temporarily blind. She turned the windshield wipers on and could see again. The rain, she thought, was a bad omen.

They were driving in an abandoned part of the city now. It made little sense to her that Hauck would hide out there. Yet, the car stopped at an empty house. Camila shuddered at the thought that soon the chernobog would be let out of the cage.

Time to go in for the kill.

.

CHAPTER TWENTY-SIX

The Weapon

The Instructor was in full-blown werewolf form now. He attacked the bars again and again. He howled, he spit, he paced. The night was upon him, and he had no choice but to embrace it. The bars, indeed the whole cage, was bolted down so that he couldn't move it, but he shook it. Titanium steel was the material of construction, so there was no chance of his bending or breaking the bars, but in his werewolf form, he didn't care. He was in a constant state of rage, running at the bars and throwing his body at them, snarling and beating his chest when they didn't yield to his rage.

In the other cage, Sasha had changed into a monster again and was doing much the same thing as the Instructor was doing in his cage. Only with his clawed feet, he was climbing up the cage and hanging upside down from the top, bellowing his anger and his rage at whatever was keeping him locked up.

It was a good thing that both cages were encased in soundproofed material. Even so, with the constant howling, some noise escaped. It was doubled with the two of them roaring at the same time.

****

Sveta was seated in her sniper's nest while the two monsters were howling, oblivious to the rage, unable to hear them this far away. Her leg was slightly stiff and painful as she sat there. She grunted and achingly stretched her leg out some. Flexing it and pulling it back and forth, she got some circulation going in it.

The waiting was the hardest part of any operation, especially when you were the target. Always sitting quietly, keeping an eye out for trouble when there wasn't any until there was. You grew tired of it. Still, Jimmy had the computer to tell them when there was trouble coming, but she didn't trust the computer. Too much could go wrong with it and you only got one chance at getting it right. She couldn't wait all night, though perhaps she could go to sleep now and that way she would be awake when they came. The problem was, she didn't feel in the least sleepy. This was a difficulty that she couldn't overcome. She had never mastered the art of just falling asleep whenever she wanted, signaling her brain to just shut off.

Already, she was bored and her leg hurt. Would this never end? Why couldn't Meridian's men show a little courtesy and just show up? But in her mind, she knew that would not be good. They would come at them full metal jacket, with everything that they had. Sveta estimated twenty men, and that would be on the low side. They had what, four against twenty, plus everything that Jimmy and Hauck were planning, but was that enough against twenty plus armed men? She doubted it. If they came tonight, as expected, then this could be her last night alive.

Sveta thought about that. She thought about impulsively kissing Hauck and wished she hadn't done that. On the other hand, the thought of her dying made her certain that she wished she had done more than that. It was funny. She hadn't been with a man in many years. They hadn't met her standards. But Hauck was different. He was definitely a handsome man. He was also one cool customer. Perhaps too cool. Of course, when she had injured herself, Hauck had been right there all the time to see if she needed anything. Something to think about—if she lived through this.

If she lived through this? She definitely needed an attitude adjustment. It was a hard enough mess that they had gotten themselves into without short calling the outcome.

She checked her rifle for the umpteenth time. It was good to go. The optics were good, the alignment was good, and the trigger pressure was good. Now all she needed was a target. Perhaps Meridian himself would be so good as to step into her sights. But he would more likely remain off site and wait for a call saying that they were successful.

Trying to sit in a more comfortable position, Sveta adjusted herself yet again. She couldn't seem to get comfortable. Waiting for Jimmy's computer alarms to go off that they were under attack just seemed fruitless to her. Yet she was tired. She had to admit that perhaps she would go to sleep for a while. She would have to try.

****

Yuri was holding a connecting cable to the Tesla tube when Hoke and Tricia returned from Brittany to investigate.

"Hey, we've almost got the tube ready to reconnect. You're just in time for the grand unveiling," said Yuri.

"Excellent," said Hauck with a burst of enthusiasm. "I can't believe we missed that in the first place."

"Yeah, well, it wasn't Jimmy's fault. We didn't find a diagram of what the tube looked like when it was functioning until after he had already used it."

Just then, Jimmy appeared, fresh from checking all the circuits from a motor control panel.

"Hauck," he said. Then, "Hey, Tricia."

Tricia went over and hugged Jimmy, who pecked her on the cheek.

"You come to oversee the final connection, Hauck?"

"No. I mean yes. But we have to check out the tube first. It seems there's a secret compartment to see if it has the decoded book is there."

"Well, don't let us stop you," said Jimmy.

"You mean the book with the secrets to everything?" asked Yuri.

"That's the one," affirmed Hauck.

"What are on earth are you waiting for, then?" asked Yuri.

Hauck decided he liked Yuri better when he was unknown to him. A digital phantom who just gave orders. No, that wasn't true. He like Yuri just fine. It's just that it suddenly occurred to him that here he was going after a book of secrets when his son was locked up in a cage.

"I think I better go tell Sasha that there is hope for him. If this connecting cable works out as it should, then he deserves a warning," said Houck.

153

"There would be a good idea," said Jimmy, "because we are almost ready to go. Why don't you wait a few minutes, though, at least until we test the circus before you tell him? Better not to get his hopes up until then. It'll just take a few minutes until we know for sure."

Hauck thought about it and then nodded. He caught Tricia looking at him, almost with pity in her eyes, until she noticed him looking back.

"Good," said Jimmy, "just hang on. Yuri, is the cable connected?"

"It is."

You could see it in the Russian's eyes. A certain expectation, and a certain pride at the role he played in it, thought Hauck, even though all he did was connect the cable. Hauck was excited to see that they had finally found the problem. At last, he thought, my son will return to normal. I hope that is.

"Everybody step back off of the platform," said Jimmy, "while I go back to the motor control panel and fire it up." While Tricia went with Jimmy, Hauck and Yuri stepped back off of the platform. An eerie silence descended on them. Finally, Yuri broke the quiet.

"You think it will work?" he asked.

Hauck considered it for a moment and then answered.

"How would we know? The only monitoring devices are at the motor control panel where Jimmy and Tricia are," said Hauck. "And how would we know what they meant, anyway?"

Just then, Jimmy's voice cut across the distance, coming out from the motor control panel.

"Ready? Here goes nothing."

Jimmy threw the switch, and suddenly the lights dimmed slightly and Hauck heard a crackling noise coming from the chamber. The light inside the tube flickered and then exploded with a steady luminosity such as Hauck had never seen before. He and Tricia looked at Jimmy, but Jimmy was busy watching gauges and needles.

"Is it working?" he called out.

Jimmy gave him a thumbs up.

"So far it's holding steady, and the output is unbelievable, simply unbelievable."

Hauck breathed a sigh of relief. At least he could tell his son. That took a tremendous burden off his shoulders. Suddenly, the machine powered down.

"What?" asked Yuri

"I don't know…" said Hauck.

"Everything is okay. I'm just putting the machine through its paces, that's all," called out Jimmy.

For the second time in as many minutes, Hauck breathed a sigh of relief. When he looked at Yuri, he saw that he, too, had been concerned.

"I'm going to tell Sasha," said Hauck.

"I'm going with you," said Yuri. "This is exciting."

Hauck and Yuri set out for the long trek to the cages, with a positive sense this time. Things were going to be all right. Yuri, in particular, seemed genuinely excited.

"Man, wait until Sasha hears what we've done," he said. "He'll be excited to get out of that cage."

"We don't know it all work yet," cautioned Hauck. "We'll have to try some experiments first."

"On what?" Yuri asked incredulously. "You know we don't have any pets to try it on. In fact, we have nothing to experiment on. Why am I telling you all this? You already know that."

Hauck stopped for a minute and Yuri stopped with him.

"I guess we're all shooting in the dark now, aren't we?" Said Hauck.

"Kind of, yes," said Yuri.

"But we're a good team, aren't we?"

"Yeah, I think we are."

An awkward silence ensued, broken by Hauck looking up at the cages. They were too far away to hear the werewolf howling, but they could see the lead blanketed cages which covered the sound suppressing material. Like strange guardians of this world, they stood atop a hill.

"Come on," said Hauck. "Let's get going."

Yuri shook his head in agreement, and they started walking up the ramp that led to the cages. Ramps led all over the complex like a series of spiderwebs, but they stuck to the one and eventually wound their way up to the cages. This close, they could hear the virtually nonstop howling.

"Yep," said Yuri. "That's definitely a werewolf."

Hauck withdrew a key from his pants pocket and unlocked the gate that led to the sound suppressing material. As he opened the door, a fetid smell came from it, and Hauck gagged reflexively. He kept one hand over his face as the creature slammed the cage wall. Snarling and yapping like a diseased dog.

"Just look at that thing. The smell," said Yuri, loud enough to be heard over the racket.

The thing with the six arms kept crashing against the bars like a crazed animal. Hauck was amazed at how big it was. It scrambled up to the top of the cage and bellowed out his anger.

"I'd say we have to wait for Sasha to turn back into a man before putting him into the tube," said Yuri.

"I think I agree with you, Yuri."

****

Charlene was bewildered by the hole she had made with the weapon.

"Awesome," she mouthed.

She walked over to stand directly beneath the hole. It was roughly four feet in diameter. It led into what looked like the sewer system. Charlene estimated it had to cut through five feet of rock to get there. She walked around in circles, admiring her handiwork. Looking down at the tube, she considered the magnificent power she held in her hands. If it could do all of this, then just what did the rest of the equipment do?

She decided to find out.

There was some big stuff here, but she decided to investigate the small things first. They were more her size. Besides, when she considered how she would get them down to Hauck, that was another matter. She could take maybe one or two — possibly three — but that was all. There was only one tube, so she looked around for something else. She settled on a table full of gadgets and walked over to them. They look like ordinary pistols with adaptions to them, but there were also round globes with hand straps on them and strange projections.

"I wonder what these are?" she said.

Slipping her fingers through the hand-holds, she looked for a power switch and found one. She was about to fire it up when she

156

remembered the effect of the last one, and aimed at a faraway point on the ceiling.

Well, here goes nothing, she thought.

She flicked the power switch to the on position and held her breath. The hand-held sphere came to life. At first, nothing happened. Charlene saw that five buttons of different colors had also turned on when she flicked the power switch to life. They were a stretch away from her, but she extended her index finger and pressed the one that was lit up green. Immediately, she was surrounded by a shield of green that projected a good three feet away from her. She was stunned.

Cautiously, she extended her free hand toward the light that surrounded her. She was just about to touch it when she thought, *I better not. You never know what the reaction could be.*

She knew she should wait to touch the thing, but curiosity got the best of her, and she extended her hand again and, after saying a brief prayer to all that was holy, she touched the green light. It was a solid wall. She pushed against it, but the light was unyielding.

"Well, I'll be damned. It's like a solid wall. Shit," she said.

Charlene tried to walk around in the ball of green light and found out that she could. The actual test was when she would bump into something. She found an empty table, walked towards it, and was stopped at the limits of the green light.

Satisfied, she excitedly pushed the blue button and found herself lifted off the ground a good four feet.

For a moment, she forgot about Hauck. She forgot they were soon to be under attack. She was flying, after all. Her feet were off the ground, floating above the floor. Now if she could only control the thing. After a moment of just standing there, trying different things — leaning this way and that — she was about to give up, when she hit upon the idea of the three remaining buttons. She pressed one and was immediately rewarded with a motion to the left, solving the problem of how to navigate the green ball. And suddenly, she was off and flying around the room.

She flew in a wide circle, seeing the wonderful weapons and gadgets laid out below her like a smörgåsbord. Finally, she came back to where she had started from and hovered a minute. Unaware of how much time had passed since she started, she let the green ball of light containing her down. Then she pressed the buttons that made the green ball disappear.

The table before her held several things to be explored still. There was one thing that looked like a pistol, but not quite. She was about to try it out, when far in the distance she heard Brittany's voice shouting.

"Warning, warning: the distant perimeter has been breached. Six vehicles are approaching the entrance at a rapid rate of speed. Warning, warning: the distant perimeter has been breached. Six vehicles are approaching the entrance at a rapid rate of speed."

Charlene hesitated, then shoved the pistol like apparatus down the front of her cargo pants, and started running toward the exit.

CHAPTER TWENTY-SEVEN

The Penetration

The six cars pulled up to the house and formed a semicircle around the truck, which backed up into the driveway. Doors opened, and men with semi-automatic weapons got out. Doors opened in the van and the men surrounding the back door parted for Akim. Lastly, the doors opened and Camila and Akim got out of the cars. They walked to the back of the van, and Akim's men cleared the way by stepping aside.

"You will go in first with your men," said Akim.

Camila nodded, thinking that he had said never to go in front of the chernobog. He didn't have the chernobog set free yet, and she noted that. Though how Hauck and his team could not have noticed six vehicles pulling up to the house and all the men getting out was beyond her. She turned to Akim. All the lights in the house were off. The entire home looked to be abandoned.

"You're sure that he is inside?" she asked.

"The chernobog is never wrong."

She divided the men into three teams. Six around the back of the house, six for the front of the house, and the remaining six covered the garage entrance to the house. When everyone was in position, she performed a radio check. That satisfactory, she said into her microphone, "You will enter the house on the count of three, two, one go."

The men blew down the doors with explosives. Flash bangs and stun grenades were rolled in before them, and they entered with rifles up and laser pointers on. They were met with no resistance. There was no one home. All around the house was a smattering of broken furniture.

"All clear," said one man.

"You've encountered no resistance?" Said Camila.

"There's no one here."

It was as Camila expected. The chernobog was wrong. There was no one home. Camila felt foolish. But suddenly, the radio crackled again. It was from the man at the side door to the house.

"There's a door here beside the entrance that's locked," said a man.

"Say again," said Camila.

"I said there's a door here beside the entrance that's locked."

Camila frowned.

"Open it."

"It's a master lock," said the man.

"Blow it," said Camila.

"It would seem," said Akim, "that we are not to enter that door."

"Oh, we'll enter it all right."

"We're in," said a voice in her ear.

"What does it look like?"

"You'd better come look."

Camila, recognizing that Akim was on the same frequency as herself, walked forward.

"Camila?" said Akim with an enigmatic look.

She stopped.

"Yes?"

"Be careful," said Akim.

Camila said nothing.

The six men were joined by the other six men from inside the house and the six from the back of the house. They all gathered around the door, which had been blown off its hinges. Inside was another door at the back of a small room. The second door was made of a titanium steel alloy that appeared to be thick.

"Shit," said Camila.

"What should we do?" asked one of the three leads.

"I'm thinking," she said.

Would explosives even dent the titanium steel door? Camila

doubted it would. Acids? No.

"Get me a cold laser and cut a hole into the locking mechanism. That should get us in."

Four of the men got ready to go for a cold laser.

"What is the hold-up?" asked Akim, who had appeared suddenly.

"The door appears to be a titanium steel. We have to cut our way in," said Camila.

"I don't understand the difficulty."

"We need a cold laser. I was just about to send men out to get one."

"Then what are we waiting for? Time is precious."

****

The four men returned with the cold cutting laser nearly three hours later. Then they loaded it on the back of the SUV and took it to the door, past Camila and Akim. By this time, Camila was clearly fuming, but there was nothing to be done about it. They got out of their cars and followed the men over to the door, where the men were assembling a tripod. Finally, they were done.

Camila put a halt to the man who was about to cut through it and then thought better of it. She and Akim stood near the front of the garage, out of the way of the eighteen men. The men huddled around the cutter, ready to break the doors down.

"Now we shall finally break through," said Akim.

Something was bothering Camila, however. She was overcome with eagerness to get through that door and get it done. As a laser beam cut through the titanium steel, it was made up of a bluish white light. The person manning the controls wore goggles to protect his eyes, and the others looked away from it. They had given Camila and Akim a pair of goggles to wear, and they were wearing them.

The laser had been successful in cutting a five-foot rectangle in the door. While it was still smoking, and the men were waiting for it to cool down, Camila wondered again about that nagging feeling.

"Kick it open," said Akim.

Men hurried and moved the laser. They folded it up on its tripod and moved it to one side of the garage. Then men made to kick the slab that they had cut out of the way. It was as a man's foot was lashing out to kick it that Camila recognized the door hadn't fallen in. Something was holding it up and she—and then the door exploded outward.

It had been held in place by an explosive net, and now, with a single kick that dislodged it, was released to go flying into the man would kicked it. The men who stood behind him were in for a shock when it came shooting out. It erupted in orange light and the smell of burnt flesh. The noise was unimaginable in the confined space, and the spreading out of the concussive wave flattened eight of the men that stood nearby. Akim and Camila were stunned by the detonation; too stunned to do much but dive for cover, at which time it was too late.

Camila got up to her knees, coughing and wiping the dust from her eyes. Her first thought, though, before Akim, before the safety of her men, was whether the police would be on their way soon. She didn't know, though, because the ringing in her ears was so intense. Akim was faring no better, as he was sprawled out on the driveway, his head bleeding and his right arm at an odd angle. Camila felt blood dripping down from her scalp and over her forehead and past her eyes, and she realized she was wounded.

She looked over her men, and saw them slowly getting up, all except for four, maybe five that were quite dead. The carnage was unbelievable. Hauck must've wired the door with enough explosive to blast anyone trying to forcibly enter to Hell and back. Pieces of the garage were scattered everywhere. It was a good thing that the garage was empty or there would have been flying projectiles like nobody's business.

The piece cut out of the door had smashed into the back of the van. The doors were twisted and one hung by a single hinge. But inside the van, the steel box that contained the chernobog was unharmed. Camila gave a sigh of relief at that. She didn't want to imagine if, for example, the chernobog's box had sprung open in the blast.

Camila got painfully the rest of the way to her feet. She ached all over. Where the hell with the sirens? Where were the police, the fire department, and the paramedics? For that matter, for a blast of this magnitude, they would normally be all over the place. Wait, her hearing was returning. She could hear sirens, but they were going in an opposite direction from their location. What the hell was going on?

It was almost as if they were being misdirected to where the location of the explosion had come from, somewhere in the opposite direction.

Akim got to his feet, too. He seemed groggy, disoriented.

"That son of a bitch," was all he could say repeatedly.

"What should we do?" she finally interrupted him

The garage was still issuing forth a thin stream of smoke, but it was going down in volume.

"What should we do?" screamed Akim. "We should go in, that's what we should do. But back the cage of the chernobog up to the door. The chernobog must go in first."

CHAPTER TWENTY-EIGHT

Getting Ready

Hauck turned his head around at the sound of Brittany's blaring voice.

"Let's go," he said Yuri.

The two of them abandoned the cages and ran for the Tesla tube up to Jimmy's control room, where Jimmy and Tricia and Brittany waited for them. Hauck, when he had gathered his breath again, spoke into his radio.

"Sveta, are you there?"

"I'm here."

"You heard the alarm?"

"I heard it. I was just going to sleep when it went off."

"I'll give them three to five hours to cut through the door. The explosives will go off when they try to kick it through, and then all hell will break loose."

"Got it. Anything you want me to do?"

"No. Just be careful, Sveta."

"I will, Hauck. You and the others, too."

Hauck signed off and looked at the others.

"Yuri, you head to your place. You keep your head down, you understand?"

"Yes."

"You wait until they are inside before firing, got it?"

"Got it."

"Good. Get going. Tricia?"

"Yes?" she said.

"You've got to hold them off at the throttle point with Sveta. Can you do that?"

"I'll try."

"That's all I can ask. Now go."

Hauck watched Tricia wind her way through to her sniper's perch, and he worried after her. But there was no time. They had all the men they were going to have tonight. It would have to be enough.

"Jimmy, you understand what we have to do?"

"What about Sasha?" asked Jimmy.

"He's turned again, so will have to proceed without him. You'll have to shut down the tube."

"Okay, so we go with Plan B?" grinned Jimmy nervously.

"Yes, we go with Plan B."

"I've been itching to try out Brittany's full capabilities for a while. This will have to be my experimental run."

Hauck nodded.

"Yes, I'm afraid that, once again, we don't have time for experiments. What do you have for me?"

"The door is rigged with explosives, that much you already know. And I'm ready for your images to confuse the other side. I don't know if that will work, though, honestly, Hauck because I've never tried it before. And one thing."

"Yes?"

"I found the master control for the lights."

"What?"

"I said, I've—"

"But that's magnificent. You go pass out the night vision goggles to Yuri and Tricia, and I'll pass them up to Sveta. Go."

"Yeah, I'm sorry I didn't remember them before but—"

"Just go."

Jimmy took off and Hauck got his pair of night vision goggles, plus a pair for Sveta. He left on the run for Sveta, thought twice, and instead he stopped and called her on the radio.

"Sveta?"

"Yes?"

"Jimmy's found the master control for the lights, so I'm bringing you a pair of night vision goggles."

"Don't bother. I've already got two."

"Oh."

"I've got everything in this nest that a girl assassin could need."

Hauck smiled. He felt immensely relieved with Sveta there, but immensely anxious for her, too.

"All right. Be alert."

"I will. And Hauck?"

"Yes?"

"Quit worrying, okay?"

Hauck walked back to Jimmy's desk. He had to be ready, and he was, but something kept nagging at him. Charlene. That was it. He hoped she would be sequestered somewhere out of sight. It was important that he didn't know where she was. This was for her own safety. No one knew where she was hiding, and that, too, was for her safety. What no one knew, no one could tell if they were captured. He just hoped that she was somewhere where she couldn't be found.

And the Instructor's and Sasha's well-depended on it. They had to get out of their cages when it was all over. They would slowly starve to death if not. And that was unacceptable to Hauck. Charlene had to get out. They all had to live to see another day, otherwise, this was all for naught.

Jimmy came back from passing out his night vision goggles.

"Done," he said.

"Good," said Hauck. "Now you were saying before we had to pass them out what new things you had discovered."

"Oh, yes. Let's see, we covered the door with explosive devices and the controls for the lights. Next, we've got to cover the deployment of multiple images of you. Like I said, I don't know if this will work. It may not fool them at all, but we'll try."

"It'll have to do."

"Okay, just so you know. The projectors, we've got eight of them all total, are all set in place. Now, under special effects, Brittany has the capability of setting off explosions around the place."

"What?"

"Yes," said Jimmy. "She can set off real charges—we have ten of them—or to set off fake explosions."

"Explain that."

"Well, she can make fake explosions anywhere around the place. For example, you want an explosion in quadrant one, right? Brittany can make the sound of explosions and throw them anywhere you would like."

Hauck thought about it. That could really come in handy.

"Go on."

"Would you like a demonstration?"

"Yes, but first let me contact the others."

Jimmy waited patiently for Hauck to notify everyone of the coming explosion. When Hoke was finished contact them, Jimmy said, "Is there anyplace in particular you'd like me to demonstrate? Anyplace that we have a speaker, that is."

Hauck considered. Finally he said, "Behind me. Anywhere behind me."

"Brittany, you heard the man."

Suddenly Hauck jumped with the sound of an explosion not one hundred feet behind him. He dove reflexively for cover.

Jimmy laughed. He laughed so hard that he doubled over. Hauck emerged from beneath the table, scowling.

"I warned you," said Jimmy.

"I never thought it would be so authentic," said Hauck.

"I can make it less so," said Brittany.

"No Brittany, it's just fine the way it is; you caught Hauck by surprise," said Jimmy.

"Anything else?" said Hauck, hoping to change the subject.

"Brittany can emit lasers from twelve points around the cavern. Would you like a demonstration?"

"Wait a minute," said Hauck. "Let me notify the others."

When he had finished warning everyone, he gave the okay. He gave the nod to Jimmy, who fired the lasers upward. The flash was stunning in its brilliance. It was an array of red-colored lights that went up in beams of light and then vanished.

"That was impressive," said Hauck.

"Thanks," said Jimmy. "Brittany, do we have anything else for Hauck?"

"Not working at this time, doctor," said the AI.

"All right, thank you, Brittany. Well, there you have it, Hauck. The explosive rigged to the door, the sound of explosions, the images of you and the lasers. Is that going to be enough?"

"It'll have to do," smiled Hauck. "But doctor?"

"Yes?"

"I want it clear that you must stay safe."

"Of course."

"No, I mean above all else. You are the only hope that Sasha has."

"Certainly."

"No, please, hear me out."

"Okay," said Jimmy slowly.

"You've got to say safe, even if it means Tricia is in danger. Just as I must stay safe even if Sveta is in danger. Do you understand?"

"But—"

"There must be no buts about it, Jimmy. None. Tricia and Sveta are too far away for us to help. You can help them the most by manning your computers. You're the only one who can do that."

"I understand, but... but I—"

"There can be no buts about it. You have to stay and man your computers. That's all you can do. Believe me, I would lie down my life for Sveta, but I can best help her by concentrating on and killing her opponents. If you aren't there to guide my movements, well, I'll be lost, and where will we be then?"

Jimmy opened his mouth to answer, but slowly closed it. Hauck was right, of course, but he didn't know if he could idly stand by while Tricia was hurt.

"You've got to be my eyes and ears, as well as the eyes and ears for everyone else. It's not possible to concentrate on one person. You just can't. There are three of us to direct, and I will need directing most of all. Can you do that, Jimmy? I have to know that I can count on you."

The seriousness of their situation was sinking in.

"You can count on me," said Jimmy.

Hauck studied him carefully for a minute. Then, at last, he nodded.

"Good. Thank you, Jimmy. Now, where do you want me?"

"As far away from the Tesla tube as possible. In fact, if you're up to it, we should lay it on its side so it doesn't get shot. I've got two more, but I'd rather not have to use them to completely build a new model if we don't have to."

"Lead on. I don't know how much time we have, but let's put it to good use."

They went down to the Tesla tube, and carefully, very carefully, laid it on its side. It looked just like a giant discarded cigar tube.

"Let's put it behind the platform," said Jimmy. "Less chance of a stray bullet hitting it."

"Agreed," said Hauck.

Grunting, they disconnected the cables and maneuvered it down off of the platform and out of sight. It was strange how empty the platform looked without its towering presence there.

"Well, that's it," said Jimmy. "Let's go back up to the computer and get a look where to position you."

As they walked, Hauck mentally ticked off all that could be done in his head. It seemed he had accomplished all that could be reasonably expected of him in a short time. The rest was in God's hands.

Once again, he was in the place that was soon to become a battleground for all those people that he held dear. Sveta, Yuri, Tricia, Jimmy, and Charlene. At least Charlene would be safe during the upcoming combat. As for the others, he would just have to let it go. He couldn't think about what might happen to them. What was it that he told Jimmy? Concentrate on taking out as many of the bastards as he could. If they had twenty-five, he could count on the door blast killing or putting out of operation three of them. That would leave twenty-two of them to deal with. He could count on Sveta killing at least five of them, which would leave seventeen, and he would he could take out four or five, that would leave thirteen or twelve. If Tricia or Yuri could take out three each, that would leave six to be killed. Or they would get one of them, or all of them. The math just didn't work out.

Of course, all that didn't take it take into account Jimmy's computer system. That was the unaccounted for variable.

"Hauck?"

"Yes?"

"I think you should initially be close."

Hauck stopped walking, and Jimmy did the same.

"Explain."

"You should be concealed, and when they are all in, you will be able to pop up and kill them where they stand. As a counterattack, you can fall back. But I think initially you should be close enough to get them. I'll distract them with fake Hauck's, which should be all over the place. They'll waste their bullets on them."

Hauck thought about that. It was risky, but it just might work.

"Okay, time for me to quit talking and get my guns in. It sounds like a plan that if it works, I should be able to take out a few more men and if not... well, I prefer not to think about it. Let's go."

CHAPTER TWENTY-NINE

The Breakthrough

Akim and Camila stood to one side as the truck backed through the now dissipating smoke. When the truck had backed up sufficiently, Akim seem to think. He hesitated, and then said to Camila, "I was wrong. Your men must go in first, just to see what is there. The chernobog will go in only if we need him. Have them go now."

Camila, who was at first taken aback by his command, then nodded at her regrouped men.

"Go," she said.

The men nodded, and then wound their way past the truck and into the opening they had cut. It was nothing but blackness ahead of them, so they had their night vision goggles on. The lead man, named Roberto, was a Mexican from the drug cartels. He was a short but deadly man well versed in the ways of killing. He led the way, and two other men followed, Jay and Steve. They were big men. Jay was bearded and covered with tattoos and Steve was clean-shaven with a baldhead and a cap covering his baldness.

Roberto stepped through carefully through the laser cut door and through to the other side. He looked around and could see a stairway up ahead. He motioned for the others to follow. Six men came through after Roberto, Jay, and Steve. They moved silently, as still as death. Nine men went through and ten more to go. From what Roberto could see, they were in an immense cavern. He held up his hand to the others to stop their forward momentum.

The stairway extended on for what seemed like a long way, and they were exposed the whole way. Roberto didn't like it. There didn't seem to be anyone there, though, but they could be hiding. In fact, they probably were hiding. This damnable long stairway, though. His radio clicked on. It was Camila.

"Report," she said.

"We're in a big, spacious cavern of some sort, on a stairway that stretches a long way. I can't see the end."

"Hold," she said.

Roberto kept on eyeing the darkness, his gun up.

"What's wrong?" said Jay.

"The lady said to hold."

Jay grunted in response.

"Okay," Camila came back on the radio, "proceed with caution."

"You've got it," said Roberto.

The sooner he got off this creepy stairway, the better. He led the way down the stairs, came to a platform, and then halted and looked around. The full contingent of men were behind them now. Fifteen other men were on the catwalk, and no one had taken a shot at them yet. Just three more to go. Roberto could suddenly see it clearly; they were waiting for them all to line up and then take the shot. He held up his hand to stop the last three men from coming in. He got on the radio.

"Camila," he said.

"Yes?"

"I think they're waiting for us all to lineup on the stairway to take the shot."

"Hey what's the holdup, man? We're sitting ducks up here," said Jay.

"Quiet," said Roberto.

"How you want to play it?" Said Camila.

"I want to send some men back," said Roberto.

Akim suddenly came on the line.

"Do it," he said. "Just do it."

Roberto got on the open channel.

"I want the last five men in line to go back to where you came from."

"Say again," said one man.

"I said I want the last five men in line to go back up to where you came from. Now."

The men started back up again, and Roberto led the men further down the stairway. Now the place was coming into view. It was filled with fabulous equipment that Roberto did not understand what it was for, but he really didn't care. He was looking for hiding places for shooters, and what he saw was a nightmare of havens for people that could hide. Literally, what were they waiting for? They could open fire at any time.

That's when it hit Roberto. He had chosen the right strategy. They had too few shooters. This might be a big cavernous place, but they had too few shooters to fill it up. That was when the stairs blew up in a conflagration of smoke and fire.

The men on the stairs screamed as it exploded, but their screams were lost in the noise. The stairs literally disintegrated, sending fragments everywhere. The men on the stairs were immediately ripped to pieces, or fell the remaining sixty feet to their deaths.

Camila shoved the remaining three men to the side, ran to the doorway, and looked out into the havoc greeted by the fire and explosion. She looked over a vast area blurred by smoke and dust. Holding her palm over nose and mouth, she waved the smoke away as best she could to see.

"Roberto?" she called into her radio.

"What is going on? What the hell was that?" said Akim.

"It was an explosion, you idiot. We just lost almost all of our men," said Camila. Then into her radio again, "Roberto? Roberto? Answer me, dammit."

Camila heard a coughing come over her radio

"Roberto? Is that you?"

Another coughing fit, this one stretch on for minutes. While the coughing continued, Camila scanned the other channels to no avail until she finally got Jay.

"Jay? Is that you? Jay? I repeat, is that you?"

"Oh my God, I think I broke my back. I can't move my legs. I am paralyzed from the waist down," Jay moaned.

"Look, that's okay, Jay. We'll get you out of there. Did anyone else make it?"

"No," said Jay, almost in a whisper.

"That's all right, Jay."

But Camila didn't know if it was all right at all. Getting Jay out would be impossible.

"No, please don't, please don't," came Jay's voice from the radio.

"Jay?" said Camila.

There came an indistinct sound, a muffled noise from the radio.

And then a voice.

"Jay and the other survivors didn't make it. I put a bullet in their brains."

"Hauck?" whispered Camila.

But the voice on the line had gone silent, like the digital phantom that he was.

CHAPTER THIRTY

The Agression

Hauck put his CZ pistol back into his custom-made holster that allowed for his suppressor. A third man had lived, but Hauck put him down to. That made three men that Hauck had killed. There were maybe fifteen to eighteen on the bridge when it exploded. Maybe only ten or twelve. It was hard to tell. That meant probably twelve to fifteen dead. Hauck didn't expect any ID on the bodies of the three men he had dispatched, but he searched them anyway. He chose Roberto's body to frisk first—what was left of it. Roberto had been pretty broken up in the fall. He assumed from the way he lay, he had a broken back. The hole in his head where Hauck had plugged him with the bullet didn't make him any prettier.

The man, as expected, didn't have any identification. He wore a crucifix around his neck and had tattoos plastered on all available surfaces. The portable camera that was strapped to his head was shattered. Hauck moved on to the next man, glancing up at where a frustrated Camila stood looking down. He assumed she couldn't see him, but he didn't take any chances.

Satisfied that she couldn't see him, he checked out the second man. He had a broken arm and two broken legs from the fall, and from what Hauck could see, a head injury, and the inevitable hole in his forehead, with the back of his head being blown out by Hauck's bullet. Hauck kicked him over and rifled through his clothes for any kind of identification at all, but he could find nothing.

Hauck pulled the same trick on the next man, although this one had endured more damage from the fall on the staircase in the blast from the bomb than the others. His head was twisted and on an angle, and before he died, he had been breathing stertorously. Hauck had really done this one a favor by putting him down. He went through the pockets of his clothing and came up empty.

He stood up and vanished behind the giant gauge. There was no sense being out in the open anymore than he had to. He was accustomed to the green-yellow light of his night vision goggles. But he had to get used to the visionary distortions that they caused.

"Sveta," he said into his radio.

"Here," came the response.

"That took out twelve or fifteen of them," he said.

"I'll have to remember to congratulate Jimmy," she said.

"I figure an additional three with the exploding door trick, and that's got to thin the herd down."

"I think you're right, Hauck. It's all down to how many they had to begin with."

"Agreed."

There was no way, of course, to know how many men that Professor Meridian had come with. Hauck estimated twenty to twenty-five, but really, that was just a guess on his part. They could have had forty for all he knew, but he didn't think so.

"So, what's next?" asked Vienna.

"I don't know. Wait to see how they get down without a stairway, I suppose. That's where you come in to pick them off, one at a time. As they come down, you've got to shoot them."

"Hauck?"

Jimmy came on the radio.

"Speak."

"Brittany's picked up their private radio transmissions. It seems that even though they were encoded, we can easily break them."

"Really?"

"Really."

"What do they say?" cut in Sveta. "How many men did they have?"

"I think they only had twenty-five, so with however many you killed, plus those didn't survive the bridge, plus the ones we got with the exploding door, that they only had five left."

"Five?" Said Hauck.

Five they could take.

"Wait, there are six more men, sorry, but they are special, but Hauck?"

"Yes?"

"Have you ever heard of something called a chernobog?"

Hauck thought about it. No, he decided he'd never heard of it. Although, something about the word seemed familiar.

"No, I can't say that I have. What about the rest of you?"

Neither Sveta, Yuri, or Tricia had ever heard of it, either.

"What is it, Jimmy?"

"That's the damnedest thing. They haven't said either. But one of them, Camila, I think her name is, seems damned afraid of it. Anyway, they're about to turn the chernobog loose on us."

"What?" said Hauck. "Say again?"

"I said, they're about to turn the chernobog loose."

"That can't be," said Yuri, suddenly.

"No, serious as a heart attack," said Jimmy.

"What is it, Yuri?" Asked Hauck.

"Well, I remember what a chernobog is suddenly. It's a myth the old women used to scare children into good behavior. You know, like if you don't behave, the Chernobog is going to get you, and that kind of shit."

"Yes, but Yuri, what exactly is this chernobog?" asked an impatient Hauck.

He kept an eye on the elevated door for signs of movement. As far as the professor and his men knew, that was the only way in. They surely couldn't know of the way in through the sewers. Besides, Jimmy had that alarmed.

"Like I said, a chernobog is a myth. It was supposed to be some kind of... vampire or something like that. It had the powers of turning into a mist, could become the bat, or a rat, but mainly he could suck the blood. But that, as far as I knew, was a myth. Why?"

Jimmy, are you saying they actually have a chernobog?"

Jimmy fell silent for a minute.

"Jimmy? Jimmy?" said Yuri.

"Quiet. I'm listening to Brittany relay messages between Camila and someone named Akim."

"Oh," said Yuri.

"What are they saying?" asked Tricia.

"They are telling the chernobog minders-six of them I think—to open the chernobog's cage and to stand back, so he can... so that he can have untrammeled access to the broken in door. He will... something... something... his responsibility is to kill all life in this cavern. Oh, shit."

"A vampire?" said Hauck. "That's crazy. Tell Brittany to find any weaknesses they have."

"I don't think they have any Hauck," said Yuri.

A moment's silence and then Jimmy spoke.

"There seems to be a paucity of records on the chernobog. One says among Slavic people, there is a belief that they kept in their drinking festivals and feasts. They at the same time bless and curse the names of their gods, respectively, in the name of a good one and an evil one, saying that good things come from good god and evil things come from the evil one. In their language, they call the evil god chernobog, or black god. Chernobog is a Slavic deity whose name means black god, about whom much has been speculated but little can be said definitively. The only historical sources, which are Christian ones, interpret him as a dark accursed God, but it is questionable how important or evil he was really considered to be by ancient Slavs.

"Another says only that the chernobog is the mysterious black god of evil and swearing. His name means black God. He is a dark demonic deity, a hideous shadowy figure dressed in black, who only appears at night. The Lord of evil, the chernobog causes calamity and disaster, bringing bad luck and misfortune wherever he turns. There is no hidden agenda—he just enjoys being a black-hearted villain. He is the Darth Vader of Slavic mythology. His opposite number is Belobog, the way God of goodness. The two of them are in eternal conflict.

"The chernobog was feared all over Russia as a being of pure nastiness, in the same evil club as Ahriman and Satan. Few would pray to such a deity, but one early passage reveals that people would spit curses into a bowl during feasts to keep him at bay.

"The chernobog is so utterly malevolent that few writers dared to jot down details of his foul deeds. All we have are shadows and rumors and hints. It's almost as if early priests invented him as a Slavic Satan figure to keep the locals terrified.

"That's only the things listed on the Internet. Everything else is fanfiction. I'm sorry."

"What about how to kill a vampire?" said Hauck.

"Just a sec," said Jimmy. "Let me patch Brittany in—it's easier. Okay, Brittany you're on."

"Yes, doctor."

"Okay, so everyone can hear what you say are ways to kill a vampire."

"You can burn them with direct sunlight," said Brittany. "Which is impractical because there is no direct sunlight below ground."

"Go on," said Hauck.

"You can pound a wooden stake through its heart or you can douse it with holy water."

"We don't have any wooden stakes or holy water," said Sveta.

"You could take off his head at the shoulders," said Brittany.

"Now that we can do," said Yuri excitedly. "We could shoot it off."

"It's most commonly done with a sword. I don't know what effect bullets would have on a vampire," said Brittany.

"Anything else?" said Hauck.

He was nervously checking the blown high-set door.

"You can kill a vampire with silver. But that doesn't seem practical, because I don't think anyone has silver down here," said Brittany.

"And?" said Tricia.

"You can kill a vampire with fire."

"I can rig up a flamethrower or two, depending on how much time we have to do it," said Yuri

"Then get back here and do it," said Hauck.

"I think I can help," said Jimmy.

"Good. We'll see if the three of us and Brittany can hold off this… vampire. Brittany, are you ready to throw images and sound explosions?"

"Yes, I am Hauck. But Hauck?"

"They are letting loose the vampire now."

"You hear that Yuri? Everyone?"

Everyone acknowledged.

"All right, listen everyone, we go for the neck and head shots only if you can. We've got to separate his head from his body, if it's at all possible," said Hauck.

"But what if that has no effect?" said Tricia.

"Then I've got to find a sword. I think I know just where to get one," said Hauck. "It's in the Instructor's things."

"I'm going to trust in my rifle," said Sveta. "If that fails, I've got a large knife for backup."

"All right," said Hauck. "I'm going for the sword now."

As Hauck ran, he hoped to God that Yuri and Jimmy were able to put together a flamethrower or two, because he sure didn't want to face a vampire with only a sword. Garlic was out, except for what little they had as a seasoning for food. Holy water was a nonstarter. Where were they going to get either holy water or sunlight down below ground? And besides, there was no time.

He passed Jimmy and Yuri and ran to the Instructor's room. He got down on his hands and knees near his bed and pulled out a long case—the Instructor's sword.

A chilling, inhuman sound split came from far away. Hauck looked up sharply. What was that? The chernobog. It had to be. Hauck hurriedly threw the case on the bed and opened the box. The Instructor's sword lay inside. Hauck picked it up and hefted the enormous blade in his hands. With one last look around the room, he wished the Instructor was here beside him instead of locked up in a cage. He turned and ran outside of the room.

Hauck stopped at Jimmy and Yuri, who were frantically assembling parts for a flamethrower.

"How are we doing?" he asked.

"Leave us alone, we're busy," said Jimmy tersely.

"You got the sword," said Yuri. "You have to stay and protect us while we are assembling this thing."

"But I've got to help the women," protested Hauck.

"You want us to finish the thing or not?" said Yuri. "Hauck, we're defenseless here without you."

"Hurry," said Hauck.

While Jimmy and Yuri sweated it out on the two flamethrowers, Hauck kept scanning the place. That was the one thing about the lights out and wearing the night vision goggles, was that in order to cover the place, you had to keep moving your head. So far, Hauck saw nothing, but that didn't mean anything. The vampire could be stealthily approaching him from Hauck's backside, and Hauck wouldn't know it until it was too late.

Jimmy grabbed a wrench and began tightening down the two tanks that would supply the fuel onto a harness that he had put together. Yuri did the same thing with a harness he had contrived. It was painstaking work assembling the things within the confines of a green-yellow world. Hauck didn't know how they kept their sanity while doing it.

The vampire screamed again, a hideous sound. Closer now, as Hauck estimated it. But not much. Brittany had all the imaginary Haucks running around. Hauck didn't know how convincing they were, but if they were convincing at all, they must be giving the vampire fits. He could see at least six of himself running around, popping up, and then disappearing.

He realized then that Sveta and Tricia were all that they had between themselves and the vampire.

CHAPTER THIRTY-ONE

The Chernobog Released

Akim entered the truck and unlocked the door to the chernobog's box. He flung the door open and stepped back. The chernobog slowly stepped out. It was all dressed in black and was a formidable presence. Its black eyes looked eerily hungry.

"Now, you will go down into the belly of the beast, and destroy every man, woman, and child that is down there," said an enraged Akim.

The chernobog smiled.

"As you wish," it said.

"And then you will return to me," said Akim, "when they are all dead."

"And then you will release me?"

"Go. Now," said Akim, pointing with his left index finger imperiously.

Camila and her remaining men were off to one side of the van. The six movers who carried the chernobog's box stood to the other side, leaving the chernobog a clear runway to the door.

"As you wish," said the chernobog, licking his lips.

The chernobog walked to the doorway's edge and looked down. Then he looked back. He turned to the door again, and, giving an inhuman scream, he stepped off into the darkness.

Camila rushed to the hole cut in the door and looked out at the chernobog. At first, she could see nothing. But then, in the green-yellow light of her night vision goggles, she saw the faint form of the chernobog hitting the ground gracefully. He looked around himself and started walking.

"Don't worry, my dear, the chernobog will finish what your men could not do. But you must send your men in after him. Have them fast rope to the ground."

"But you said that the chernobog would kill them."

"Yes, but first they must flush out their opponents," smiled Akim.

Bait, thought Camila. He was using them as bait, but she looked at her three remaining men and gave them instructions. If the men were nervous, they didn't show it. Frederico, Ivan, and Igor were their names, and they geared up silently. They put their harnesses on and secured the ropes to the bumper of the truck. Camila watched them, certain that they were going to their deaths. She felt Akim's eyes upon her, but refused to look back at him.

"We are ready," said Ivan.

Camila hesitated only a second before she said go. She realized why they were unafraid. They thought the chernobog was on their side. Too bad, she thought, that when all was said and done, they would be a meal for the chernobog.

"Next you," said Akim.

She gulped, hoping against hope to slip away.

"But, I would be—"

Camila felt Akim come up behind her as he spoke.

"You will go now and direct the men from the cavern."

She nodded, got into her harness, and connected with her rope. Camila looked back at Akim. Maybe she should shoot him right there, but for some unaccountable reason, she was afraid to. She looked back at him one last time, then went out past the door and leapt.

The ride down was fast through the darkness, and she hoped she would not get shot on the way down. She hit the floor and disconnected herself from her harness quickly and crouched down.

"Ivan, are you down?" she asked over her radio.

"Yes, I'm here."

"Igor, are you down?"

"Yes."

"Frederico, are you down?"

"Yes, I am here."

"Ah, I can see you all now. Listen to me. Spread out and try to be careful. We don't know how many people they have, but we assume the number to be small," said Camila. "Any questions?"

"No," said Ivan. "Wait, we shoot to kill, right?"

"Everyone that moves that the chernobog doesn't take down first."

A sudden gunshot split the darkness.

"Shit," said Igor, "I thought I saw someone. I guess not."

Normally, Camila would've shot Igor herself, but she had too few men to risk it.

"Okay, move out."

When the men had moved out, Camila went to the back wall and worked her way around it, trying to be obsequious in her movements, hoping not to be seen. She was trying to get as far away from the chernobog as possible. It was out there, somewhere, of that she had no doubt. The question, though, was where? This place was a nightmare warren of places to hide.

It was silent, though, and she didn't like that. No, she didn't like that one bit. In all of her times as a hired assassin, silence and darkness had been her friend. She had never been in a situation like this, though. Deserted alleys, yes. Abandoned warehouses, yes. Empty streets and penthouses that she stretched high above the city. But nothing like this.

As she moved along the wall, her SIG Sauer automatic at the ready, she felt the wonder of the place. Painted in hues of green and yellow in the night vision goggles, the giant tubes, the pipes, and floating globes, the gages and dials and motor control panels, she felt intimidated by it all. Yet, at the same time, she was acutely aware that every nook and cranny of the place could be a hiding place for a shooter. She grasped her rifle tighter.

The place was so large. She felt confident if she could just make it to the cavern's far wall, she would be safe from the chernobog. She was so intent on looking for people that she almost ran into a locker. Stopping and going around it, she looked first to see if there was a shooter there, and, seeing no one, she kept going. She passed a huge globe that was at ground-level and stopped. A monstrous cry split the darkness, and Camila was sure that the chernobog was hunting.

She saw a figure emerge from the darkness and run along an aisle. Raising her rifle to shoot, she loaded quickly. The man just disappeared. It was an eerie feeling. How could he just disappear into thin air? Was that Hauck? If he had the ability to do that, then they were in trouble, and she was glad that her plan was to stick to the wall and go to the far side of the cavern.

Progressing a good deal further, she was surprised to come face-to-face with an armed man. She fired with her SIG-Sauer at the man, who wavered a moment, then was gone. Camila was stunned. She had just fired at point blank range, and he had simply vanished. He wasn't real. He was just an... image. Probably computer-generated. But... it had seemed so real.

Came another cry from the chernobog, and this time she heard a man scream.

CHAPTER THIRTY-TWO

The Battle Begins

Sveta could feel the sweat trickling down from her forehead. She had missed the fast ropers because they had been too fast. She had fired, but her shots had been where they were and she cursed. They had landed behind some vessels and now they traveled unseen. But that wasn't what bothered Sveta.

"Tricia?" she said into her microphone.

"Yes?"

"Did you see that thing that came down before the four?"

"Yes."

"What did you make of it?"

"It seemed like — like a man, but it sure wasn't like any man I'm familiar with."

Brittany came on the line just then.

"That was the chernobog," she said.

"I was afraid of that," said Sveta. "He just basically flew down."

"I'm nervous," Trisha said. "Aren't you?"

"We've got the imaginary Hauck's popping up all over the place, and Jimmy and Yuri are working on flamethrowers. All we got to do is hang on — "

The sound of a silence gunshot came over Tricia's radio. It was two pffts and then silence.

"Tricia?" asked Sveta.

"I'm here," answered Tricia. "It was just one of the four gunmen who fast roped down sneaking up on me."

"Keep an eye out for the other three. With all this machinery in the way, they're hard to see."

"Got it."

Sveta considered. It was a game of cat and mouse. Sveta considered herself the cat, and the three remaining men were the mouse. Except for the chernobog.

"Where are you, Tricia?"

"I'm over near the wall."

Sveta was dead center of the cavern. She was up high on the catwalk between two gargantuan pieces of machinery. It was eerie with the lights turned off. She found the popping up of digital Haucks distracting. She would almost be ready to pull the trigger when he would vanish. Hopefully, the enemy found it as distracting as she did.

Another scream came out of the darkness. Where was that? Where did it originate from? She scanned the darkness for an answer, but there was none. Damn the darkness. It was a two-edged sword. Difficult as it was to be seen in the darkness, it was more difficult to see. The night vision goggles helped, but their view of something so large as the cavern was limited. Everything was distorted in the ghostly green and yellow light.

She saw someone moving. Was that Hauck, a digital image of Hauck, or someone else? Sveta trained her scope on the person, but they ducked out of sight. She kept scanning the area, hoping against hope that they would pop up. But what she saw instead was a black shape coming up fast. Sveta tensed and readied a shot. It was the chernobog.

Brittany had said that one method of killing a vampire was to separate its head from its body. Sveta tried to get a bead on the juncture between its neck and its head. It was moving too fast, though. She could get a bead on the body, but that was not enough. If she fired now, she would give her position away. Or would she? She took the shot.

Just then, she hesitated, for the chernobog came upon the other man. Sveta could clearly see now when the man turned at the coming of the chernobog.

Got you, thought Sveta.

But to her surprise, the chernobog turn into a black mist, also surprising the mercenary. The man didn't seem to know what to do. With a speed that impressed Sveta, the black mist surrounded the man, wrapping around him like a blanket. The man was like a fly trapped in a spider's web. Sveta watched, stunned that the chernobog was attacking their own man. It was horrifying to watch how the black mist surrounded him. The man struggled, but couldn't get free. He fired off bursts from his weapon, but to no effect. They merely ricocheted off the surrounding pipes and equipment.

The chernobog's face materialized out of the mist, jaws descended. Sveta fired a round at his head. A digital image of Hauck appeared not three feet from them, startling the chernobog, who immediately materialized and leaned forward in a threatening posture. Because of this, the bullet struck harmlessly to one side, flattening against an oblong piece of steel. The chernobog leaped at the Hauck image and went completely through it. Confused, the chernobog looked back at the image just in time to see it fade away. He gave a bloodcurdling scream filled with rage.

Meanwhile, the man whom the chernobog had attacked fired his weapon at the chernobog while Sveta watched through her high-powered scope. The bullets should have ripped the chernobog to shreds. Instead, with each successive onslaught, the chernobog only jerked back, the holes that should have been fatal, merely slowing down his movements. Sveta felt a chill go down her spine, and a feeling of dread settled over her just watching. The chernobog turned into a black mist rapidly and enveloped the man again. The man screamed as the chernobog's face appeared in the brume, but before Sveta could get off a shot, the chernobog had descended on the man's neck. Sveta was reduced to watching as the chernobog fed on the man. He was trapped in the smoking mist, twitching as though he was being electrocuted. The chernobog's face was pressed against the man's neck, and he was sucking the life force out of him. Sveta watched in horror as the man shriveled before her eyes and became visibly smaller.

The urgency of separating the chernobog's head from his body became impressed upon her, and she angled the scope around, but she could not get a clear shot. As the poor man's life force was drained from him, though, the chernobog cast the man aside. What was happening? Why was the chernobog devouring their own men?

Sveta took careful aim. She got the crosshairs of her lens on the chernobog's neck and fired. He turned to mist and was gone in the blink of an eye, and, once again, the bullet bounced harmlessly off a piece of thick steel.

She moved the lens back and forth, trying to reacquire her target. Trying harder, she expanded her search, but to no avail. Sveta felt a trickle of sweat escape her. The chernobog was gone. Vanished into thin air. She felt genuine fear when the darkness closed in around her. The chernobog's feeding on their own man was what did it. The feeding was horrible enough, but to do it to their own man?

As Sveta scanned the area with the lens, she tried to figure it out. Did the chernobog make a mistake? Impossible. It was just killing everyone, everyone that stood in its way. Could that be how it was? To what end? She was concerned for Hauck, Tricia, Jimmy, and Yuri on the ground. It was not realistic to see what was happening with these night vision goggles on. She had made the mistake of choosing a sniper's nest with the lights on, but with the lights off, and the green-yellow light of the night vision goggles, she just couldn't see as clearly. Should she ask Brittany to turn the lights on, or keep them off?

The chernobog didn't have any night vision goggles on. He could see in the dark that much was clear. And he didn't have that tunnel vision effect so common with night vision goggles.

"Hauck?"

"Yes?"

"I just saw the chernobog eat one of its own."

"Say again?"

"You heard me. I just saw the chernobog eat one of its own."

"Did you get a shot at it?"

"Negative. He always had the man between me and him or it or whatever it is and everybody else listen up — I just saw him turn into smoke and vanished."

"Oh shit," said Yuri.

"Exactly," said Tricia.

"Hauck," said Sveta, "I don't think we're doing ourselves any favors by having these lights turned off. I can't see the chernobog in the night clearly. I am okay going for a body shot with the lights off and using these night vision goggles, but to get a shot cleanly at the juncture of a neck and a head at this distance, I don't think I can do it."

"What are you suggesting, Sveta?" asked Hauck.

"That we turn the lights on."

Hauck thought about it for a minute. If they turned the lights on, they would be like sitting ducks. In the dark, at least they had cover.

"Hauck, there's one other thing."

"Yes?"

"The chernobog sees in the dark. Maybe his eyes are light sensitive," said Sveta.

"We don't know that, Sveta," said Hauck.

"I know that, Hauck."

"We'd be risking a lot."

"What would we be risking? The professor only has three men left. We don't have to worry about them. The chernobog will take them out, and it's the chernobog we have to worry about. And I'm telling you, Hauck, he can see in the dark."

"Jimmy," asked Hauck, "how much time until we are ready with the flamethrowers?"

"We're ready now."

Hauck knew that if they threw the lights on, that the men with the night vision goggles would be temporarily blinded. Sveta would be safe up high, but he thought Tricia would be exposed.

"Tricia, how far are you from us?"

"Ten minutes, tops," said Tricia.

"All right, be careful, but make a run for us. We'll cover you as best we can. Go now."

"Got it."

"Sveta, have you got that? Cover her as she runs. When she gets here, take your night vision goggles off, and we'll turn the lights on."

"Okay, she's in my sights."

"I hope so," said Hauck. "Yuri, Jimmy — put your flamethrowers on, and get ready to use them at a minute's notice."

While Jimmy and Yuri put their harnesses on, Hauck stood watch with his sword, ready for anything. He didn't know if the three remaining men of Professor Meridian's or the chernobog would find them first, but he had to be prepared. That's why he kept his sword in his right hand and his H&K MP7 slung over his left shoulder and his left hand on the trigger.

"Okay, we're ready," said Jimmy.

"Then we wait. She should be here in five minutes," said Hauck.

"She's still in my sights," said Sveta.

Suddenly, a man stood up, and was about to fire a shot at the running Tricia, when a digital image of Hauck appear directly in front of him. Startled, the man fired at him. It just went through him. The man assumed he had missed and fired again, but Sveta, ever watchful, put a bullet into the man's head. He dropped to the ground without a word. The digital image of Hauck vanished.

"Nice work, Brittany," said a relieved Sveta. "I think that just leaves one or two of them left."

"Thank you," said Brittany.

Tricia's head appeared in Hauck's sight moments later. He breathed a sigh of relief.

"Come on," he said under his breath. "You can make it."

Tricia dodged machinery and quartz oscillators, glass rods, and wires in her mad run to Hauck and the others.

"I'll go get her," said Jimmy.

"No," said Hauck.

"But — "

"No," repeated Hauck. "Can't you feel it?"

"I've got to help her," said Jimmy, and he took off running.

"No," said Hauck, and he reached for Jimmy, but he was too late.

Jimmy was already running for Tricia.

"You want me to go get them, Hauck?" asked Yuri.

"Yes," said Hauck.

And Yuri took off, too. Hauck watched him go with a feeling of dread.

"Sveta?"

"What?"

"Have you got Tricia in your sights?"

Yes."

"Watch carefully. Jimmy has taken off after her, and I've sent Yuri after Jimmy."

"Got it."

Hauck saw Jimmy arrive to meet Tricia, and Yuri get there just a few moments later. The three of them started up toward the platform, when they stopped and looked around. A hideous scream rent the darkness. The three of them began running again. They made it as far as two minutes away when they stopped again. A black mist suddenly appeared before them. Jimmy raised his flamethrower and pulled the trigger. Just as the chernobog's face appeared from the mist, a jet of liquid fire blasted him.

"Go," yelled Jimmy.

And the three of them began running again.

Come on, mouthed Hauck silently. He raised his sword to the ready position.

Jimmy and Tricia were in the lead, while Yuri was back a little way, fumbling with his flamethrower. The black mist appeared again, and with a vengeance, it wrapped itself around Yuri. The chernobog's face appeared above Yuri's and Sveta fired a round. It was a clean shot, but it only got part of the chernobog's head. Immediately, it vanished completely. Yuri gagged and began running for the stairs leading to the platform, which Jimmy and Tricia had made it to already. He was on the fifth step when the obsidian colored smoke appeared before him and grabbed him again.

"Now, Brittany — turn them all on," yelled Hauck.

Suddenly, all the lights in the entire cavern came on. This time, Sveta was ready, and timed her shot almost perfectly. When the chernobog's face appeared, she fired a round right into his face and the chernobog screamed and vanished. Yuri scrambled up the remaining steps and joined his friends.

He fell on the platform and threw up.

CHAPTER THIRTY-THREE

The Actual Battle

Hauck looked down at Yuri and then looked up for the chernobog.

"You're all right, Yuri?"

Yuri coughed and sputtered for a minute.

"That son of a bitch—"

"He's okay," said Tricia.

"Thanks for coming down," said Jimmy.

"What? Oh, no problem. You would've done the same for me. Thank God for Sveta, though."

"Where is it? Where is the chernobog?"

"He is moving away from you," said Brittany.

"How do you know that?" asked Hauck.

"Why, I can track his movements by the sensors scattered all around the cavern. I thought you knew."

"Sorry, Hauck, I meant to tell you," said Jimmy. "But things got so hectic that I—"

"Don't worry about it," said Hauck. "Brittany, where is he now? And I would guess you can tell me the location of the other man, too."

"Yes. The chernobog is heading toward the center of the cavern and the other man is moving along the wall away from everyone."

"Moving toward the center? What would he be moving there for?"

"That is where Sveta is, I assume," said Brittany.

"What? Sveta, are you hearing this?"

"Yes, I heard it, Hauck."

"Be careful, Sveta."

"I know."

Hauck fretted about Sveta's safety. How could he just leave her there.? It was one thing against gunmen—she could hold her own against any gunmen, but against the chernobog, against the vampire with unknown powers? And if he went after her, what would that accomplish except putting the others in danger? Besides, he didn't even know if it was going after her or not, but he had a dreadful feeling…

"Brittany?"

"Yes, Hauck?"

"Deploy as many of my images as you can around the chernobog."

"But—"

"Just do it."

"Certainly, Hauck."

"What do you hope to accomplish?" asked Jimmy.

"I hope to distract him."

He peered out over the machinery in the tube to see Sveta, and he finally found her. She had crawled up two stories higher than she had originally been located.

"Hauck?"

"Yes, Brittany."

"We have seven more men fast roping down."

"What?"

"We have seven more—"

"I heard you, Brittany. I was just thinking this could not be at a worse time."

"One man is odd, Hauck," said Brittany.

"Odd?" said Jimmy. "Odd in what way?"

"It's difficult to say, but he doesn't appear to be living. He, like the chernobog, has no heat signature."

A frustrated shriek pierced the still air.

"Brittany?"

"Yes, Hauck?"

"Set off as many explosion noises as you can."

"Yes, Hauck."

The air thundered all around in the cavern with monumental

explosions and the machinery fairly shook with them. The chernobog screamed again and his scream cut through the air like a jagged knife. It looked around wildly, and Sveta took another shot at it. It struck home, and the chernobog screeched an earsplitting sound and vanished.

"I got him in the head again," said Sveta, "but it didn't seem to make any difference. He just vanished. I've got to take his whole head off at the juncture of his neck and his head."

"Stay where you are," said Hauck.

"I'm bloody well not going to climb down with that thing down there."

"I've got to go get Sveta," said Hauck.

"What?" said Tricia. "Excuse me, but that's insane. Sveta safest where she is now."

"But for how long? How long until the thing finds her? It's hunting her now. I've got to go."

"I'll go with you," said Yuri. "It's safer if the two of us go. I've got the flamethrower, and all you got is that stupid sword."

"I can't ask you to do that, Yuri."

"Yeah, well, you don't have to."

"Jimmy, will you be okay?" asked Hauck.

"Go," said Jimmy, "we'll be okay. I've got the other flamethrower and Tricia's got the gun. But hurry will you? I've got a bad feeling about this."

"Hauck," said Sveta, "don't do it. This is insane."

Hauck nodded, and he and Yuri took off on the run.

He ran, dodging around the equipment, not caring that said Sveta was yelling in his ear, not bothering to check if Yuri was right behind him. All he could hear in his ear as he ran was Sveta blasting at the chernobog, and he ran harder. He didn't care if he was a target. In fact, there were multiple images of himself in his way, but he ran through them. The explosions crashed around him; he didn't care where they came from, but he knew they were the phony sounds created by Brittany. But were they? Maybe they were from somewhere else, but he didn't care. All that mattered to him was that Sveta was in danger, and he had to help her.

In the distance, up ahead, he could see her, perched high above the floor of the cavern, and he saw the flashes and the sounds of her SIG Sauer blasting away at the chernobog. It had now seen her, and it was rising, floating towards her. Hauck screamed and kept running.

Suddenly, he went down from a shot out of nowhere. His leg was bleeding, and he lay on the ground, holding his sword in one hand. He was in pain and he writhed on the floor. Dimly, he heard Yuri running and returning fire, and then silence, punctuated by faux explosions that Brittany let off. Yuri knelt beside him, his flamethrower rattling as he did so.

"Hauck, Hauck, are you okay?" said Yuri.

"I'm okay. They just nicked my leg muscles. Guard me while I make a bandage to stop the bleeding."

In between the background of the explosions, Hauck could hear the firing of submachine guns. He laid his sword and his gun down on the ground, and with his knife, ripped a hole in his pant leg. The bloody mess that he saw made it hard to determine the extent of his injuries. He wiped off his leg with his torn pants. What was exposed was a bullet wound that cut through his meat, but that was all. Hauck tore his pant leg, wrapped it around his leg, and cinched it off painfully with his teeth. He grabbed his SIG Sauer and, leaning on it, he got to his feet and, in a crouched down position, retrieved his sword.

"Can you move?" asked Yuri, firing off another burst from his FN P90.

"I think so. What do we have?"

"We got two men pinning us down over behind those motor control panels. We can't make a move to get out of here without getting shot."

"They think I'm down, right?"

"I guess so, but I wouldn't count on it."

"We've got to get to Sveta. We just have to."

A sudden cry split the air, and Hauck risked a look. One man was wrapped in the chernobog's black smoke and the other was frantically trying to shoot it, but with little luck because he was afraid of hitting his own teammate. The chernobog buried his head in the man's neck and was greedily devouring his life. Sveta took the opportunity for another shot, but got the other man instead. The chernobog raised his head and growled like a dog deprived of a piece of meat. He looked around and screamed his rage. Sveta fired another bullet, but the chernobog tossed the man aside and moved too quickly for the shot to hit him.

The chernobog reappeared about five feet away from where he was, and looked around, searching for the source of the offending bullet. But then he looked up. He saw Sveta in her perch, and he smiled, turned into smoke, and began to rise.

Hauck cried out to Sveta, but another round of bullets flew near him.

****

The lights came on, and Camila stumbled and fell. She didn't get the night vision goggles off, and she was blinded by the sudden burst of light.

She took off the night vision goggles and scrambled to her feet. Camila moved quickly through the maze of apparatuses and contraptions. The only thing she cared about was getting out of the range of the chernobog. She heard several blood-curdling screams and roars, and that made her move faster. She stuck to the wall of the cavern as closely as she could. Passing by locker rooms, dials and gauges, and test tubes of all sorts and sizes, from the giant to the tiny —she just kept going. The cavern was immense in size and she felt dwarfed by it. She ran out of breath at a point where the cavern went up, and she had to stop for a moment to catch a lungful of air. It wasn't clear to her just what the range of the chernobog was, but the professor was correct on one point, she just had to get as far away as possible. The chernobog was busy eating everyone he came upon, and she was afraid he would run out of people to eat before long and come after her.

She got moving again, climbing over a fallen mess of wires. There must've been something that happened down here. Some kind of wild, giant animal must have gotten loose to wreak this kind of panic. Finally, she clawed her way through and was free of it. She was even with two giant cages, from which she could hear muffled sounds coming, like howling and/or baying.

Up high enough now, she could see in the distance two tiny

figures on a platform. She didn't have a shot, though, and she couldn't care less. The chernobog would finish them. She just had to get far enough away so that when it was done with them, he wouldn't get to her as well. From inside of the giant twin cages came more muffled sounds. She should run, but her curiosity got the best of her. She looked for a way into the cages, but found both locked, with immensely sized locks. Finally, she gave up and started to run again. She may have been curious as to what was locked in the immense cages, but she was more concerned about staying alive.

Up and a over a hill that was in her way, and then down again. She tripped and fell over some machinery, then scrambled up to her feet again. The damnable equipment was in her way. She felt like she'd been running forever.

****

Tricia fired at one of Akim's men and scrambled for cover. She just got behind a file cabinet when the file cabinet was sprayed with bullets.

"Jimmy," she called, "are you hurt?"

"No," came the response. "I'm down here."

Tricia looked and saw Jimmy laying on the floor with an FNP 90 clutched in his hands.

"Jimmy, I—"

Another burst of fire and Tricia huddled down. At her first opportunity, she stood up and fired back. Their opponents were down at where the Tesla tube was before they dismantled it.

Without warning, Jimmy stood and began firing his FNP 90 at the men. His aim was off, and he hit the platform that they stood on instead of the men. The FN jammed and, rather than trying to unjam it, Jimmy ducked down just as one man fired a quick burst at him.

"What are you, nuts?" cried Tricia. "Just stay down."

"Sorry, I was just trying to help," said an out of breath Jimmy.

Jimmy got the FNP 90 to unjam, but it was out of bullets. He threw it aside in disgust. Instead, he picked up Hauck's Mossberg shotgun. It felt right in his hands. It felt good, like it belonged to him.

"Doctor?" said Brittany.

"Yes, Brittany?"

"I think I can distract the two men long enough for Tricia to shoot them."

"How?" asked Tricia.

She didn't see how that was possible, but pinned down by the men's gunfire, she was willing to listen to anything.

"I have a digital image of Hauck appear to them. They are right near a projector. When Hauck appears suddenly, they will be distracted and you can shoot them."

Tricia thought about that for a minute. She really didn't have much choice, though. It was that, or nothing.

"Okay, do it."

"Now," said Brittany.

Tricia stood and fired.

"Tricia," said Brittany.

But it was too late. For Akim stepped from behind Tricia, and stabbed with his khylsty dagger, and he twisted it until Tricia groaned and dropped.

Jimmy screamed.

CHAPTER THIRTY-FOUR

The Battle Continues

The chernobog rose.

Hauck grabbed his SIG Sauer and fired. The chernobog turned, snarled, and went into a dive at Hauck.

"Oh shit," said Yuri, "he's coming straight at us."

He dropped his own submachine pistol and brought up his flamethrower. He checked the tip to make sure that it was still lit, and it was. The chernobog's speed was tremendous, coming straight for them, when Yuri let loose a stream of liquid fire. The chernobog dodged out of the way and tried flying behind Yuri. Yuri turned with it, continuing to spray the fiery liquid after it. Hauck was firing at the chernobog, too, but couldn't seem to hit it. The chernobog disappeared in a cloud of smoke.

Yuri spun around, looking for him, but he couldn't find it. He shut off the stream of liquid and kept turning in circles.

"Where is it? Where has it gone? I can't see it anywhere," he said.

"I don't know, but we have to keep searching."

It was hard to hear over the fake explosions. Hard to see over the laser lights that strobed through the globes that lit the cavern. And the images of Hauck that appeared and disappeared were confusing to even Hauck.

A shot came from overhead. Sveta was shooting at something now. Hauck wondered what it was, but he kept scanning the surrounding area, looking for the chernobog.

"I can't see it, Hauck."

"I know, Yuri. Keep an eye open for it. It's got to be here someplace."

Then, suddenly, when Hoke was looking one way, the black cloud formed around Yuri. He frantically depressed the trigger and released the liquid fire, but the chernobog was too close to him. Hauck turned at the sound of the ignition, the spraying of a liquid jet stream of flames.

"Hauck, help me," cried Yuri.

Hauck let loose a quick burst of bullets at the chernobog's head, which had just formed from the mist. The chernobog snarled and uttered an unnerving cry, but dropped Yuri. Hauck raised his gun to fire again, but it jammed. Yuri started a stream of fire, but it missed. The chernobog rushed in a black mist and engulfed Yuri, who sputtered and cried out. Hauck let his SIG Sauer dropped on its sling, and took his sword and swung at the chernobog's head. But the chernobog again dropped Yuri and escaped Hauck's vicious swipe from the Instructor's Katana.

"Jesus, God," yelled Yuri.

He took up his flamethrower again and spun around in circles, looking for the chernobog. Meanwhile, Hauck worked frantically to unjam his SIG Sauer. It was while Hauck was trying to unjam his submachine gun that the chernobog struck Yuri again. He grabbed him from behind, and before Hauck could turn around even, he had sunk his fangs into Yuri's neck.

"No," screamed Hauck.

Before he could even switch to his sword, the chernobog backed rapidly away, a cloud of swirling dark smoke, his face buried in Yuri's neck, sucking away his life's blood. The chernobog worked rapidly, keeping Yuri's body in the way of Hauck's now live sword. Every which way that Hauck tried to get in to save Yuri, the chernobog simply yanked Yuri's now lifeless body in the way. At long last, as Hauck watched in agonized frustration, the chernobog threw Yuri's shell aside and rapidly backed away.

Hauck charged the chernobog, but it simply danced out of the way, floating through the air like a wraith. But a bullet caught it in the shoulder, and it looked up to see Sveta and it transformed into smoke. It rose up into the air. Hauck took a swing at the smoke with his sword, but fell short, even when he jumped. He cursed the chernobog, and he cursed Professor Meridian. He jumped wildly in the air, swinging his sword at the chernobog, but could not reach him.

Yuri lay on the ground, discarded like so much used clothes. His body was crumpled. His face was drawn in a rictus of death, a gasping grimace, a gaping hole where his mouth was open. The flamethrower lay by his side, its primer still burning. Hauck wanted to go down to his friend's body to properly mourn it, but there wasn't time. He disengaged the SIG Sauer from around what was left of Yuri's neck and swung the strap over his own neck. Looking quickly away from Yuri's body, he felt tears sting his eyes. He looked around for the chernobog and finally found him going up after Sveta.

He fired as many rounds as he could at the ascending chernobog, but to no avail. This time, it was paying no attention to Hauck. He was not coming back after him; he was going after Sveta. Hauck screamed his frustration as he climbed the steel rungs that would take him to where Sveta was, high above the ground. She was firing at the chernobog to no avail, and some shots came damn near Hauck, but he didn't care. He kept climbing.

He made it halfway up the catwalk, when the chernobog pulled up level to where Sveta was. It was smoke now, and this infuriated Hauck and made it impossible for Sveta to get a shot in. One half of the way up, he screamed at the chernobog and shook his fist. Sveta was spinning around, trying to get a shot in at the chernobog, being laughed at for her efforts. Hauck saw the chernobog's face forming out of the mist behind Sveta, and he yelled. Sveta turned around just in time to see that black mist closing in. The chernobog's mouth was wide open for the kill when a green ray of light slammed into it from nowhere.

Hauck, open-mouthed, followed the ray to its origin and saw a girl flying through the air. He couldn't believe what he was seeing. The blast from the ray had blown a hole in the chernobog two feet wide where its head once was. The chernobog squealed at the impact, and incredibly, it spiraled out of control. Hauck couldn't believe his eyes. He looked at the reeling chernobog as it descended, bouncing off the footway as it did, until finally, it crashed into the bottom. It lay there, still as death itself beside Yuri's body.

When he looked up, he saw Sveta and the girl, carrying Sveta in one arm, descending in a ball of light. He was flabbergasted to see that it was Charlene. When they came to where they were even with him, he still couldn't believe it.

"How—" he started.

"Later," said Charlene. "See you at the bottom."

And with that, Charlene and Sveta continued on the way down. Hauck scrambled to keep up with them. Down the rungs that led down to the ground he climbed, hand over hand, with the Instructor's sword and Yuri's SIG Sauer rattling from his chest by their respective straps.

When he finally reached the bottom, he found, after looking around to make sure that they were safe, that Sveta and Charlene were in shock at Yuri's death.

"I can't believe it," said Sveta. "All this time..."

Charlene was actually crying.

"Shouldn't we get a blanket or something to cover him up?" she asked.

She wiped the tears from her eyes as she said it.

"Charlene, how did you... I mean, where did you..."

"I found a way out of this place," she said, wiping her eyes once again. "You can go through the ceiling."

"Yes," began Hauck, "but where did you—"

"It's an attic full of weapons. I was climbing up, and I saw this strange, I don't know, when I found a concealed way out."

"Yes, but how is it possible that you fly?"

"Oh, that," and she showed him the ball. "It puts up this protective shield around you and it, well, it enables you to fly. This tube is a ray gun. It—"

"I know," said Hauck, "I saw what it can do."

"Charlene, where did you find this?" asked Sveta.

"Above the place where I was hiding. I was thinking about the air ducts in this place—I mean, there have to be some, right?"

For a moment, she just stared at Yuri's body.

"You found air ducts in the place? I never found any, and I looked," said Hauck.

"You just didn't look in the right places."

"We've got to get going," said Sveta. "Tricia and Jimmy may need our help."

"What about Yuri?" asked Charlene. "We just can't leave him here."

"That's the best we can do for him for now," said Hauck. "We don't even have a blanket to cover him with. But Sveta's right—Jimmy needs us."

Still, Hauck looked at the body of the chernobog, which had faded to dust before his eyes, and he shivered.

"Come on, let's get going," he said.

****

Tricia crumbled to the ground. Akim took his knife out of her smoothly. Jimmy just stood there shocked for a second, and then shot of jet of liquid fire out as Akim, who dove out of the way. He ran to Tricia to see if he could help, keeping an eye on where Akim had disappeared.

"Tricia, Tricia. Wake up, Tricia," Jimmy said.

Akim attacked Jimmy again, but again, Jimmy sprayed the liquid flames at him and Akim disappeared.

"Jimmy?" said Tricia, who lay on the ground moaning.

"You're going to be okay," said Jimmy.

"I don't know about that," said Trish weakly.

Jimmy and Tricia heard machine gun fire and Jimmy stood to take them on, but it was Hauck, Sveta, and Charlene.

"Oh, thank God," said Jimmy.

Hauck said to Sveta and Charlene, "You watch for the second chernobog or whatever he is."

He knelt down by Tricia and rolled her over. There was a knife wound just above her kidney, that was bleeding.

"Get me some compresses," he said to Jimmy.

"From where?"

"I don't care, just get them," snapped Hauck. "Tricia, can you hear me?"

"Oh God," she breathed, "this is too much to bear."

"Hang in there, Tricia. It doesn't look like he got your kidney."

"Hauck, I don't see him," said Sveta.

"Keep looking."

Hauck didn't see that the man had nicked a femoral artery, and that was good. The blood flow wasn't right for that. He held his hand over the wound and pressed.

Tricia screamed.

"What are you doing?" she gasped.

"I'm applying pressure to your wound, Tricia. You are going into shock; just bear with me, please. I don't know what other internal organs are damaged. I don't think, though, that he got anything in the way of an artery, though, and that's good."

Just then, Jimmy arrived with a bunch of bandages, scissors, tape, and a first aid kit.

"How is she?" He asked.

Hauck only shook his head and got to work ripping her shirt and swiping down the area around the stab wound with alcohol.

CHAPTER THIRTY-FIVE

The Werewolf

Hauck patched up the wound as best he could.

"I think I got the rest of his men," said Sveta. "Fortunately, Charlene got the chernobog. I don't know what I would have done without her."

"I got lucky, is all," said Charlene. "Where is that other thing?"

"Chernobog," said Sveta. "I think he's one, too. He's called the chernobog."

"Tricia?" said Jimmy. "Are you okay?"

"I'm—"

"She's going into shock, Jimmy. I've stopped the blood loss, though."

Hauck checked all the symptoms; cold and sweaty skin, weak but rapid pulse. She had the irregular breathing, and the dilated pupils. She was definitely headed into shock territory.

"What do we do?" asked Jimmy.

That was the question. What were they to do?

"I think there's just one man left, Hauck," said Sveta.

But Hauck wasn't convinced that the one person left was just a man.

"Where is he?"

"I don't know. He just vanished into thin air."

"I think she's hyperventilating," said Jimmy.

"He's nowhere around here," said Charlene.

"Keep looking," said Hauck. "And Jimmy, that's normal for someone going into shock. We're going to have to move somewhere we're less sitting ducks, though. Can you move her?"

"If you help."

"Sveta?"

"Yes, Hauck."

"We're going to have to move somewhere where we can see everything. Jimmy and I will carry Tricia, and you and Charlene will have to be on point, okay? You take Jimmy's flamethrower. Charlene can carry her ray tube and anything else she thinks she needs. Got it?"

"Yes."

Sveta took the flamethrower from Jimmy. It was bulky, but the strap could go around her neck and that made it less so. She hung the SIG Sauer around her neck, too, and was ready to go.

"Ready to go, Hauck. Charlene?"

"I'm ready to move up, too. Where are we going?"

Hauck rolled that around in his mind while he put one shoulder beneath Trisha's and Jimmy did the same. She got painfully to her feet.

"Charlene, you go first and Sveta, you back us up. We're going up, so that we can have a fair fight. Or we have to find the level that Charlene found that has the weapons in it. So let's go."

Another look around, and they didn't see Akim, which was fortunate, for Akim was feeding on his two remaining men. They were firing their submachine guns as they died, wriggling their bodies horribly as he fed on them. And with his incisors extended, he bit into their necks and lapped up the blood as though we were a hungry dog.

Charlene led the way carefully, the ball with the handhold shoved in a pocket. The only weapon she had out was the tubular ray gun from the attic. She wondered how long the device would function, though. After all, it hadn't been fired in how long? She wasn't sure if it would go on working forever, or if it would peter out when she needed it most. She wished she carried a SIG Sauer, too.

"Tricia," said Jimmy, "how are you doing?"

She didn't answer at first; she was trying to catch her breath.

"I'm okay. Would you quit asking me that?"

"Sorry," said Jimmy.

"I love you, Jimmy," said Tricia.

"I love you, too, Tricia," said Jimmy.

"Hurry up," said Hauck. "And quit talking."

They took the same path the Camila had taken, winding their way up. Hauck had a sudden thought.

"Jimmy, what happened to Brittany?"

"A stray bullet got her and put her out of commission," said Jimmy. "I got to stop for a few seconds."

"A little bit further," said Hauck. "When we draw even with the cages, then we'll stop for a minute."

They climbed over the machinery and the steepening slope of the ground. Hauck looked around and back at Sveta. She was having the most difficult time of all climbing backwards as she was, keeping an eye out for Akim, which she didn't know exactly what he was. So, she had to look up, too, to see if he was going to attack from above. Charlene led the way, while Hauck and Jimmy carried Tricia along. She was growing more tired and heavier every step of the way. Jimmy kept checking on her to see if she was all right. The bandage was holding, for now, but Tricia looked paler. But he was still worried.

At last, they reached the cages, and Hauck and Jimmy laid Tricia on the ground. Sveta and Charlene stood guard, watching for Akim. They weren't really sure what they were watching for, so they watched for anything.

Jimmy was exhausted, but he held Tricia's hand.

"No more adventures for you, kid. You had enough," he said.

"Oh, shut up," she said.

From one cage came the sound of a howl.

"I wish the Instructor wasn't locked up in that cage," said Hauck.

"If wishes were horses..." muttered Sveta.

"I see nothing," said Charlene. "I mean nothing at all. Maybe he's gone."

That was when Hauck first saw him. Trailing them. Walking along the path that they had taken to get up there.

"There," said Hauck.

Charlene and Sveta saw him then. Striding along. Not carrying any burden like Tricia, he was making fast time over the machinery and gauges and motor control panels. Gaining on them with every second they waited.

"You three go on," said Hauck, "I've got an idea. It's crazy, but it just might work."

"Hauck—" began Sveta.

"Go," said Hauck. "I don't have time, Sveta. Take Tricia and go."

Sveta was about to argue, but she looked back and saw Akim coming. Jimmy took Tricia over one arm and Charlene the other, with Sveta backing them up.

"Be careful," she said, over her shoulder.

Hauck didn't in reality know what he was doing. He was about to unleash a werewolf. He was going to unlock the Instructor's cage. But he had to give them a fighting chance. He had to let them get to the ladder, that would get them high enough above the ground that they could escape both Akim and the unleashed Instructor. There just might be enough time. But he would have to hide some place, too, if he was to have any chance of escaping. Someplace where the werewolf wouldn't be likely to find him.

He looked around and then up. It was possible, yes. He could unlock the two padlocks and then climb up to the top of the cage, but it would be too slow. Akim was getting closer. His black form was coming after them, getting to where Hauck didn't know if he had time. He looked around for anything to climb upon, and he settled on a crate that could be moved to one side of the opening of the cage. Pushing it over to the cage, he evaluated where it was and moved it over some more. If he could just kick it over, he would be fine, he hoped.

Hauck looked at Charlene and the others and saw them climbing up the scaffolding, with Jimmy and Charlene helping Tricia up. She slipped, and Sveta caught her. Hauck saw her boost her up to where Jimmy and Charlene could get hold of her and take her up again. He breathed a sigh of relief. They would make it up before Akim got to them if he could slow them down. It would all come down to a matter of timing.

He unlocked the soundproofed enclosure. Looking back, he saw Akim was close now. He hesitated at first. What the outcome of letting loose a werewolf that was the Instructor could not be determined in advance with any degree of accuracy. Really, he was just we relying on a wing and a prayer. He looked up one last time at Sveta, judged that they were far enough away to be safe, took a deep breath as he saw where Akim was, and opened the soundproofed cage. Next, he went inside, where the werewolf viciously attacked the door.

Hauck didn't think of that. He had to get the werewolf away from the gate before he could unlock it. Frantically, he looked over his shoulder to see where Akim was. Just then, the werewolf ran back to the distant part of the cage, where he beat on the bars. Hauck didn't hesitate. He unlocked the inner door of the cage, ran to the outside and scrambled up to the top of the cage, kicking the crate over as he did so.

Akim drew even with where he was, smiled at Hauck's supposed hiding place on top of the cage, when the werewolf, free of his confinement at last, burst forth in a rage. Snarling and snapping its jaws, he saw Akim at the same time as Akim saw the werewolf, and his eyes grew wide. The werewolf let out a tremendous roar and attacked. Hauck should've hidden away, but he couldn't help but watch.

He saw the flashing teeth of the werewolf going in for the kill. Akim moved to one side, fast as lightning, and bared his own teeth. Hauck was shocked to see his incisors extend, sharp and pointed, and unbelievably long. He wondered if he could escape, now that they had seen each other. Looking toward Sveta, he saw them just as they were making it still further up the scaffolding. He looked back, and saw the werewolf circling Akim, angry at his captivity, and snarling and snapping. Akim looked fearsome, tall, and vicious. His fingernails had become claws. But they were all over the place. Hauck didn't see ant way to get down without getting caught right in the middle of them. They closed and clinched, with flashing teeth and claws raking at each other.

The werewolf was awe-inspiring. His muscles rolled beneath his fur, and his jaws—with the extended teeth that with one grasping motion would have torn out Akim's throat. He moved so fast that he fairly blurred.

Akim was quick, too, though.. He disappeared in a cloud of smoke that left the werewolf baffled, looking around crazily for Akim. Suddenly, he saw Hauck. He was about to attack him when he was engulfed in a cloud of black mist and Akim bit him on the neck. The werewolf roared and reached back, grabbing a hold of Akim's head and throwing him away from him. He roared and closing in for the kill, but Akim, at the last possible moment, vanished in a cloud of vapors. This time, Hauck ducked down on the top of the insulated cage and waited while holding his breath.

It wasn't long before he heard the werewolf's enraged cry and looked up to see Akim and the werewolf engaged in a life-and-death struggle.

Hauck took his chance and dropped from the top of his cage and ran for his life. Over the machinery, he ran. He tripped once and got up, limping, but gritted his teeth and ran. Hauck was bleeding, and he didn't even know it.

Behind him, he heard Akim and the werewolf at each other's throats, gnashing and snapping and growling.

CHAPTER THIRTY-SIX

The Werewolf versus the Chernobog

Hauck was limping badly by the time he got to the scaffolding. He was bleeding down the right leg, had lost a lot of blood, but he started climbing. Behind him, the roars of the werewolf and the snarling and spitting of the chernobog assaulted his consciousness. He felt dizzy, paused, and continued on.

He risked a look back, and what he saw shocked them. The werewolf and Akim were lying on the ground, rolling back and forth, biting at each other with a ferocity that was terrible to behold. Hauck began climbing again.

Charlene saw him and scrambled down to meet him halfway.

"Here, come on," said Charlene.

Grunting in pain, he had to stop for a breath. He looked back again at the werewolf and Akim. They were locked in mortal combat, slashing each other with their long nails and biting. Hauck gathered up his strength, gave a nod to Charlene, and continued his long climb.

The screaming of the two was almost unbearable. Hauck had made it two-thirds of the way up with Charlene's help, but he had to rest again.

"Sorry," he said, "I'll be okay in a second."

"It's okay," said Charlene.

Hauck saw her, too, looking past him at the battle raging between Akim and the werewolf. It was urgent for them to get to the upper floor. He could see Sveta looking down nervously. Her own leg was bothering her too badly to come down. She was looking at the strange sight of the two fighting wildly for supremacy.

Hauck glanced back at the tube before gathering up the strength to go on. One of the two would kill the other, then go after him. In Hauck's mind, the Instructor had to win, and he didn't want to be around when the kill was accomplished. He was leaving a blood trail for them to follow, but it couldn't be helped. He struggled on, with Charlene helping him when she could.

Surprising Hauck, a bloodcurdling scream cut across the way. It was the werewolf. He was injured. Akim must be getting the upper hand. Hauck grimly undertook the last leg. Charlene and Sveta pulled him up on the last part of his journey, and he lay there panting.

"Where are you hurt?" Asked Sveta.

"Right leg—I must've hurt it when I took a tumble at the pile of machinery," said Hauck.

Sveta examined his right leg. She cut away his pants to get a better look.

"Whoa," she said, "that's quite a cut."

They didn't have any first-aid supplies, so she hobbled together a bandage out of his torn pants, and tied it off. Hauck bit his lip.

"There," she said. "That's going to have to hold."

She brushed his hair out of his eyes, so that he could see. It was a touch filled with tenderness, but Hauck didn't notice.

"We've got to kick out the scaffolding and I can't do it," said Hauck. "Jimmy, you and Charlene are about the only able-bodied people we've got left to do it."

Another howl, and this time it was not from the werewolf. This time it was a sound of pain, and this came from Akim.

"Got it," said Jimmy. "Come on, Charlene."

A horrible scream came through the air, and Hauck hobbled over to the opening to get a look. He hung himself half out of the opening and looked back at Akim and the werewolf. His eyes were met with a horrible sight. The werewolf had Akim by his head and one shoulder and bit down ferociously on his neck.

"Go, go," said Hauck to Jimmy. "You've got to break apart the scaffolding soon, or he'll be up here after us."

Jimmy's eyes widened, and he descended the constructed rungs of steel with Charlene hot after him. Hauck watched them as they scrambled down the superstructure of the scaffolding, looking for a place to break it loose. He looked at the werewolf and Akim, sure that Akim was finished now, but Akim stood up, lifting the werewolf that was fixed on his neck and plunged his long, sharp fingernails into the werewolf's throat. The werewolf howled and let him go, bringing his paws to his neck in disbelief.

"Oh, shit," said Jimmy. "Where are the pliers? I've got to have pliers to break this."

Tricia's weak voice said, "Hold on, I think I've got a pair in my pants pockets."

"You just be quiet and I'll get them," said Sveta, who hustled over to get them.

"They're right here," said Tricia.

"Hush," said Sveta, and went through Tricia's pockets and finally came up with the pliers. "I've got them."

"Well, bring them over here," called Jimmy, who was already climbing up to retrieve them.

"I brought a couple of extra tools in case you need them," said Sveta. "That girl of yours is a regular goldmine of tools."

"Is she okay?" Said Jimmy.

"I don't know," said Sveta. "That's just an honest answer."

Jimmy shook his head, then descended the scaffolding to where Charlene was waiting for him. He passed out the meager supply of Tricia's tools, and they went to work.

"I hope they've got enough time," said Hauck, looking nervously at Akim and the werewolf.

Akim was bloodied by the battle. Hauck couldn't make out the extent of his injuries. He squinted down, but the motions were too quick to see as the werewolf raised both of his hands and full out attacked. Akim met him head on and they wrestled, claws raking, blood flying, and snapping at each other. They knocked against the motor control panel, knocking it completely down. Akim screamed again as a motor control panel dug into his back. And the werewolf pressed his advantage. He attacked mercilessly and tore Akim's left arm to shreds.

Meanwhile, Jimmy and Charlene were doing their best to

dismantle anything below them so they could kick the assembly away from them. Jimmy tried to get a screw those, but it would not budge. Charlene tried a screw, but that, too, was rusted in the place.

Finally, she gave up.

"What if I just blasted it with my tube gun?" she asked.

"You think it would cut it in two?"

"Hell, yes, I think so."

"Well, what are we waiting for then?" said Jimmy.

Charlene grinned and led the way back up to the opening. Hauck was waiting for them. He raised an eyebrow.

"The screws and bolts wouldn't loosen, so I got a better idea," said Charlene.

"What's that?"

"She's going to ray gun it," said Jimmy.

Hauck smiled, and Sveta gave her a thumbs up. Charlene got the tube while Jimmy moved out of the way. She stopped and gave a look at Tricia, who smiled weakly back at her. She climbed on the stairs leading to the scaffolding, then turned around and gave a thumbs up. At that moment, a bloodcurdling cry of rage and triumph echoed through the cavern. Charlene twisted around to see the werewolf with his foot on Akim's body, howling a terrifying scream of victory. Suddenly, Charlene's body went cold. They were high up and yet the only chance of the werewolf not coming up after them was if she cut the scaffolding.

Like a laser beam, his yellow eyes alighted on her, and the werewolf stared at her for a full minute. Charlene found herself unable to move, such a hypnotic effect he had. She felt that if she was still, he would look away. It was as though if she remained still, he couldn't possibly see her. But all her hopes were shattered when, giving forth a tremendous scream, he ran straight for her. Leaping over the machinery as though it wasn't there, he bore down on her with extraordinary speed. It was as though he had already healed from his incredible battle with the thing that was Akim — but that wasn't possible.

Whereas Charlene and the others had Tricia to carry and Sveta could only limp alongside them, the werewolf was making inconceivable speed across the same expense. It bounded across the tubes and cages as though they weren't there.

"Hurry," called Hauck.

"I'm trying," yelled back Charlene.

The problem was that the tubular device could be fired from a standing position, but she was damned if she could figure how to fire upside down. She finally angled enough to where she could get a shot, but she missed.

The werewolf reached the bottom of the scaffolding, where it roared yet again. Charlene looked on in fright. His roaring made her hair stand on end. Jesus, he was fast, so incredibly fast. He was a quarter of the way up the scaffolding by the time she had aimed a second laser blast at it. This time she was more fortunate to have hit it square on. But it didn't separate it as planned. It hung by one of the four struts and swung crazily in place. She tried kicking it, but it wouldn't budge. The werewolf made it to the halfway mark, and Charlene began to get genuinely nervous. She could see now its bright yellow eyes and slavering teeth, and the claws it was using to gain handholds on the scaffolding.

She was genuinely crying because she didn't want to fail the others. There was one last chance at the single strut that was holding the scaffolding in place, and she took it. It was a clean shot and cleaved the scaffolding in half. The werewolf was almost up to that point when it started to waiver under its own weight, and it stopped, looked around, and roared. The scaffolding was bending.

Undeterred, it leapt the remaining distance to where Charlene was. She gasped, and she heard everyone above calling her name. The werewolf's claws were extended in eager anticipation. It clawed at the air eagerly and snapped his teeth as he came, but to Charlene's surprise, he fell short by a good two feet. He fell, waving his arms madly for purchase of any kind, but he fell a good seventy-five feet to the ground below. Charlene watched him falling.

She was oblivious to the cheering that went on above. Instead, she watched him impact the ground. She was waiting to see if he got up, or if she had killed the Instructor. That was, of course, why she didn't simply blast him with the ray gun. Because she felt confident that she would have finished him off. Or would it? Suddenly, she saw movement below. The werewolf was sitting up. It shook its head and sprang to its feet, emitting a hideous howl as he did so. It looked up at her, rage in his yellow eyes, and it roared again.

Looking down at the killing machine that had just fallen seventy-five feet and survived it, she felt lucky to be up as high as she was. She turned around and, putting the tubular ray gun to one side of its strap, she began the long climb back up. Just four or five more hours to go until daylight, but what a welcome relief that would be. Because when daylight came, the Instructor would no longer be a werewolf. Now they just had to get down.

CHAPTER THIRTY-SEVEN

The Disaster

Camila was relieved and out of breath. She looked around and saw a virtual museum of equipment. Some were so many odd shaped things she couldn't conceive of what they did.

But she was frightened by all the horrible sounds that came from behind her. One time, she stopped and climbed up a mountain of unused equipment, and seen something that terrified her more than her wildest dreams. She had seen Akim in his true form, battling with a werewolf. She was mesmerized by the titanic struggle and couldn't move. It was as if she were spellbound. The sight of them tearing into each other was beyond description.

Eventually, though, she got down from the pile of equipment, but she fell and snapped her arm. She rolled in the dirt in agony. How could she have been so stupid? Her arm was literally on fire. It was her right, her gun arm. Camila lay on the ground, gasping for breath. How could this have happened to her? She moaned and sat up, her arm throbbing with pain. She held the broken right arm with her left. The pain was so intense, she almost passed out.

She got to her feet and looked around. The SIG Sauer automatic machine pistol was slung around her neck. Fortunately, in the fall, it had not been damaged. She just needed some place to hide. She stumbled around and found a motor control panel, but she couldn't open it with just one hand. Try as she might, she just couldn't. Where could she hide?

Silence fell all around her, then the mighty victory cry of the werewolf. It was horrifying and chilled her to her bones. That beast was no longer tied up with Akim. It was free to roam where it would. She spotted a raised platform with steps leading up to it, but her arm was throbbing so badly that she had to stop for a minute and grab her breath, painful though that was. She decided she must've cracked a few ribs when she fell. It hurt to take a deep breath, and she winced. Finally, when she had a few calming breaths under her belt, she trudged up the steps to get a look around and see if there was some place she could hide from the werewolf. To her surprise, she saw it was moving with tremendous speed towards her. Her breath caught in her throat until the werewolf took a turn in direction and she saw he was really headed towards some scaffolding that extended to the roof of the cavern. High on the scaffolding was a woman trying to use a laser beam on the scaffolding to cut off a path that the werewolf could follow upwards. Camila could not believe her eyes as the werewolf climbed. She decided she had to find a place to hide.

The stairs were blown up to the door, and she couldn't get past the werewolf in any event. She could try, but if he saw her, she was dead. She just couldn't take that chance. No, she had to find some place to hide that was nearby, that was close. Looking around, she saw a possibility. She immediately came down the stairs holding her arm and made for it. She looked behind her and saw that the werewolf was speeding up the scaffolding toward the young woman. But she saw that the woman, cutting it very close, blasted through the remaining part of the struts that held it in place.

Camila came to a dressing room cabinet that just stood there in the middle of an empty patch of ground. The door was open, and it was filled with stuff, which Camila immediately started to, one-handedly, remove. As she was pulling it out, she heard the werewolf scream in rage, and she was startled enough to move faster. She got the bulk of the junk out and tried to fit inside. It was a close squeeze, and she took even more out. She had to take off her SIG Sauer machine pistol to squeeze inside. Once inside, she forgot to retrieve it; she was simply in too much pain to care.

Finally, she was satisfied. Camila squeezed into the storage cabinet and closed the door behind her. She was never so relieved in her whole life. Her arm was still broken and felt like hell, but at least she was safe, and that was something. She would sleep in the storage cabinet until six hours or so it passed, if she could with sleep with her broken arm, and then try to figure out a way to escape.

She took a medical kit from a pants pocket and quickly shook out two pain pills. The soldier's friend was what they called them. She swallowed them dry and waited for them to take effect. As she waited, she considered the werewolf. Where had it come from? It made little sense, but she was glad she was in the storage cabinet.

Camila ripped a piece of her pants off—a long strip and used that to make a makeshift sling. Now the trick was getting it around her neck. She tried once and banged her broken arm against the inside of the storage cabinet, and even with the pain pills that really hurt. A scream escaped her lips. She lay up against the side of the storage cabinet for a minute, clenching her teeth and waiting for the pain to subside. Finally, when it quit hurting, she tried again, this time more carefully. This time, she was successful. She breathed in a sigh of relief, thinking that things were for the moment going her way.

At last, the pain pills kicked in fully and she fell asleep. It was a troubled sleep, filled with vampires and werewolves, but she couldn't help it.

About an hour and a half or two hours into her sleep, she awakened in a panic at the sounds of scratching at the door to the storage cabinet. She blinked her eyes and held her breath. Slowly, she reached for her SIG Sauer automatic weapon, but it wasn't there. She panicked for an instant until she remembered she had abandoned it outside. Slowly, she reached for her Smith & Wesson M & P Shield with her good left hand. Withdrawing it in the cabinet's darkness, she checked it to see if the safety was off. It was.

Still, the scratching persisted. Suddenly, a massive roar assaulted her ears like nothing she'd ever heard before, and in response, she scrunched against the back wall of the storage cabinet. The pistol was clutched in her left hand. The door to her cabinet slowly opened, and she saw her worst nightmare. She fired off an entire clip of ammunition in a matter of seconds, but it didn't seem to faze the beast. Instead, he roared all the louder and grabbed her by her feet and threw her outside of the enclosure. She landed with another painful crunch, this time to her left shoulder.

Trying to get up, her left arm gave out, and she collapsed back onto the ground. The werewolf grabbed her left leg and hauled her up until she was even with its face. Camila screamed just as the werewolf's jaws clamped down and bit through her neck.

****

Charlene climbed back up to the level that Hauck and the others were on to backslapping and cheers all the way around. She gladly accepted the thanks until she saw Tricia and Hauck.

"You guys okay?" she asked.

"They're — how do you say in English — they're okey-dokey," said Sveta. "The main thing is that we're alive."

Jimmy was running his fingers through Tricia's hair in a tender gesture. He stared at her with a reverence that Charlene found hard to describe — it made her wish that she had someone who cared as much about her.

"Now we've just got to find a way down," said Charlene.

"There's two more ways down, and one way up," said Hauck. "There's two more scaffoldings like this one, which I've seen, and look, you blasted a hole in the ceiling with that tubular laser. The sewer system is just above us."

"Oh," said Charlene.

"He's just sore because it hurts to walk," said Sveta.

"I miss Yuri," Hauck said, and the genuine sadness in his voice was hard for the others to mistake.

Sveta laid a hand on his shoulder and squeezed.

"And I'm going to miss him too," she said.

"Yes, but right now, we got to get out of here and get Tricia some medical attention."

"Okay, help me get some boxes to climb out of here via the sewers," said Charlene. "I can make it if I have something to stand on, I think."

Jimmy got up, kissed Tricia's forehead, and began assembling a confused hodgepodge of desks and chairs and tables that were just precarious enough that they took Charlene aback. She stood looking dubiously at the mound for a moment.

"No, I think I'll just pass," Charlene said.

"What? It's perfectly safe," said Jimmy.

By way of an answer, Charlene pulled the little ball out of her pocket and smiled.

"I think I got an alternative method of transportation. I'll throw it down to you after it takes me up."

"Ah," said Hauck, "clever girl."

****

Professor Meridian waited all night long and received no word of Hauck's demise. Round four o'clock in the morning, he got worried. But by five o'clock, he was really getting worried. By six o'clock in the morning, he began to get angry. What happened to Akim and his chernobog? What happened to Camila? Where was everybody?

He fumed, but by the morning, he knew he would never see them alive again. Hauck and his men had emerged victorious. He slammed his fist on the desk. How could that be possible? Who could defeat a chernobog and twenty-six armed men not counting Akim?

He thought back and couldn't remember if Akim had told them they were going. Or, for that matter, he hadn't told Camila either. The professor was all alone in the empty warehouse, because all of his men had gone after Hauck. Failure. He had been an utter, abject failure. How could this happen? He didn't know where to begin, but he vowed then and there that he would get Hauck if it was the last thing that he ever did.

****

Tricia, Hauck, and Sveta saw Gennady. He was the closest thing to a doctor that Hauck knew. He worked on Tricia feverishly for the better part of four hours.

"You know," he told Hauck after the surgery was complete, "it was close. He stabbed through one kidney and twisted the knife so—you understand? Good, another three hours I don't know what I could've done for her."

"Thank you, Doctor," said Hauck.

Jimmy was in the next room worrying about her.

"You know, you don't have to compete with Sveta for matching wounds, yes?"

"Point taken. You know, Yuri didn't make it."

Gennady's smile vanished.

"I'm so sorry, Hauck."

"So am I, doctor. Yuri was a good man."

Next came his attention to Sveta's injuries, and after much arguing, he applied a fresh bandage to her leg. She looked for all the world like a mummy.

"How are you doing?" asked Hauck.

"Just shut up. Thanks to you, he had to apply a whole new bandage to my leg."

"Charlene and I are going to get the cars moved from the front of the house and tidy things up a bit, so it won't look like a whole team tried to break into the house. And we'll close the door while we're at it."

"I'm coming with you."

"Sveta, I'm not sure you—"

"Seriously, I'm not listening. Let's go."

Hauck sighed, but still, it was good to have her back. But he was just wondering about the next attack by Meridian. They would have to abandon the underground lab and go back to his apartment. That meant that Sveta could pick up her enormous wolf Rasputin. He would be glad to see Sveta. Problems, problems, but at least they were alive to solve them.

Everyone except Yuri.

He would have to go down in the cavern to retrieve the Instructor and his son. Details. He normally loved them, but he was a bit overwhelmed by these problems. Like he could lock up the Instructor, but what would he do with his son?

Maybe staying with the lab would be for the best.

He looked at Sveta and then at Charlene and said, "Let's go. That place will not clean itself up."

"What will we do about the Instructor?" asked Charlene.

"Make him put some clothes on," said Hauck. "And then we'll have a good long talk about neutralizing Professor Meridian once and for all."